SHERRIE

SHERRIE

Evelyn Culber

This book is a work of fiction.
In real life, make sure you practise safe sex.

First published in 1995 by
Nexus
332 Ladbroke Grove
London W10 5AH

Copyright © Evelyn Culber 1995

Typeset by TW Typesetting, Plymouth, Devon
Printed and bound in Great Britain by
Cox & Wyman Ltd, Reading, Berks

ISBN 0 352 32996 3

SHERRIE

Foreword

Sherrie stood in the stark reception area, blinking as the spotlights suddenly bathed her in their harsh light. Even though she was subjected to exactly the same procedure every time she reported to Headquarters, she still felt nervous. She looked down at her feet to make sure that she was standing on the mark, noticing that it was getting a little scuffed and needed touching up. Obviously quite a few pairs of feet had shuffled anxiously on the spot since her last visit.

She straightened her shoulders, tightening the silk of her blouse against her full breasts. Her nipples tingled. She concentrated on them, taking deep, slow breaths so that they rubbed softly on the smooth material and the pleasure intensified. She stared at the far wall, deliberately avoiding eye contact with any of the four video cameras which focused unblinkingly on her. She waited.

'Strip!' The disembodied voice made her jump. It always did. But, glad that the waiting was over, her hands flew to the buttons on her blouse and she undressed with only the slightest nervous fumbling, removing every stitch of her clothing. Standing with her hands on her head and her feet wide apart, she closed her eyes and savoured the cool air on her skin as the unseen examiner operated the remote controls of the cameras, sweeping over her body from head to toe.

'Turn round.'

She did so and the tingle started up in her buttocks as they became the main object of attention.

'Bend over.' Her breathing sounded louder in her ears.

1

'Open up your bottom.' Her hands reached behind her, gripped the softness and moved apart, slowly enough to let her enjoy the exposure of her most intimate areas.

'Excellent. You are in great shape. Go to room number three for your briefing.'

Pleased at the compliment, she waited until the hidden door slid open and then walked briskly down the corridor and into the room. As usual, there was only the small desk, a leather-topped stool and the one file on the top of the desk. She sat down, holding her breath at the first touch of cool leather on her warm, bare bottom and got down to work.

The moment she closed the file, the voice broke into her thoughts.

'What do you think, Sherrie? Is he a suitable candidate?'

'Yes,' she replied, 'the problems with his Group are fairly straightforward. In fact, he would probably straighten things out on his own – eventually. But he has got to act quickly and he doesn't seem to be in the right frame of mind. We don't appear to have much in the way of personal detail. What makes you think that we can convert him?'

'It's in the file,' the voice answered briskly. 'The report from our financial journalist.'

'Oh . . .' Sherrie flicked through the pages. 'This bit about his eyes following his PA's bottom when she walked out of the room?'

'Yes. You should have spotted that. You will be punished.'

'Yes, Sir.' The cheeks of her bottom started to tingle and she trembled in anticipation.

'Right. Now, he has planned a major world trip in three weeks' time. I suggest that we use the aeroplane ploy again. See to it. He won't be easy, Sherrie. He is utterly dedicated to his Group and has been incredibly successful. Obviously we want you to open his eyes to the pleasures of the flesh but not distract him. He probably does more to help the economy than any other man, so go carefully. I've booked you and Patricia into the Cottage for all of next weekend

2

so that she can update you on the economic forecasts. Oh, that reminds me, she needs disciplining. I'll leave that to you ... Well, good luck, Sherrie. I know that you won't let the Organisation down.'

'Thank you, Sir.'

'Right. Now for your punishment. Bend over the stool.'

She did so with all her normal grace and her naked buttocks felt as soft and vulnerable as ever as they curved upwards, ready for the first bite of the rattan. The lights dimmed and the single spotlight focused on her bottom, so that everything else faded into shadow. She could almost feel its warmth on her skin. The door opened and she closed her eyes as he walked silently across to her and halted by her left hip. His hands roamed all over her buttocks, kneading them, patting them and smoothing them, assessing the quality of skin and flesh. She held her breath as he prised them open to examine her anus. Then she felt the cool touch as he rested the rattan cane across the centre. She took deep, slow breaths and forced her muscles to relax. And waited.

With luck, he would give her the maximum – eighteen of the very best.

Chapter 1

Sir James MacGregor found himself taking several deep breaths in a reasonably successful attempt to control the surge of anger. He stared wordlessly at the red-faced Operations Manager who was the unfortunate recipient of the basilisk stare which had reduced many a better man to a quivering wreck.

'I thought that I made it quite clear that this trip is absolutely vital and that the aircraft was to be fully serviced beforehand,' he said coldly. 'Now you tell me that it's out of action. Terrific.'

'I know, Sir James,' the man tried to placate him. 'We are all very sorry. But hydraulic leaks are a bugger to sort out and the Service Manager won't let you take off until it's been fixed. But we've been lucky. I've found a replacement.' He smiled, clearly pleased with himself. 'It's a long-range HS125, available for the duration of your trip and even more comfortably equipped than the Boeing. It's ready now, Sir. To be honest, I don't know the operators but I have managed to find out that the holding company is Consolidated – and they're reputable enough. The plane's immaculate. They showed me their servicing schedules and everything's bang up-to-date.'

'My dear fellow, why on earth didn't you say so before?' Sir James said genially. 'Well done.'

'Thank you, Sir James. Please follow me.'

The tycoon strode through the hall, quickly passed through the Customs formalities and then into the car which took him the short distance to the sleek, surprisingly small plane. He shook hands with the Operations man, skipped up the short flight of stairs, ducked into the main cabin and whistled at the opulence of the appointments. Then he noticed the girl smiling a quietly assured welcome.

He did not react to her dark beauty. A sweeping glance took in the general details of her appearance – crisp white blouse and knee-length skirt, neat hair and subtle make-up – but he nodded his approval at her air of calm efficiency.

'Better than the average floozie they seem to land me with,' he muttered to himself as he settled into one of the four luxury seats which provided the main feature of the cabin. He buckled his seatbelt with the brisk efficiency of long practice and, as the girl slipped forward out of the cabin, opened the worn briefcase and set to work on the first of the many files crammed inside it.

The take-off was smooth and Sir James raised his eyes from the papers long enough to enjoy the sensation of power as the plane rocketed into the sky. It was the only part of flying he enjoyed. He heard the muffled thump as the undercarriage locked itself into position, sighed wearily and addressed himself to one of the most turgid Marketing Reports he had ever faced. He found his mind wandering. He undid his belt, stood up, removed his jacket, stretched, paced up and down and then resumed his seat and tried again. It was no good. He put the thick report back into the briefcase, rummaged around and brought out another, 'Ohio Metals Inc. – Background & Current Status.'

'Hell's teeth,' he muttered, 'I should have read this days ago. I'm meeting them on Thursday. What's happening to me?' With an air of grim determination, he settled down to it.

Sherrie eased open the connecting door and studied her charge. The photos in the file had not done him justice. Over six foot, pretty fit, broad shoulders, nice mid-brown hair with a distinguished touch of grey at the temples. As one would expect from a Chairman of an International conglomerate, he was immaculately and conservatively dressed. He wore very little jewellery – just a signet ring and a stainless steel Rolex. That figured.

He looked terribly tired and Sherrie could see that he was having difficulty in concentrating on whatever it was he was trying to read. With growing certainty that their research had been accurate and Sir James was ripe for treatment, she pushed the door open and walked slowly into the main cabin. He frowned up at her, obviously displeased at the interruption. She treated him to her best smile and his expression softened.

'I am sorry to break in Sir James, but can I get you anything?' she asked.

'Thank you. A coffee? Help to keep me awake!'

'Yes of course . . . but if you'll forgive me for saying so, you look as though a break would do you far more good. How about a nice long Buck's Fizz? We've got plenty of fresh orange juice and the champagne will do no more than give it a bit of a kick.'

'Brilliant. Thank you very much.'

Sherrie was relieved to see him toss the report onto a spare chair and sit back with a sigh of relief. She walked back to the galley hoping that he was following the movements of her skirt as it pulled tight across her bottom.

Sir James did notice, but only vaguely.

'Bugger it,' he said to himself, 'the girl's right. I'm not taking anything in.' With only the slightest pang of guilt, he put the file back in the briefcase, shut it, settled back in the luxurious chair and closed his eyes. His neck and shoulders were stiff and the beginnings of one of the headaches which often plagued him nagged away behind his eyes. He started the deep breathing exercises which his masseur had taught him and the tension eased. Then the girl reappeared, carrying a beautiful crystal goblet. The deep orange contents glowed in the subdued light. He reached out for it and took a long swig while she waited for his approval – or otherwise.

It was delicious and he immediately began to feel better. For the first time he really looked at the girl and realised that she was probably the most beautiful woman that he had ever met. No, she was more than beautiful – stunningly attractive was a more accurate description.

7

'Perfect! Thank you . . . No, don't go,' he said hurriedly as she appeared to be about to leave the main cabin. 'Sit down and keep me company. I'm sorry, I don't even know your name.'

'Sherrie, Sir James. I'd love to. What were you trying to read just now?'

'Oh, just the history of a Company we've just taken over. They became a bit dozy, so we've got to decide what to do. We may try and drag them into the 1980s, but will probably just keep the best bits and sell the rest off.' He took another long sip of his drink and found himself wondering why on earth he was discussing his affairs with this young woman. Not because she was female, as there were already several excellent women managers in the Group, but because as an air hostess she could hardly be expected to understand the problems of running an International conglomerate.

'Why?' she asked. He looked at her in surprise. She was leaning forward, her elbows resting on her knees and her chin cupped in her hands, her forehead furrowed in intelligent concentration.

'Because they're not profitable enough,' he replied.

'But if they've survived this long, they must be basically sound,' she reasoned. 'Besides, I can't help feeling that we've had our fair share of the boom and that the bust is not too far ahead. Look at house prices in England . . . something's got to give. How long will interest rates stay this low? Surely now's the time to consolidate. To look at the longer term. And you said that they are making a profit.'

Sir James opened his mouth, intending to use the choicest of the several put-downs which came to mind, and then hesitated. She could well be right. He leaned forward and they talked for an hour or so, after which he had gained a thorough respect for her brain and the breadth of her knowledge. He sat back, looking at her thoughtfully.

'Well, Sherrie, you've given me food for thought. A banquet, no less!' He chuckled quietly to himself. 'Tomorrow's meeting will certainly be intesting. Anyway, that's enough business for now. I want to rest my weary mind. I know, let's have another drink. And please join me this time.'

'With pleasure, Sir James.'

She seemed to be rather longer than he thought reasonable, but he rapidly forgave her when she returned carrying a large tray. On it there was an open bottle of vintage Krug, his favourite champagne, a plate filled with smoked salmon, and another piled with thin slices of brown bread, slices of lemon, salt and pepper.

'Excellent! Here, let me help you.' He rose, taking the tray from her and setting it on the table.

They ate and drank in growing contentment and the conversation moved smoothly from the general to the more personal.

'Are you married, Sir James?'

'No. I've had a couple of near misses but there always seemed to be some urgent business cropping up at the wrong time.'

Some time later he said, 'I hope that you have made the usual arrangements with Customs and Immigration at Kennedy?'

'Of course, Sir James.'

'Good. If there is one thing I really love about my position it's not having too much trouble with Airport authorities. Mind you, I'm always a very good boy and don't take any chances. But there's something about Customs Officers which gives me the creeps.'

'I know what you mean,' she replied. She was looking at him very intensely and he was again struck by her extraordinary beauty. Focusing on her big, dark eyes, he saw something in their depths which sent a tingle running right through him. Work could bloody well wait – some sixth sense told him that talking to Sherrie would be far more productive.

'The atmosphere reminds me of interviews with the Headmaster!' he quipped.

'Yes. You're right,' she said huskily. 'You know, to a few people, that's a turn-on.'

'You're joking! No, you're not, are you? Tell me more.'

9

She looked at him, a wicked little smile on her lovely full mouth and he felt a rare stirring in his groin.

'Settle back, Sir James, and let me tell you a sexy little story. After all, my full name is actually Scherezade – the teller of tales!'

The last flight from Paris – and the last flight that day – had just landed at Heathrow. The plane was pretty empty and the senior of the two Customs Officers on duty wanted to clear up some paperwork, so asked his young assistant, Janet, if she would mind handling the flight. He would, of course, be available should there be any problems.

'Not at all,' she replied, pleased to have been given the responsibility.

The passengers – twelve of them – arrived. None of them particularly caught her attention until the very last one appeared. She was an elegant, beautifully dressed woman in her mid-thirties and our heroine only noticed her because she had entered the Hall in a distinctly shifty way. She had looked straight at Janet, the waiting officer, and her relief at the sight of an inexperienced young female in sole charge was obvious from her expression. She then marched briskly towards the exit, but seemed unable to help the occasional darting glance in the general direction of authority.

Smiling to herself, Janet stepped forward. 'Excuse me, Madam, could you come to the counter, please.'

'Is anything wrong, Officer?'

'Just routine, Madam. Is this your luggage?'

'Yes.'

A thorough search revealed nothing untoward, but the woman seemed so nervous that Janet's suspicions were fully aroused. She asked her to wait, moved across to the internal telephone and told her boss what was happening.

'Search her,' was his immediate response. 'If she's clear, lock up and get off home. If you find anything, come back to me. You've done well. Good luck.'

Peering round the corner, Janet studied the woman. She was very attractive and suddenly Janet felt an inexplicable flutter of excitement. She returned to the counter and politely informed the other woman that she was not satisfied and was therefore going to conduct a personal search. She thought that she saw a flicker of relief in the woman's eyes, but dismissed the notion as patently absurd. But there was no sign of reluctance as they moved into the Interview Room.

The woman took off her jacket, skirt, blouse and slip without a murmur of protest. Leaving her in bra, knickers and stockings – and looking quite gorgeous – Janet carefully went through the outer clothing, having decided that if she was smuggling something, precious stones would be the most likely choice. Absolutely nothing, so she turned back to the woman who was waiting patiently. She smiled gently at her and Janet felt another little flutter.

She really was special, this one. Lovely firm boobs, long and very shapely legs, no flab anywhere and a flawless skin. Immaculate honey-blonde hair, big blue eyes, gazing at her now with disturbing steadiness, and a full, wide mouth. Then those lovely lips parted, the glistening pink tip of her tongue emerged, ran slowly over them and slipped back inside. Suddenly Janet understood what was going on and her tummy contracted at the realisation. The woman was actually enjoying herself!

Janet stared into her eyes, wondering what to do. Should she be professional and bring the thing to an immediate halt? Or go along with the woman's obvious desires? The yearning in her eyes and that lovely body were irresistible. Janet pointed at the bra. With studied deliberation, the woman took off the bra. Janet's gleaming eyes stayed fixed on the quivering movements of the breasts as they swung into full view, pert and rounded with pinky-brown nipples puckered in excitement. She took the proffered bra, ran her fingers expertly round the seams, dropped it on the growing pile of discarded clothing and stared at the naked breasts.

'Some years ago, Madam,' she said slowly, 'there was a case of a woman who smuggled heroin in a beautifully made false torso. I am not sure what it was made of – some sort of latex, I imagine – but apparently the join was so fine, it matched her skin so well and the breasts were so realistic that the deception was only discovered after a fairly detailed search. I think that I had better examine your breasts, Madam, just in case.'

They were thrust out in clear invitation and Janet's hands reached out and gently cupped them, thrilling at the way the nipples stiffened noticeably at her touch. The woman's skin was satin-soft, her flesh firm. Janet squeezed and stroked. She placed her hands on the under curves and lifted the warm mounds, making them wobble. She ran her thumbs over the nipples and was rewarded by a gasp of pleasure.

'Well, they feel natural enough. But no one can disguise the taste of rubber. Brace yourself.'

She bent down and sucked the nipples into her mouth, first the left, then the right, gently nibbling the tense little projections. She could hear the woman's heavy breathing whistling through tightly-clenched teeth above her . . .

Sherrie paused momentarily and looked at Sir James. His eyes were closed and he was obviously enjoying the images which her words were conjuring up. Smiling to herself, Sherrie continued.

The woman's hands pressed down on the back of Janet's head, forcing her face into her flesh until she had to straighten up and catch her breath. They looked deeply into each other's eyes. The woman's yearning was clearly etched in her face and Janet allowed her studied severity to soften as she came fully to terms with the situation. She stepped back and admired the full length of the near-naked body in front of her, her gaze travelling down over the subtle curve of her tummy, with the deep little button holding her eye for several moments, then to the small, white silk knickers, outlining the pubic mound and downwards to the entrancing sight of the stockings, their tops indenting the flesh of her naked thighs.

In the meantime, the woman, whose name was Mrs Delmes, was in seventh heaven. Her breasts ached at the memory of those nice lips and skilful hands. The girl was perfect. Young, pretty and with an ideal air of severe authority. Her mouth was much more seductive now that it had relaxed from the rather grim tightness which was obviously part of her professional 'look'. A quick sweep of her body with her eyes confirmed her initial impressions of a biggish bosom, narrow waist, deliciously curvy hips and neat calves. Mrs Delmes felt a strong desire to see her naked but could see no way of arranging it. Their eyes met again.

'Take your stockings and suspender belt off, please,' Janet said, her voice unsteady. The woman's breasts swung as she bent to her task and in no time at all, there were three further items to be examined. Janet's gaze returned once again to the near-naked body.

'Your knickers, please. Right off.'

There was hunger in Janet's eyes as she watched the slow movements of the hands up to the waistband; the careful insertion of the thumbs between elastic and silken skin; the slow exposure of a neatly-trimmed triangle of dark gold hair which thinned out to reveal the darker slash of the cleft between the plump lips of her sex. Mrs Delmes eased her knickers off and handed them over, standing up straight and making no attempt to cover herself.

The completely naked woman was even more delectable than the fully-clothed version and Janet's eyes swept hungrily up and down, pausing only to linger on the key visual points – eyes, mouth, nipples, tummy-button and pubic hair, all of which served to highlight the gleaming whiteness of the woman's skin. The only sound was the heavy breathing – until the woman spoke:

'If it's possible to make false breasts, surely one could also find a way of making false buttocks?'

For a moment, Janet was taken aback. Bottoms had not featured particularly prominently in any of her encounters but suddenly the prospect of examining that part of the woman's anatomy tempted her.

'So you think I should examine your buttocks?' Janet asked slowly.

'Yes . . . please,' she whispered.

With a slow, purposeful tread, she moved round the woman and for the first time in her young life, carefully studied a bare female bottom. She immediately wondered why she hadn't done it before. This one was truly a lovely example. The woman standing before her might have been no longer in the first flush of youth, but maturity simply added a rounded voluptuousness to what had obviously always been a striking feature. With a quiet sigh of pleasure, Janet squatted down and looked at it really closely, loving the smoothness, the plump curves, the tight division between the cheeks and the nice deep folds where thighs and buttocks met. She reached out to touch it and was amazed at the way the flesh yielded to the gentlest pressure of her fingers, belying the apparent solidity. Her skin there was almost as smooth as on her breasts and it felt deliciously cool.

Janet pressed the tips of her fingers and thumbs as far into each cheek as they would go. Smiling at the distortion in the hitherto smooth, firm shapes, she kneaded away, eyes fixed on the movements of the cleft as the neighbouring mounds bulged in and out. She patted the roundest parts, loving the rippling quiver it caused. She enjoyed herself immensely and, judging from the sighs from above, so did the woman.

Janet stood up and moved back round until they were again eye to eye, noting with satisfaction the signs of arousal – the parted lips, the soft flush on the cheeks and neck, extending down to a point just above the breasts. Looking at the open mouth, with the perfect white teeth just visible, Janet felt an almost overwhelming urge to lean forward and kiss it, to inhale the woman's breath and to slip her tongue into the moist warmth, but knew that the game was not yet over and the intimacy could spoil it for them both.

'I am not fully satisfied, Madam. I am going to give you an internal examination.'

The older woman's eyes closed momentarily and a shudder made her naked breasts sway.

'You mean . . .?'

'I mean that I am going to push my middle finger up your vagina. As far as it will go. And then I shall repeat the manoeuvre up your bottom.'

'My *bottom*? Oh ... I suppose people do smuggle things in their ... um, in *there*. But *I* wouldn't dream of it. I promise!'

'I'm afraid that it is standard procedure whenever we have the slightest doubt. I understand that it will be humiliating for you, but I assure you that it will not be painful as long as you stay reasonably relaxed. Well, not too painful!'

As she spoke, Janet studied the woman carefully. For the first time, she was showing signs of nervousness and Janet guessed that the thought of having to present herself for the digital penetration was worrying her a little. Apparently, being made to strip naked was as far as her fantasy had gone. Janet felt a warm glow through her middle. In spite of her sexual inclinations, she had not really enjoyed the few internals she had had to carry out, but this was very different. The sense of power over this lovely woman was intoxicating and her smile was suddenly cruel.

'I have always been told to start at the bottom. Turn round!'

Breathing heavily, the woman did as she was told. Her full buttocks quivered nicely as she came to a halt. Janet moved closer, squatted and palmed the plump cheeks thoughtfully.

'Bend forward.'

Her splayed fingers spread all over the tightened flesh and her thumbs sank in on either side of the groove, easing it open until the slightly wrinkled, pinky-brown surround of the woman's anus popped into view. She paused at that moment. Never having examined this particular and especially intimate orifice before, Janet wasn't quite sure whether she would like it. She took a deep breath, moved her hands another inch or so further apart until all was fully revealed, peered closely and found that she did like it. Very much indeed.

And so it was with even greater anticipation that she moved decisively towards the climax of the examination.

'Yes, I'll definitely start with your bottom. Go over to the examination table.'

Janet's education advanced a bit further as the naked woman walked across the room. Admittedly she was very aware of being watched and added an extra sway and wiggle to a walk which was naturally graceful, but even so, the young girl was surprised at how sexy it was.

The woman reached the upholstered table, hesitated and then rested the upper part of her body on the clean white sheet. Taking hold of the far edge, she spread her legs wide, bent her knees in, and waited.

Janet gazed at her, wide-eyed. If the woman's bare bottom had looked tempting when she was standing, seeing it jutting out towards her, the central groove parted just enough to show a glimpse of the usually well-hidden hole and with the lightly-furred sex showing just below, all in such startling contrast to the creamy-white skin around it, was all far too nice to dismiss with only a passing glance. So she looked long and hard from a distance before treating herself to a closer view.

Squatting down with the object of her attentions only inches from her face was certainly an improvement, highlighting not only the satiny texture of the woman's skin but also enabling her to see that the slit between the plump lips of her sex was slightly open, as if in sympathy with the bottom-cleft above. Pearly little drops of moisture clung to the surrounding hairs and the heady scent of feminine excitement filled Janet's nostrils. Concentrating on the matter in hand, she soon decided that, for all the aesthetic charms of the position, the woman was insufficiently accessible. She stood up.

'I'm afraid that isn't quite good enough – I want your anus fully exposed. Please kneel up on the top of the table, knees well apart, face resting on the pillow and your bottom sticking as high as you can get it.'

She watched the re-positioning, moving around to keep the woman's rear in view all the time, fascinated by the changing perspective as she clambered up, knelt on all fours, lowered her head and spread her knees before finally arching the small of her back downwards.

'That's much better,' Janet said briskly. 'Not too un-comfy, I hope?'

'No I'm fine,' the woman replied, her voice muffled. 'But this has got to be the most obscene position I've ever been in.'

Janet would not have argued. The drum-tight cheeks, with the two holes between and below them, were deliciously obscene!

'I can imagine,' she replied drily.

'Are you a bottom girl?'

'I am now!'

'Thank you.'

Janet smiled, straightened up, walked briskly over to the cupboard, unlocked it and reappeared at the head of the couch, placing two pairs of surgical gloves and a tube of lubricant just in front of the woman's widening eyes.

Mrs Delmes watched Janet's preparations with some trepidation. She was kneeling up in relative discomfort, her bare bottom horribly prominent and her defenceless anus tingling in anticipation of its imminent penetration. She may have engineered the entire confrontation and had often fantasised over this particular scenario, but although the reality had so far lived up to her dreams, her open vulnerability was beginning to make her wonder if actually having a finger firmly thrust right up her virgin back passage wouldn't ruin the whole thing. Her eyes followed Janet's deliberate movements rather unhappily.

The right-hand glove was carefully extracted from the sealed packet, the hand steadily inserted and the glove tugged into the tightest possible fit. Then the middle finger was extended and lovingly coated with a glistening layer of jelly. As the hand and its owner disappeared from view, her anus began to twitch in earnest and she closed her eyes and concentrated fully on her imminent ravishment. Then, as suddenly as they had come, her fears left her. She had noted the glint in the officer's eyes; her pretty face was alight with enjoyment and as she focused her full attention on her bottom-hole, Mrs Delmes felt a surge of lust. She stuck her bottom out even more and held her breath.

Janet once again took her time and moved slowly from front to rear studying the pleasing side view, from the slightly dishevelled hair, via the flattened breasts, the gently-curving tummy, the upward sweep of the back, the prominent hipbone to the egg-shaped jut of the nearer buttock. As she approached her target, the profile of the further cheek loomed into sight, revealing the width of the dividing cleft between the twin mounds. She moved right round until she was standing by the woman's left hip, with her left hand resting on the small of her back, the extended thumb brushing the stretched skin covering the little bulge of her tailbone. She bent at the waist to look straight into the very exposed little hole, marvelling at the way the tiny muscular ring stood proud of its immediate surroundings. Placing her finger on the exact centre, she held it there for a minute to build up the tension and then she firmly thrust in, right up to the knuckle.

There was a gasp from the woman and a delicious little squirm from the assaulted behind as the shock of the stretching of her anal muscles sent a wave of prickling fire up the woman's back passage. Then she seemed to realise that it was not painful, as Janet quite clearly heard an 'ooooh' of pleasure.

Janet played with the willingly proffered bottom-hole for several minutes before removing her finger completely and taking another look at the spectacularly displayed rear. Her bare left hand smoothed firmly over the tight buttocks, the forefinger ran slowly down the full length of the yawning groove, lingering on the pink anus, which glistened with the residue of the jelly.

'Well, you're obviously not trying to smuggle anything up your bottom.'

'Are you absolutely sure, Officer?'

The slight breathlessness in the voice, plus a waggle of her hips provided a clear indication of the woman's desires and, in case Janet failed to get the message, she pumped her bottom-hole in and out.

For a second Janet was tempted to ignore the request, but she had so enjoyed the feeling of the tight, clinging warmth round her finger, that she was quite happy to repeat the exercise. She had the woman wriggling her hips desperately before she finally withdrew, took off the glove and re-arranged her panting victim.

In no time the woman was lying face up, her bottom just over the edge of the couch and one foot resting on the back of each of the two chairs placed about half a metre from the end of the couch. Her legs were therefore raised, apart and reasonably comfortable. Janet placed a stool between the two chairs and, before getting to work, surveyed her new target.

The neatly-furred pubic mound offered an arresting focal point at the junction of the rounded thighs as they sloped downwards and inwards from the raised knees. It was beautifully supported by the surprising amount of tightly-divided bottom flesh visible below it. Walking back up to the head of the couch, Janet's eyes moved up the soft white plain of the tummy and onto the soft breasts before locking onto the other woman's eyes. By now each was as turned on as the other and so Janet hurriedly wriggled a new glove on to her right hand and went back to the stool.

She ran her left hand quickly up and down the inside of each thigh, tickled the tip of her forefinger up and down the tight groove between the dimpled bottom-cheeks, then slowly prised the plump lips of the neat little sex apart, fully exposing the coral-pink, glistening folds inside.

Mrs Delmes' thighs were quivering with tension as Janet poised her extended finger at the entrance to the dark tunnel and, as she thrust it smoothly in up to the knuckle, she bucked and writhed. Simply to maintain the little game for a few seconds longer, Janet wriggled her finger around, as though checking for contraband. Placing the tip of her left forefinger on the hooded clitoris, she rubbed away gently and rhythmically as her gloved right hand pumped steadily in and out.

Suddenly the recipient of her expert favours yanked her knees backwards, wrapping her arms round them to hold them well out of the way, with the result that her anus popped into view. It was too good to resist and Janet halted the proceedings while she adjusted her hands to enable her to slip a spare finger into the panting lady's bottom.

In less than a minute, the sounds of the woman's climax echoed round the bare walls. And that was only the first. Janet gave her a short breathing space and carried on, loving not just the feel and taste of her gorgeous body but also the heady pleasure of being in complete control.

'Kneel on the table and stick your bottom out,' she commanded breathlessly. 'More than that. Better . . . Now turn over and spread your legs!'

Before too long Mrs Delmes was clearly shattered and, rather reluctantly, Janet told her to get dressed, at which point the game was obviously over and they could be themselves. They kissed, gently and affectionately.

'I haven't done anything to you, Janet. Do you mind?'

'Of course I do, but it wouldn't have been very sensible for us both to be naked.'

'I feel awfully guilty at having taken up so much of your time.'

Janet was on the point of dismissing the thought when the memory of that beautiful bottom stopped her in her tracks. She looked deep into the woman's eyes and saw that the longing had returned. She reached behind and smoothed a hand thoughtfully over the curves beneath the dress.

'So you should be . . . naughty girl . . . *very* naughty girl!'

'Do you think I should be punished?' the woman asked softly.

Janet felt a hollowness in her tummy.

'Yes.' She hitched up the skirt and wriggled her hands into the knickers until they were resting on bare flesh.

'What would be best?' the woman whispered.

'A good spanking?' Janet's rigid fingers sank into yielding flesh.

'Oh yes! Will you do it to me? Put me across your knee, pull my knickers down and give me a really good spanking on my bare bottom?'

'Yes. It would do you a power of good.'

'You'd better come round to my house. We can be private there.'

'When?'

'When will you be off duty?'

'Monday.'

'4 o'clock OK?'

'Fine.'

'Here's my card. It's quite easy to find.'

'I'll be there. And when I've finished with you, your nice, white bottom will be as red as a beetroot.'

'You do like my it – my bottom, I mean?'

'Yes, very much.'

'That's good ... you won't let me down, Janet? I couldn't bear it.'

'I said I'll be there.'

Janet watched her new lover walk elegantly out of the deserted Hall and smiling broadly, got ready to go home.

Sherrie focused on Sir James' face. She had been watching for signs of boredom or distaste throughout her little story and had been relieved that he seemed to have been totally absorbed in it. When she stopped, he opened his eyes and gazed steadily at her, looking far more alert than before. She felt certain that she had got it all just about right.

'What an amazing girl you are!' He suddenly grinned at her and she grinned back with a surge of relief. 'But you can't leave it there. Did Mrs Delmes get her spanking?'

'Of course. And it was the start of a beautiful, if somewhat peculiar, relationship.'

'Tell me about it.'

Janet turned up in good time, her heart thudding away. If she was impressed with the size and opulence of the house, she showed no sign of it and she and Mrs Delmes sat down with a cup of coffee and talked about nothing in particular for a while. Janet had softened her appearance somewhat, although her dark suit and plain white blouse still gave her an air of quiet authority, perfect for the occasion. Mrs Delmes was in a simple, short-skirted dress which gave her an appropriately youthful look. As they finished their coffee, Janet looked casually around the room and noticed a very suitable, armless chair by the desk in the corner. Since their

21

confrontation at Heathrow, she had given a great deal of thought to how best to approach this second meeting and smoothly took control. Her voice was deliberately low, steady and authoritative.

'Right, Mrs Delmes. Stand up. Put your hands on top of your head. Look at me when I'm talking to you. Now, you know why I'm going to punish you so there's no need to say any more. I take it that you've had your bottom smacked before?'

'Yes . . . quite often.'

'Good – it certainly doesn't seem to have done you any harm! Now please fetch that chair and put it in the middle of the room. There. Yes, that will do . . .' She sat down on it. 'Across my lap, please. Up with your tummy so I can pull your skirt right out of the way. Really, Mrs Delmes, these knickers are not exactly decent, are they? At least half your bottom is showing. Not that it matters, because I'm going to take them down for you.'

She began to do just that, revelling in the prospect of seeing the other woman's bare bottom again. Mrs Delmes played the game to the hilt and protested volubly at the shame of it all.

'Oh no, please don't – it's so embarrassing . . . Oohh!'

'Stop wriggling around!' Janet shouted. 'A ridiculous fuss . . . down to your knees they go, my girl! I'll just tuck your skirt up – I don't want it slipping down . . . that'll do nicely. Now, Mrs Delmes, make yourself comfortable because I think this'll take quite a long time –' Smack! her hand came down on the bare buttocks.

Janet had never spanked anyone before, but in no time at all was beginning to realise what she had been missing. Mrs Delmes' bare bottom was definitely a sight for sore eyes in any circumstances and looked especially attractive peeping out between the drooping knickers and rucked-up skirt. The way it wobbled at each spank, the sound her hand made, the feel of the flesh as it yielded under the impact, the sight of the spreading pink stain – it was all very sexy.

After a bit she realised that it would be all over too soon

if she carried on at the same pace, so she eased up, lightening the force of her spanks and lengthening the interval between them, concentrating on changing the blotchy red to a more even colour. Janet loved being in complete control, especially of this older and much more sophisticated woman. Each jerk, every little kick and heave made her heart beat faster. The noise of her hand and the squeaks and cries from her victim were music to her ears. After some five minutes, short of breath and with her hand stinging like mad, she paused and stroked the warm, soft cheeks.

'Well I hope that that's taught you a good lesson.'

'You haven't finished, have you? I was just wondering when you were going to stop warming my bottom up and start spanking it properly!'

Janet only just managed to stop herself laughing out loud and played lasciviously with the naked behind in front of her for a moment or two while she tried to think of a suitable reply.

'You saucy little minx! Well, we'll soon have you regretting your impudence. Your bottom may be quite red now, but by the time I've finished with you, it'll look like a beetroot. A big, fat beetroot.'

'I haven't got a big, fat bottom.'

'Oh yes you have. It wobbles like a jelly when I smack it. Like that. And that. And *that*.'

In another five minutes, Mrs Delmes' bottom was beetroot-red and she was crying real tears, but by this stage, Janet was beginning to understand her and although she couldn't believe that even this extraordinary woman could take any more, she firmly told her to keep still for the final six blows.

She landed each one on the lower curves. The sitting part. And by the end the bottom half of each buttock was even redder than the rest and Mrs Delmes was howling lustily. But as soon as Janet relaxed the pressure of her left arm on her waist, she clambered to her feet, rubbed frantically away at her burning rump and her tears dried up immediately.

'Janet, that was fantastic! Come on. Up to my bedroom and you can kiss it better.'

But before the kissing started, Mrs Delmes had to strip naked and admire herself in the full-length mirror, with Janet watching in amusement. After which one red bottom was posed with due care and Janet found that kissing this part of a woman's anatomy was surprisingly nice. She then had an inspired idea.

'Right, you naughty girl – it's time for the second part of your punishment. Kiss the hand that spanked you . . . that's right, now the thighs which supported you so solidly . . . of course you have to bare them . . . and now the bottom which supported us both . . . Ohhh, that *is* nice . . . you want me to bend over? Oh, you want to look at the hole . . . Is that all right? Can you see it? . . . Oh my god . . . what was *that*? Your tongue? But . . . Oh, it was *fantastic* . . . Do it again! Hang on, I'll kneel up and stick my bottie up . . . Ohhh yessssss!'

When they eventually curled up to sleep, Janet thanked her lucky stars that fate had arranged for her to be on duty on that particular shift. She eased the middle of her body away from her new lover's curving rump and stroked the soft, warm bottom with a slow gentleness which was so unlike her usual brusqueness. She then tucked her pubis back against the roundness, pressed her breasts against the smooth back, kissed the nape of the neck and settled down to sleep. As she drifted off, her last thought was after all that, she really should find out Mrs Delmes' first name!'

Sir James stared out of the window thoughtfully. 'It's funny, there's something oddly appealing about the thought of two girls enjoying themselves in that way . . . Do you like it?'

'Yes.'

'Would spanking one excite you?'

'Yes.' Sherrie smiled serenely.

'And being spanked?'

'Yes.'

'But you're not anti-men?'

'Certainly not.'

'I see. Well, Sherrie my dear, you've certainly entertained me – and taken my mind off things for a while. Umm . . . will you be on board for the whole of the trip?'

'If you want me.'

'I want you! Now, I really must do some work before we land, but we're off to L.A. after New York – a nice long flight. I'm looking forward to it already.'

'So am I, Sir James. Some more orange? Coffee?'

'Oh, some coffee would be perfect. Thank you very much.'

He settled down with renewed dedication and gradually Sherrie's earlier remarks about the dangers of the over-heated economy in the West made more and more sense. He heaved out his lap-top computer and began the major task of re-structuring the Group to see it safely through the potentially troubled times ahead.

Every now and then his mind drifted off for a little rest and liquidity analyses were replaced with images of the fair Mrs Delmes sprawled over Janet's lap, her bared bottom quivering under a volley of crisp spanks. Then it substituted Sherrie, first in one role, then the other. He lingered over the memory of her lovely face, the slight hint of olive in her skin, her darkly shining hair, big brown eyes, her full mouth. He found himself wondering whether her breasts were as lovely as the rest of her. Then he recalled the sway of her skirt as she walked away. He shook his head and got back to work.

His ears popped as the sleek little jet eased into its landing pattern and, for the first time in ages, he began to look forward to the battle ahead.

Chapter 2

They left JFK airport on time and settled down to the long haul to Los Angeles. Sir James had smiled cheerfully at Sherrie as he skipped up the short flight of steps into the cabin and had then immediately belted himself into his seat, plonked his briefcase on his lap, extracted several files and was soon flicking through them, pausing every so often to speak briskly into a portable tape-recorder.

Unaware that Sherrie was watching surreptitiously, having heaved a huge sigh of relief at the obvious change in him, he completed his summary of the meetings. He packed away his papers and was reaching for the button to summon her when she appeared, again carrying a large tray. Most prominent – and most welcome – was another bottle of vintage Krug champagne, the glistening drops of moisture bedewing the dark green glass showing that it has been chilled to perfection. A little balloon of froth bulged rather rudely from the opening and he found himself grinning to cover up a little flare of embarrassment at his immediate train of thought. He recalled the delights of her first bizarre story and found himself actively looking forward to another. Before then, though, there was the first glass to savour and a bowl of Beluga caviare to ease any hunger pangs. He then noticed that she had only brought one glass.

'Is my company so unattractive to you that you don't want to join me?'

She smiled down at him and walked back up the cabin to fetch another glass.

They sipped and nibbled in companionable silence, then she asked him how the meetings had gone.

'Very well. The more I thought about it – and the more we discussed it – the more certain I became that your feelings were right. We are reducing our borrowing and have backed out of a couple of big property deals. We've decided to accept bids on several of our own properties rather than hold out for more. Needless to say, I faced some opposition . . .'

'And needless to say, the opponents soon retreated with their tails between their legs!'

He grinned in a way which clearly showed the steel behind the gentlemanly facade.

'Talking of tails, your Mrs . . . er . . . Delmes . . . did she really get a kick out of being spanked?'

'Yes of course.'

'It seems strange.'

'It isn't that common but far less unusual than you would think. Lots of people enjoy being sexually submissive. Male and female.'

'Fair enough,' he conceded, 'but I find it hard to understand how something which is basically a form of punishment could turn anyone on.'

'Ah, Sir James, the main thing was that it involved her bare bottom! Let me tell you another little story, which may throw a little more light on the subject. Why don't you take off your jacket and relax. Let me pour you some more champagne . . .'

Let's go back to the eighteenth century, to an independent State in what is now Germany. Corporal punishment was an integral part of the penal system. Prisoners were beaten for any transgressions while they were inside and apart from that, were subjected to a whipping at the beginning and end of their sentences – known as the 'Welcome' and the 'Farewell'. Fairly obviously, the idea of the first was to warn them what to expect and the second to remind them of the consequences of offending again. Mind you, in those days crime was almost the only alternative to grinding poverty and most prisoners just regarded a flogging as one of those things. We'll start at a dinner party. The new Governor of a prison for female offenders is entertaining some of the local 'quality', all of whom are usually invited to witness punishments, seeing it, of course, as part of their civic duty! The conversation soon moves on to the various methods traditionally used to whip the women.

'I hope, Governor, that you will re-introduce the birchen rod,' one woman said. 'Your predecessor preferred the bull's pizzle and I confess that this is not to my taste.'

'The *what*?' Sir James' eyes snapped open.

'The Bull's Pizzle,' replied Sherrie with a shudder. 'It was literally a bull's penis, dried and stretched to make a vicious whip. Rather like the South African Sjambok. But even worse.'

'Good God ... not to my taste, either! Sorry, Sherrie, please carry on.'

'I agree,' said the Governor. 'One must, of course, be firm with these unfortunates, but both my good wife and I are in full accord that Justice should be tempered with mercy. But does it not concern you that the birch demands an uncovering of the lower person and –'

'Please forgive me for interrupting, Governor, but that is a vital part of the punishment.'

The speaker, Frau Schmidt, was the forceful wife of the Deputy Mayor. A large woman with a magnificent bosom, steely-blue eyes, strong views – and sensual appetites. She emptied her wine glass and continued. 'Most of the prisoners are of the poor and therefore have not been brought up with the modest attitudes that are second nature to us. Even so, speaking as a woman, I assure you that having one's hindquarters laid bare in public must affect even the most hardened of the women. And to those of a better background, the sense of shame would be overwhelming.'

There was a pause as the guests reflected on the thought of womanly buttocks displayed naked. Then the Governor's wife spoke up from the other end of the table.

'It will be my duty to take charge of the chastisements.

I was, after all, a Governess before my beloved husband met me, so am not without experience. I have devoted considerable thought to the subject and hope that you will all be present to observe for yourselves.'

The guests' eyes lingered on her. She was by far the most beautiful woman present. Her golden hair and bare, white shoulders shone in the flickering candlelight; her blue eyes gleamed with fervour and two of the men – and one of the women – had exciting thoughts at the idea of bending to her will. She was pressed to tell them more of her thoughts and plans but smilingly told them to wait until the morrow, when she would be 'opening her account'.

At noon on the following day all was ready. The weather was exceptionally fine, so the ceremony was to take place in the open courtyard and the wardresses had been organising things with their normal efficiency. The prisoners were standing in a tight group, some way behind the eight comfortable chairs for the visitors and with a clear view of the ominous whipping block, although the visitors naturally had the best possible view of the action.

The block was new. The old one had been a simple bench with stock-like brackets at each end to secure the hands and ankles. This was higher, shorter and with a step at the end on which the victim presumably would have to kneel.

The distinguished guests emerged from the Governor's house and took their places. A very aristocratic and elegant lady firmly established herself in the centre seat, to the visible annoyance of the Governor – and of Frau Schmidt.

The atmosphere was surprisingly festive. One can quite understand that the guests were filled with anticipation, but the prisoners were also looking forward to watching their sisters' imminent ordeal. It was a cruel and sometimes brutal age; they had all been flogged at least once and the prospect of watching someone else being dealt with was regarded as an entertaining interlude in a pretty grim existence. Whispered recollections of the first victim's familiar rump mingled with interested speculation on the shape and form of the second's – a newcomer, receiving her 'Welcome'.

Four wardresses appeared from behind the crowd. Three were carrying buckets containing an impressive quantity of birches and on sighting these, the buzz of excitement grew in volume. They were going to get it on their bare bottoms. Much more fun than the whipping drawers to which the pizzle had traditionally been applied, even though these were nicely tight and showed off the curves beneath. The fourth was carrying a stool, on which was another bucket with the neck of a bottle of wine clearly visible. There was a puzzled silence at the sight, then a louder buzz.

At last the Governor's wife strolled calmly up to the bench, smiled at the occupants of the chairs and then nodded in the general direction of the building behind them all. There was another pause and the audience studied her with interest. Her beauty was in no way diminished by the strong sunlight and her gown set off the slenderness of her body to perfection. Her golden hair was tied up in a neat bun, adding a touch of severity to her appearance.

It was several moments before one of the more quick-witted prisoners voiced the thought that it looked as though the Governor's wife was actually going to administer the punishment! This was unheard of. It didn't seem right – and she looked far too frail to do the job properly. From what they could see of the birches, they seemed much too light for mature bottoms used to adult treatment.

The disappointment – and disapproval – was clear from the tone of the whispers. They wanted blood. And the chief wardress was the best person to provide it. Meanwhile, the main attraction was being dragged out to meet her fate. They heard the scuffling clatter of her clogs on the stones, her bitter cursing, the grunts of the wardresses as they pulled her along. This was quite normal but there was something different about the quality of her protests. Something which made the convicts crane round to see her emerge. All became clear when she was led past them to the block. She had been stripped down to her shift and the tail of her one remaining garment had been pinned up to leave her bottom completely and humiliatingly bare. There was a collective gasp and several amused giggles at the sight of this big woman being unceremoniously dragged along, red in the face, her breasts bouncing freely under the thin material covering them and her naked rear end wobbling voluptuously as she struggled.

No wonder there had been a note of despair in her voice. It had always been the custom to wait until the last minute before baring the victim. To be paraded like that must have been horrible. Even to Birgitte, who had been whipped more often than most.

When the little group reached the bench, they halted and the two main participants stared at each other, the one calm and lovely; the other panting, her face red and twisted with fear and hatred.

'Let go of her.'

Hands dropped away, leaving pink imprints where fingers had dug into the upper arms and wrists. The two women stood alone as the wardresses took their places behind the chairs. Silence fell.

Obviously, there was always a tense atmosphere as a whipping was getting under way but on this day, it was even more marked. Every eye in the audience was fixed on Birgitte's shamefully displayed bottom, some with a tinge of sympathy at her plight, a few with ill-disguised lust and all with interest. In the meantime, the object of everyone's attention just stared miserably down at the cobblestones.

Nothing further happened for nearly two minutes and the more perceptive began to appreciate that the Governor's wife had already introduced a new dimension to the punishment. Birgitte certainly did. For one thing, she felt so self-conscious at her nudity that her normal desire to make things as difficult as possible for her tormentors by struggling with all her strength was overcome by an even more natural inclination to stay as still as possible. She was revealing enough of herself as it was. Then a soft hand stroked her left buttock. Gently. Soothingly. She felt some of the tension drain away and looked up into the lovely face.

The Governor's wife spoke.

'Lay yourself on the block, Birgitte.'

To her surprise, Birgitte found herself obeying without the slightest protest. She could just hear her fellow prisoners murmur in amazement and sensed that several were grinning broadly at her meekness. She knelt on the lower part of the platform, rested her torso on the main part, held her hands out to be strapped and tried to collect her scattered thoughts.

She was not the brightest of women and her twenty-one years had been hard and harsh, with five of them spent in various Institutions. She had been sentenced to three years in Bridewell for an unprovoked assault on a nursemaid whom she thought had been mocking her, unaware that the other girl was near-sighted and tended to smile at any vaguely familiar shape just in case they were in some way acquainted.

Her new position made her naked bottom feel even more prominent and she stared blindly at the further wall of the courtyard while her hands and ankles were strapped, waiting for the burning agony of the rod to introduce a familiar element to her ordeal.

She jumped and gasped aloud as she felt the Governor's wife touch her bottom again. Her hand was soft and it passed slowly over the whole surface, with the fingertips dipping into the cleft between the broad cheeks. Her flesh was squeezed and patted. Gently and . . . well, nicely. She felt it ripple and quiver. She frowned, puzzled and uncertain, and shifted uneasily. The voice broke into her confusion, low and with a discomfiting warmth.

'You have a pretty bottom, Birgitte. Good, firm flesh and nicely shaped. It is a shame that I now have to make it all red and sore. But it is my duty and I hope that you will at last learn a lesson from your well-deserved punishment.'

The Governor's wife had been quite genuine in her complimentary remarks. Birgitte did indeed have a splendid rump, even if a modern fashion pundit would have expressed horror at its size! But in those days, a shapely plumpness was to be admired and Birgitte was certainly both plump and shapely.

The Governor's wife selected a rod from the nearest bucket. Resting it against the expanse of white flesh before her, she adjusted her stance and then slowly administered the first stroke. She sensed rather than heard the murmur of disapproval from the rows of prisoners and smiled to herself. As she had said to her dinner guests, she was not inexperienced and knew full well that her methods were very effective. What only her husband knew for certain was that she would enjoy every minute!

She watched the slender bundle of flexible twigs bite into the fleshy cheeks, then moved forward and bent down to study the effect more closely. There was a visible pink patch right across the centre of the girl's bottom and an even closer inspection revealed that it was made up of a tracery of fine pink lines, with little spots on the further flank where the tips of the birch had bitten in. Fully aware that the pinkness would not be visible to those at the back of the crowd, she grunted in satisfaction at the evident softness of Birgitte's skin and resumed her position.

A further dozen or so flicks landed on the passive bottom. Quite obviously, Birgitte was so used to serious floggings that this childish treatment was hardly affecting her at all. She made no sound and her solid buttocks neither quivered nor twitched. Her breathing was steady and when the Governor's wife turned to study her face, she saw that her victim had her eyes closed and had a little smile on her lips. The Governor's wife returned to the business end and administered another dozen strokes, with an interval of some thirty seconds between each. By the time they had been delivered, the effects were much more noticeable. The whole bottom was a distinct pink and Birgitte was breathing far more heavily. She paused again.

As the worn-out birch was casually tossed aside and the hand which had wielded it poured out a refreshing glass of wine, the audience were able to study Birgitte's bare bottom at their leisure. The guests, with the advantage of a much closer view, were more obviously impressed than the prisoners. Several of them were nodding in approval and Frau Schmidt was beaming happily. The second dozen had

had an obvious effect. The skin was now a bright pink in colour and so Birgitte's bottom stood out in clear contrast to the pallid whiteness of her thighs and back. It was beginning to look distinctly painful and they had been close enough to see the way her hips had jerked as the last few strokes had smacked her, and to have heard her sharp little gasps as the sting grew more biting.

If the prisoners were too far away to see all this, they could hardly fail to be aware of the buckets full of new rods and it did not take a great deal of intelligence to work out that the whipping was only just beginning.

The Governor's wife bent over to inspect her handiwork before moving to the other end of the bench and crouching down.

'Your bottom is reddening beautifully. And you are being very brave. But I fear that there is plenty more to come. Please think about your life, Birgitte. You do have a most attractive posterior but do you not feel terribly ashamed at having it laid bare and whipped like a naughty child? And with a large audience watching every quiver and shake of your hindquarters? Looking on keenly as I turn them red? Remember this, my dear, next time that you are tempted to stray from the straight and narrow path of righteousness. Now, I shall continue. Be brave, and learn from your pain.'

The softly-spoken words finally affected Birgitte. If everything leading up to this stage had just confused her, suddenly she began to appreciate the real value of her whipping. Nobody had ever told her that her bottom was nice: she had never been spoken to with that sort of sympathetic warmth. Nor had she ever been caressed like that. She was certainly feeling the effects of the birching and the warm sun on her naked and smarting skin was a sharp reminder that her bottom was starkly bare. She had soon got over the shame at having her naked rear so prominently displayed and the feeling that was beginning to overwhelm her dazed mind was gratitude for the civilised way she was being whipped. Her bottom was stinging but it was nothing to the tearing agony of the pizzle and, as she heard the ominous sound of another rod being taken out of a bucket, she braced herself to offer this beautiful lady a target worthy of her best attention.

The second phase was with a shorter, bushier rod and concentrated on one buttock at a time, so that half-way through, the audience was treated to the interesting sight of a duotone bottom.

For the third, the Governor's wife stood alongside the right hip, facing the proffered buttocks and the new rod began a vertical assault. It rose, hovered and whistled down, curving round the outer curves of the nearer cheek, with the whippy little tips biting sharply into the top of the thigh. The punishment continued across the impressive breadth of the buttock right up to the inward curve of the cleft and then across the other one, before starting again.

Birgitte's bottom was now very red indeed. The audience was by this stage almost completely won over to the new approach, not necessarily by the redness of the exposed flesh but by Birgitte's reactions. Under the previous regime, a flogging lasting as long as this one would have left her virtually unconscious. In total contrast, she was now fully alert and feeling each blow as keenly as the first. Her cries and wails echoed round the courtyard; her bare bottom was dancing to the rhythm of the birch in a way which was almost sensual and very eloquent.

The Governor's wife was far too busy to react to the various comments from the audience but was able to appreciate them.

'The girl does have the most splendid and whippable bottom.' That was the upright and aristocratic lady, whose eyes were gleaming and whose own slim and elegant behind wriggled gently on her seat.

'And my wife is proving her expertise, is she not?' The Governor said, smiling.

'Most assuredly, Governor. I have never witnessed such an effective whipping. It will do the miscreant nothing but good.'

'Oooh, look, she's bringing the birch down into the middle of her arse ... That could damage 'er!' Someone cried.

'Not the way she's doing it,' replied the Deputy Mayor, 'they're just little flicks. And look at the way Birgitte's shoving 'er backside out. Opening it right up for it. Dirty cow. And listen ... she's crying. Like a baby. I never would've believed it.'

'I trust that your reservations are no longer concerning you, Your Honour.'

'No, Governor, I am fully converted to your methods. I have seldom seen a redder bottom – and yet not one drop of blood. And her contrition is quite clear from her lamentations. I have seen this one whipped before and her usual reaction is to heap a shriek of curses on all our heads. I am impressed, Sir. There will clearly be no lasting harm to her flesh, yet her mind may well remember the lesson for the rest of her life.'

'I do hope so, Your Honour.'

By this time, the Governor's wife was administering the final strokes to the outer curves of Birgitte's other buttock and, having completed this stage, she tossed the rod aside and poured herself another glass of wine, savouring it while the audience drank in the sight of the scarlet, twitching bottom. She then selected a thicker, bushier birch but before applying it, made another careful inspection of the afflicted hindquarters, running her hand gently over the skin as she did so, and then returned to the head end of the bench, bending down to raise the weeping woman's chin and look her straight in the eye.

'It's nearly over my dear. And you are still being very brave. I congratulate you. Your bottom is exceedingly sore, I should imagine.'

'Yes, Madam. It feels as though you've lit a fire on it.'

The Governor's wife smiled down at the red, tear-stained face.

'Well, that is the idea of a whipping. But although it is very red indeed, in a few days it will be just as it was before. I have not cut you. There will be no more scars.'

'Thank you, Madam. Is ... is it really nice? Me arse, I mean?'

'Yes, Birgitte, it is big, as I am sure you know, but nicely full and properly rounded. A pleasure to whip and I hope that you find a good man who will also appreciate it – and who will give it a sound spanking when it needs it. Which I am sure will be quite often!'

To the surprise of everyone except the Governor's wife, Birgitte burst into a flood of racking sobs, then quite clearly wriggled around, trying to push her bottom even further out.

The final stage set the seal on the occasion. Nobody could doubt for a minute that Birgitte had been beaten most effectively. Her bottom was an amazingly vivid colour and the movements of her body were as eloquent as her plaintive sobs and wails. And yet the sheer gracefulness of the Governor's wife, with her lovely eyes fixed firmly on the crimson buttocks, wobbling frantically by now, added a blatantly sensual element which was not lost on the watchers. In fact there were many hidden erections and feminine sexual stirrings among them!

Birgitte was not turned on. She had found the first dozen smacks surprisingly pleasant but from then on it had just been pain. But the different quality of the pain and the sympathetic approach by the Governor's wife had given here a vastly different perspective.

The more sensitive and nervous prisoners had found the proceedings very reassuring. Obviously it was painful. The blatant display of Birgitte's naked bottom had sent a shudder through most of them. But they had noted the way that the Governor's wife had stroked her. They had not been able to hear everything she had said, but the tone of her voice had clearly been warm and sympathetic. All in all, the feeling was that if they had to be whipped – and they accepted that they didn't have any say in the matter – then to be treated with a little respect and dignity made it something to be faced without feeling literally sick with terror.

The final encouragement came when Birgitte was unstrapped and they saw that she was able to stand up unaided. She tottered a bit and her crimson bottom was visibly twitching and quivering but she was soon reasonably steady on her feet as she reached back to soothe her burning flesh. She brought her right hand forward to examine it for traces of blood and, obviously greatly comforted by the absence of any red stain on her palm, rubbed away quite briskly. Then, to their utter amazement, the Governor's wife gave her a glass of wine, smiling warmly at her.

The good lady's smile broadened as the red-faced girl stammered out her thanks. She nearly dropped the glass before drinking its contents in one gulp and wincing as her attempted curtsey relit the fires in her bottom.

'Off you go, Birgitte. And remember what I said to you.'

'Yes, Ma'am . . . Thank you Ma'am.'

There was a warm gleam in those blue eyes as they followed the movements of Birgitte's cherry-red bottom as she walked off.

Sir James slowly opened his eyes and he stared at Sherrie, collecting his thoughts. Sherrie risked a quick downwards glance and her eyes gleamed as she spotted the unmistakable protrusion at the front of his trousers. He also looked down, and grinned at her, slightly embarrassed but quickly reassured when she grinned back. He leaned back and closed his eyes again.

'A strange story. It took me a bit of time to see anything remotely sexy in it, I must confess. Tell me, was the Governor's wife a liberal and kindly person, or did she enjoy whipping another woman?'

'Both. In fact, she pulled a few strings and got Birgitte a job on a cousin's farm, where she settled down happily, married one of the other workers and never got into trouble again.'

'And did her husband spank her? As the Governor's wife hoped?'

'More than likely. As I said, she had a perfect bottom for it,' Sherrie said, smiling.

'I must confess that I'm not really sure what constitutes a bottom perfect for spanking!'

'It's difficult to say, really. Size has a little to do with it, in that there is more flesh to spank if she's well-built, but

38

I find that shape is much more important. I've thoroughly enjoyed spanking some quite little bottoms when they have a chubbiness about them,' she reflected thoughtfully.

'I might have guessed that you'd know what you're talking about! I look forward to hearing more. Later. But what's puzzling me is that I found your story quite a turn on. It doesn't make sense. Let's face it, there was a young woman who had presumably been driven to crime by appalling poverty being publicly whipped on her bare bottom until she could hardly stand. If anything like it happened today there would be a worldwide outcry. Yet somehow, you made it all sound incredibly sexy. Why?'

'I suppose that that was a compliment!' Sherrie laughed. 'No, seriously, Sir James, the point is that you can't judge it by what would be acceptable today. You instinctively understood that, which is why you could "see" it through the eyes of one of the guests and therefore could find the image exciting. Look at what really happened. In an age where nudity was frowned upon – and not many people had the chance to see the relatively few paintings which featured bare ladies – a very feminine bottom was quite legitimately put on display, treated to what was not much worse than a really sound spanking, which turned it a dramatic red in colour and, at the same time, the culprit was treated like a human being, reacting to this novel experience by sticking her bottom out in a way that suggested that she was close to enjoying it. Which, compared to what she expected, she did. Her punisher was kind to her. Told her that she had a nice bottom. Went out of her way to avoid scarring her. And was also exceptionally beautiful. Birgitte had probably had little affection in her life and reacted by willingly proffering a part of her which had been praised by somebody she looked up to. The audience began to matter when she was told that her bottom was a pretty one. Then exhibitionism did come into it.

'I said earlier that the important element in spanking is the bottom. Especially for a girl. It's a much more receptive part of her body than many people realise. And I'm sure that lots of bottom men feel inhibited when it comes to admitting their feelings to their partners. Be that as it may, there she was, humiliated by having to walk to the bench with her shift pinned up, expecting to end up with a lacerated bum and with the jeers of her fellow-inmates ringing in her ears and instead, a lovely, upper-class woman finds her attractive enough to caress her bottom, to praise its shape rather than mock its size and then to whip it in a way which produced titillation as well as pain.

'And for both elements of the audience, it was a bit of a revelation. Instead of a display of callous brutality, they were treated to what was almost an erotic cabaret, with a provocatively posed and very naked bottom slowly being turned a dramatic and spectacular red. The quivering of her flesh would have emphasised the softness and her tears were moving. Not an expression of agony. The male guests obviously would have found it exciting and bearing in mind that the prisoners had virtually no contact with men, they would have been just as receptive to the sensuality.'

'Yes . . . It's beginning to make sense,' Sir James admitted.

'Does it matter if it doesn't? Make sense I mean. If the thought of a sexy bare bottom being turned red excites you, why try and explain it? The point is that you're obviously not turned on by senseless cruelty and yet you could not have got where you are without believing in discipline generally.

'I am not saying that we should go back to the past. I'm only a story-teller. Would you like to hear what happened next?'

'Of course I would.'

Sir James settled back in his seat again and closed his eyes.

The two escorting wardresses handed Birgitte over to one of the Infirmary staff, who had a quick look at her bottom and whistled in admiration.

'My God, not a drop . . . some scratches but nothing needing my attentions. Does it hurt?'

'Of course it bloody well does . . . Owww . . . sorry, Mistress.'

'It really is hot. I suppose you would prefer to leave your shift pinned up. Let the air cool it off.'

'Yes please.'

'Suits me. It's a splendid sight! Now come over to the window and watch the "Welcome" and then I'll find a wet cloth for you. That'll help with the burning.'

'Can't I have it now, Mistress?'

'No you can't. I want to see it all bare for a bit longer. Go on, over to that window and lean right out. That's good. Let's see, is anything happening? Oh, the Governor's wife is having a rest. I'm not surprised. Working over your fat bottom would've exhausted even me. Wouldn't mind a glass of that wine.'

'She gave me one.'

'I know.'

The wardress looked thoughtfully at Birgitte, who still had tear-filled eyes but whose face was soft and almost pretty in spite of the stained cheeks. Acknowledging the difference in her, she put her arm around her shoulders and squeezed, then moved her hand downwards and stroked her bottom very gently. She was rewarded by a shy smile and they turned their attention to the events in the court-yard.

Maria, the other prisoner to be whipped, was a complete contrast to Birgitte. Her background was basically middle class, and had it not been for the early death of her father, she would never have ended up in Bridewell. As it was, she was forced to take a job as a sort of junior governess/nurserymaid for one of the local merchants and had been caught red-handed stealing money. She was really lovely, with curly blonde hair which had survived the standard prison cropping in remarkably good shape, quite tall and with a perfect combination of slenderness and curves. Her sweet nature had already made her quite a favourite in the prison, although she had not found all the approaches made to her acceptable!

Hardly surprisingly, she had dreaded the prospect of her 'Welcome'. She had seriously contemplated suicide after a rather exaggerated description of the effects of the pizzle from a gloating Birgitte some days before. Having watched her tormentor's punishment from the doorway, she was not only vastly relieved that she would not be subjected to the tortures she had been made to expect, but she almost welcomed the beating to come. Her Christian upbringing had taught her all about paying for her sins and everything that she had seen indicated that her penance was going to be fair and effective.

Maria had enough self-confidence to know that her beauty would make her whipping an even more spectacular event for the spectators, so when the Governor's wife had finished her glass of wine and signalled for her to be led to the block, she straightened her shoulders and held her head high as her bottom was bared.

The wardress who carried out this simple task was one of those who had propositioned her and Maria's rather haughty refusal still rankled. Especially when the full glory of her behind was revealed. Red in the face, her eyes gleaming with lust, the wardress stroked and squeezed the plump cheeks and ran her forefinger down the cleft between them. Maria stared stolidly into the distance, refusing to give the dreadful crone any satisfaction, either by shrieking in protest or by showing the slightest sign of pleasure.

The little procession moved out into the courtyard. There was no need to hustle the victim – she walked steadily towards her fate with her pale face held up and her wide blue eyes fixed on her tormentor. She was vaguely aware of the strange feeling of warm, fresh air on her naked bottom and of its jostling movements as she walked, but most of her attention was fixed on the Governor's wife.

The two beauties faced each other. The senior one smiled warmly into her victim's eyes, sensing how she had had to summon up every ounce of courage to overcome her fear before reaching the stage where the punishment was a challenge which she was utterly determined to conquer.

'I have to whip you, my dear,' said the Governor's wife. Her voice had a throaty sultriness which took Maria's breath away. 'I have to whip you on your bare bottom. You were able to watch Birgitte's buttocks being dealt with?'

'Yes, Madam.'

'Then you know what to expect. Although as this is your first offence, I will not be quite as severe. But your bottom will be passing sore by the time I have done with it.'

'It is no more than I deserve, Madam.'

'Your attitude does you great credit, Maria. Be brave. And learn from the exercise. We do not wish to see you here ever again. As I am sure the Magistrate made clear to you, if you revert to your criminal ways, we shall be considerably more severe. Now, place yourself on the block.'

While all this was going on, every eye in the audience was glued to Maria's naked bottom. It was easily as beautiful as the rest of her. Perhaps a little large by today's standards – Marilyn Monroe rather than supermodel – but then in those days a woman was expected to have a bigger bottom than a man! Her shift had been pinned up well above her waist, so that the outward curve of her hips was clearly visible. Her cheeks were plump, firm, divided by a long and tight cleft and her gluteal folds – where the buttocks joined the thigh – were broad, clean-cut with a delightful upward curve which made her bottom look as though it was smiling slightly. Her skin was so white and smooth that it gleamed in the bright sunshine.

The preparations didn't take long and the movements involved sent lovely little shivers through Maria's flesh, emphasising the softness. And then she was strapped down and made ready. Her new position spread the target out a little, the cleft was wider and her thighs had been placed close together, so there was not even a glimpse of hair between her legs to interrupt the smooth display of bottom and thigh.

The Governor's wife helped herself to a leisurely inspection of her buttocks and quite obviously took great pleasure in it. Her slender, long fingers smoothed over the quivering mounds, assessing the texture of the skin and clearly finding it more than satisfying. Then they dug into the flesh, almost sinking out of sight as the softness bulged around them.

Maria was in a sort of trance. As she was strapped to the bench, she grew far more conscious of her bottom. The watching eyes seemed to burn into it and a most peculiar prickling tingle made itself felt on her sensitive skin. The guests noted the faint blush spreading over the surface and smiled knowingly.

Maria heard a rattle as the first rod was taken from its bucket, feeling cool drops fall on her flesh as the water was shaken from it. She held her breath as it was measured across her bottom, cool and bristly, closing her eyes and gritting her teeth as it left her. There was a faint whistle and Maria gave out a little gasp as the rod stung her. She wriggled her bottom and felt her flesh quiver as the sting spread. The Governor's wife watched and waited. Amazingly, it had hardly hurt at all. It had actually felt rather nice. A stingy tingle, which faded quite quickly. She waited for the second.

The pace speeded up, so that both birch and bottom were in constant motion. Maria was completely silent for nearly two dozen swishes, then the sting began to intensify as her skin steadily changed from light to dark pink, from red to scarlet, and her gasps and pants could be heard quite easily by the prisoners at the back of the crowd. There was a pause while the Governor's wife checked the state of her target, poured herself another glass of wine and took out another birch, a long, very slender one.

By the time she was ready, Maria was still again, forcing herself to take long, deep breaths to steady her nerves. Her buttocks were already hurting her quite considerably, but she was nowhere near tears. In fact, she was exulting in her ordeal. No other form of punishment could have made her feel properly sorry for her crime. Her bottom glowed and throbbed in a way which was almost pleasurable and although she knew full well that there was an awful lot more to come, she put all her concentration towards the feeling in her rear end. The warmth of the sun on her skin seemed to soothe the stinging in one way, and make it worse in another. She had never been so aware of this part of her anatomy and was amazed at the nagging tingle of excitement from between her thighs. Even her bottom-hole seemed to be getting in on the act and was sending out pleasant waves of sensation. She relaxed as much as she could, closed her eyes and let the novel feelings flow through her.

'Is she not utterly lovely?' The voice was female and very upper class.

'Absolutely.' A man. Less aristocratic.

'I have never seen such a perfect bottom on a girl. So deliciously plump and firm . . . and her hips swell out from her waist like a . . .'

'A cello?'

'Oh yes, Your Honour, that is exactly right.'

'And her skin is so smooth and silky in appearance. Is it so to the touch, Madam?' This last question, louder, obviously addressing the Governor's wife.

'Indeed it is, Your Highness. Less so now, of course. My rod has left a mass of small raised weals and small bumps. It is hot to the touch, as you would expect. But I can remind myself of her normal state by feeling her thighs – the skin there is of equal quality.'

As she spoke, the Governor's wife ran her right hand over the nearer column, her eyes glistening. She followed the contours round to assess the inner surface and her fingers vanished below the red flesh.

Maria gasped as the upper edge of the thrusting forefinger ran the full length of the virgin slit, stayed and then withdrew. The sweetly sour pulse in her sex throbbed even more strongly and she slowly pumped her hips in and out as the Governor's wife resumed her position, raised a new weapon and swept it firmly and smoothly down so that the supple twigs curved around the full width of the penitent buttocks, assaulting the lowest curves with a narrow band of fire and making Maria jerk and cry out for the first time.

Ashamed of her weakness, she bit her lip and turned her head to watch the Governor's wife in action. Her tears blurred the image of tall, slim elegance; the graceful upward sweep of the right arm, the downward drive, ending with a turn of the wrist and a dip of the knees. Her bottom felt as though a swarm of hornets had landed on it, but she kept silent.

The Governor's wife quickly examined her handiwork, stepped back and changed her stance so that she was less sideways-on. Then she flicked the rod so that just the tips landed on the target, covering the entire surface with little red dots which soon merged and added to the increasing discoloration.

An equally red haze was clouding Maria's vision. The pain seemed to have reached a peak and the barrage of flicks was doing no more than maintaining the existing level, which was proving tolerable at least. She was crying now. Fairly softly and as much from exhaustion as pain. She no longer struggled against the straps and was completely unaware that her bottom was pushing rhythmically in and out. She was just fading away into another trance when the pain took on a new quality, sending waves of heat right through her. She snapped into full awareness, began to jerk and heave and finally found her tongue, crying out that she was sorry and pleading for an end to her punishment.

Smiling quietly, the Governor's wife finished the series of vertical strokes with the thinnest and whippiest rod by applying it with utmost care into the cleft. The tips flicked gently against the inner surfaces, close enough to the hidden anus to send the euphoric Maria into orgasm.

It was over. The Governor's wife poured herself a final glass of wine, tossed the worn birch wearily onto the ground and stood at her victim's side while she sipped, gazing down on her twitching bottom. The satisfied expression on her face was well-merited. In spite of the considerably smaller target, she had caused no damage at all and knew that in a matter of days, Maria's delectable posterior would have regained all its previous beauty.

She replaced the empty glass on the tray and bent down to stare into Maria's face. Like Birgitte's had been, it was red and tear-stained. She stared back in a very similar way, eyes bright with tears but again, without a trace of hatred in their depths.

'Thank you Madam,' she whispered, 'that was what I needed.'

'That is good, Maria. And you stood up to your whipping with true courage. Now serve out your sentence with equal fortitude.'

'Yes, Madam.'

She straightened up and returned to Maria's bottom, running her hand gently over both crimson cheeks and slipping the tips of her fingers into the soft warmth of the cleft, trailing down the full length. Maria sighed audibly and the Governor's wife felt her bottom push against her hand.

'I will see this one again. In private,' she said to herself before signalling to the wardress to release the girl.

In an excited babble, the prisoners were herded back to their quarters and the Governor's wife rejoined the guests.

As she approached, she caught the aristocratic lady's eye. There was a strange, tight expression on her face and a silent pleading in her eyes. The Governor's wife nodded her understanding and then graciously accepted the profuse compliments of the others as she led them back for much needed refreshments. Considerable discussion on punishment followed, with a great deal of reference to the two bottoms they had just seen receiving it.

The Governor's wife was totally content. It had taken a long time for her to get her husband into his new position and everything was already exceeding her wildest hopes!

Sir James was looking Sherrie full in the face, smiling and clearly fascinated.

'What was the lady's unspoken question?'

'She wanted to be whipped.'

'Good God . . . I can see exactly what you were getting at about achieving a combination of sexiness and justice in a formal punishment but I still can't understand – well, not properly – anyone being turned on by pain. Maria's reaction made absolute sense. As a girl fully aware of her own beauty, being made to show off her bare bottom would have been oddly thrilling and the circumstances – and her

47

own conscience – would have made her far more receptive to accepting a whipping like that. And, in her highly excitable state, the Governor's wife's caresses would have touched her to the very core. Yes, I can see that. And I can understand Mrs Delmes getting a thrill from the Customs Officer. But not actually volunteering to be spanked.'

'We'll come onto that, I promise. But close your eyes and see the events as though you were one of the guests.'

'I did. And I freely confess that if you had a magic carpet and could whisk me there I'd be on it like a shot! But only because I know that there was a basic eroticism behind it. I couldn't watch a brutal flogging. No way.'

'Neither could I.'

'Sherrie, you certainly live up to your name. That was a terrific yarn. You do of course realise that the temptation to put you across my knee is growing all the time?'

'So I should hope, Sir James.' There was a mischievous grin on her lovely face which did nothing to reduce the prominent bulge on the front of his trousers – which he was doing nothing to hide. 'But we'll be landing soon, so this will have to keep you going.'

She knelt down before him, unzipped him with practised skill and he groaned aloud as his most sensitive part was enveloped in the moist heat of her mouth. He felt a hot surge of arousal and then her fingers tightened around the base of his shaft and the surges faded. She worked his trousers clear of his hips, spread his thighs and cupped his tightening balls with one hand while the other delved beneath him to squeeze his bottom. She used her lips to push back his foreskin and flicked her stiff tongue over the tip. When his gasping groans and the spasmodic jerks of his hips indicated that his climax was well on its way, she took most of his impressive length into her mouth, tightened her lips and sucked him dry.

He collapsed, limp and panting, into the enveloping seat. She kissed him and her lips were warm and soft, with a hint of promise of even better things to come. She reclined the seat, extended the footstool, tucked a blanket around him and, as he drifted off into the sleep of the just after, he heard her softly seductive voice telling him to rest. California was still a little way off.

Chapter 3

Sir James bounded up the steps and into the plane, looking fresh and alert in spite of the gruelling schedule which had kept him heavily involved in a series of meetings for the past three days. Tossing his briefcase onto a spare seat, he removed his jacket and tie, undid the collar button of his Turnbull & Asser shirt and sat down with an expectant grin on his face. Sure enough, Sherrie soon appeared with the tray, the champagne, two glasses and a plate of smoked salmon sandwiches.

'How did it go, Sir James?'

'Very well indeed. We've substantially increased our general liquidity and at the same time increased our investments in the companies with a long-term future. You were absolutely right, you know. All the major economies are beginning to show signs of stress. We'll suffer if there is a big bust, but not nearly as much as we would have if you hadn't made me think. By the way, that bottle's probably getting a bit warm!'

Smiling broadly, she put the tray down, filled both glasses, handed one to him, then bent down, picked up his briefcase and then stretched up to put it away in one of the overhead lockers. She had quite deliberately kept her back towards him and the movements of the seat of her skirt took his mind off his glass for the full ninety seconds that her actions took.

'The flight to San Francisco doesn't take that long, Sherrie and I can't wait for another story.'

'Would you like some dinner, Sir James?'

'No thanks, this lot will do fine.'

'Right.'

She gazed out of the window as the engines fired up and the plane moved smoothly along the approach to the runway. They both fastened their safety belts and watched the sprawl of Los Angeles disappear below the wing. Then her big dark eyes gazed steadily into his.

'Would you like another one about punishment with a sexy undercurrent – or punishment which is pure sex?'

'I think the former. I'm still curious about the way that serious punishment can produce pleasure,' he told her, excitement in his voice.

'Right.'

We'll move on in time, to the Napoleonic Wars and a largish village in southern France. It's 1812 and Bonaparte has invaded Russia. He had been heavily engaged fighting Wellington in Spain and Portugal for some time and the new campaign had considerably increased his need for manpower for his army. Therefore, in common with every community in France, there was hardly an able-bodied man around. The women managed to keep the farms and small businesses going pretty well and everyone was surviving. However, a fairly major problem had reared its head and the Priest, Father Dominic, caught the brunt of it.

He was in his mid-thirties, tall, dark and handsome in a way which brought out maternal rather than sexual feelings in the female members of his flock. He was a genuinely good man. Unworldly enough to be destined to remain a parish priest – because he was no good at the politics which are so much a part of higher office – but intelligent enough to have a good understanding both of Christianity and human nature. Basically, more and more women were getting more and more frustrated. Not that the worthy Father noticed anything at first. The first hint that there was a problem had come when he heard Madame Lefarge's confession. Her husband owned the local stores and had been snapped up by the Colonel of the local regiment to be the Assistant Quartermaster, on the logical assumption that there was nobody better qualified to see that the men were fed. And the Officers well-fed!

Driven to desperation by the incessant tinglings in her nether regions, Madame Lefarge confessed to having frequent sinful thoughts and then to seeking relief from her own hand.

Father Dominic was not unsympathetic – although it was a problem which troubled him seldom – and advised her to redouble her efforts in maintaining the success of her husband's business, to devote more of her energies on helping the poor and to say a dozen Hail Marys.

'Yes, Father, I shall . . . although a dozen stripes across my naked bottom from my dear husband's belt would do me far more good.'

There was quite a long silence. Both as a boy and during his training, the Father had been subjected to corporal punishment and knew full well how a reasonable application of some suitable implement to that part so obviously designed by God for the purpose did wonders to rid a boy of idle thoughts. With his normal clear logic he saw no reason why the same effect should not apply equally well to the female of the species and in his innocence, he could see none of the danger.

'I understand, my daughter. Pain can have a cleansing effect on the soul. Do you not have a relative – or a friend – whom you could ask to chastise you?'

There was a further silence, while Madame Lefarge considered the possibilities. She honestly had not meant to be taken seriously. It had been no more than a flippant remark but memories of the warm after-glow which had always been such a part of her punishments came flooding back and her plump bottom tingled.

'I do not think so, Father. Besides, if I were to approach anyone I would have to declare the reason for my request. I know that you will not pass on what is said in the Confessional but could I trust another? I think not and the gossip would be unbearable. Father . . .' She took a deep breath and felt a strange glow of exhilaration in her heart as a possible solution to her unhappiness occurred to her, 'Father, could you not punish me? You have the strength and determination of a man, and yet I know that I can

52

trust you to ... to beat me as I should be beaten. Fairly. With forgiveness as well as firmness. From sorrow at my frailty, rather than anger. As a loving father.'

'Yes, my daughter,' Father Dominic replied after several moments of deep thought. 'I shall do as you request and afterwards, you will pray for the Lord's forgiveness with the certain knowledge that you will have had mine. Wait there.'

Five minutes later, she heard him re-enter his box.

'Go into the vestry, my child. Hanging behind the door is one of my habits. Put it on and stand facing the table by the window, on which I have placed the instrument of your correction. Contemplate it and reflect on your sins.'

'Thank you, Father.'

She slipped into the appointed room, hurriedly stripped to the skin and pulled the coarse, brown robe over her head, shuddering as the rough cloth slithered over her soft skin. Pulling the hood up, she stumbled nervously over to the table and stared down at the well-worn belt which lay with casual menace on the polished surface. She shuddered at first. The prospect of the shiny leather wrapping itself vigorously around her bottom, the crack of its impact and the swathe of burning pain which each stroke would produce on her sensitive skin, was enough to make anyone shudder. Her hands stole round behind her. She ran them quickly over the twin mounds of her bottom, assessing the plumpness of her flesh as though checking its ability to withstand the imminent beating, all her awareness concentrated in her hands. At first, anyway. Then suddenly the nerves in her bottom flared into life and she felt a surge of excitement.

'A man is soon to see me in a state which only my husband has witnessed.' Her whisper echoed round the silent room. 'Bernard has always professed a great liking for that part of me. Will Father Dominic like it? But will he in fact strap me on my bare skin? He surely will – it will hardly touch me through this thick cloth.'

Her fingers sank into the softness and shifted the flesh around so that the nerves in her sex sent more waves into

53

her tummy. Her breathing quickened and she remembered seeing a sash on another hook behind the door, so she whirled round, retrieved it, quickly tied it round her waist before resuming her original position, where she took a deep breath and tucked the back of the robe up into the belt. Her bottom was now on full display and the contrast between the itchy cloth and the warm, fresh air on the exposed parts was quite delicious. Her hands dropped down again and the moist warmth of her palms reminded her so strongly of her husband's touch that she gasped, torn between desire and guilt.

'Surely my derrière will please him? Even if he has taken vows of celibacy, he can still admire my form and find me more pleasing to strap than some skinny-shanked youth.'

Suddenly weak at the knees, she bent forward until her full breasts were squashed against the top of the table. Her hands kneaded away with feverish intensity, shifting the twin cheeks this way and that, revelling in the softness under her hands and gasping aloud at the delightful tingles coming from both her orifices. Then she heard the ringing sound of the priest's boots on the flagstones in the corridor and straightened up. Just in time.

Father Dominic swept through the doorway and the sight which immediately greeted him stopped him dead in his tracks. Not having had time for second thoughts, the back of her robe was still tucked up at the back and her bare bottom gleamed at him in the subdued light. Her attentions had slightly pinkened the skin and it was quivering slightly as her legs trembled from a combination of nerves and her exertions. The good Priest's jaw dropped. His first thought was that he was surveying one of the most beautiful sights he had ever seen. His second was to berate himself for not having anticipated the obvious – that it was one thing to beat a boy's bare bottom, but to do it to a mature and lovely woman was a very different matter! Then, as he let out his breath, he felt a surge of inspiration. This was an ideal test of his moral strength. As the Lord had been tempted in the Wilderness and had overcome, so he was being tempted now and it was up to him to prove himself. He gazed at the lush buttocks quite openly, savouring the view, confident in his ability to put Satan behind him.

And so the two minds were beginning to move in the same direction, except that Father Dominic was thinking rather more clearly. Madame Lefarge's mind, by contrast, was in a bit of a whirl. In the foreground was the perfectly natural fear of the imminent consequences of her rash statement in the Confessional. There was also a feeling of guilt at having exposed herself. But, as she stood there, bare-bottomed and vulnerable, her mind seemed to lock onto the sort of emotions she felt whenever her husband dealt with her. At the start of her married life, she had only been vaguely aware of her exceptional beauty and certainly had never considered that she had a desirable bottom. Bernard had soon convinced her otherwise and now, as she stood there with the warm air playing over it, she found herself clearly remembering their last love-making . . .

A hot night . . . the bedroom shutters still open so that the cosy little room above their shop was bathed in light. She had come in from her toilette, cool in her freshly laundered nightgown and with her hair loose and gleaming after a rigorous brushing. Bernard was sitting up in their brass bed reading the '*Moniteur Universel*', gloating over the news of Bonaparte's successes in Russia – and dismissing the hints of Wellington's in Spain as impossible. She had passed in front of the window; he must have seen the dark outline of her body through the nightgown, as the war was instantly forgotten and, as she moved round to her side of the bed, he had grabbed her wrist and pulled her across his lap, an action accompanied by a happy little squeal. As soon as they had both settled down comfortably, he had begun to stroke her pouting rump through the thin covering and the feel of his hand had thrilled her as much as ever . . .

'Oh, Bernard, I have been a very good girl. All day. I don't deserve to be spanked, do I?'

Bernard, whose qualities tended towards dogged perseverance rather than speed of thought, had taken a second or two to react in the way she wanted. 'I wasn't planning to . . . Ah. I am quite sure my dear, that there is any number of things you will have done to displease me through the day. I shall not trouble to interrogate you on this occasion. I shall simply assume your guilt and administer an appropriate punishment. In a moment. First let me examine your naughty posterior.'

The hem of her nightgown had risen steadily upwards, exposing her calves, knees and then her thighs. Bernard had paused when the hem had reached the top, leaving her buttocks tantalisingly covered and presumably giving himself ample time to fully savour the anticipation. An anticipation she had also enjoyed, lying there across his thighs, eyes closed and holding her breath, waiting impatiently for him to carry on. Her whole bottom tingled. She had felt the material of her gown tighten over her cheeks as he stretched it over her behind. Then, at last, she felt it scrape upwards, flattening her flesh below it, making it bulge out as her most attractive feature was slowly exposed.

Carefully folding her gown around her waist, Bernard had studied her naked buttocks as thoroughly as ever, until she eventually broke the spell by moving her legs a little apart and cocking her bottom up towards his face in an unmistakable invitation. Sighing gustily, he had gripped a broad cheek in each hand and begun to knead them. Firmly. Shifting the flesh around. She knew that he was treating himself to a fine view of her neat, pinky-brown anus as he forced the cleft open. She had heard little squelchy sounds from between her thighs as her moistening slit opened and closed in time with her buttocks and felt a little flare of embarrassment, which had faded as the thrills invaded her. Then he reached down under the eiderdown, pulled up the front of his nightshirt and tucked his erection up so that it nestled between her hip and his belly.

Then, at last, he had spanked her. Crisply. Hard enough to make her ample bottom quiver, wobble and begin to warm up almost immediately, breaking off every so often to rub her, to part her cheeks again to look at her bottom-hole. Her 'Ooohs' and 'Aahs' were from pleasure not pain and after a while she had wriggled her left hand between them and found his rigid prick. That had been the beginning of the end as far as the spanking went as both were too excited to carry on for much longer and so, in a series of well-practised movements, she had ended up on her back, thighs raised and spread and her clothes pulled right up, giving him access to her plump breasts.

He had whisked up his nightshirt, clamped his mouth to her sex, sucked vigorously away at the exposed clitty and then moved up and slid into her in one easy movement. She had gasped and bucked as he filled her passage to bursting point, his weight squashing her hot, throbbing bottom into the bed . . .

She returned to the less pleasant – though strangely exciting – present, realising with a mixture of surprise and guilt that her nipples were stiff and her breathing was making them rub against the tickly cloth of the robe, which only made things worse. Father Dominic had neither spoken nor moved and suddenly a hot surge of shame flooded through her. She should not have exhibited herself so blatantly and was sorely tempted to let the back of the robe drop to cover her nakedness. She decided that there was no longer any point. Blushing furiously, she stared at the dust-covered window, unaware that her buttocks had clenched nervously.

It was this little movement which broke the spell. Father Dominic had been just as pre-occupied as she. The beauty of the woman's blatantly proffered bottom had held his eye like a magnet but, being the man he was, he did not lust after it or her. The rounded curves, the soft-looking cleft, the flawlessly smooth and white skin were there to receive the punishment which she had virtually begged for, which she obviously deserved and which he firmly believed would do her a power of good.

Nevertheless, he had been quite happy to stand and look at her with the same awe with which he had gazed at the magnificence of Michelangelo's ceiling in the Sistine Chapel.

Then she had clenched it. The movement had a surprising effect. As the smoothness of the curves tightened, the cleft narrowed and little dimples appeared. Slowly it relaxed, resuming its previous air of vulnerable softness and the good Father stepped forward, no longer in any doubt that he was about to give this worthy but erring woman a lesson which would set her back on the straight and narrow path of righteousness. Her bare bottom may have been exceptionally beautiful but he had resisted all temptation. He cleared his throat.

'Reach forward and grasp the further side of the table.' Heaving a sigh of relief, she did so, glad that he did not seem to be angry with her for baring her bottom in such a forward manner. She curled her fingers round the edge, turned her head to her right and rested her cheek on her upper arm. The other edge was digging into the fronts of her thighs and she eased her hips back. The only remaining problem was exactly how to position her feet. Close together, that was obvious. It would be utterly wrong to expose her femininity to that extent. And if she tucked her knees under the table the display would be just as blatant, so she slid her feet back until her legs sloped in a straight line to the stone floor. She sensed him picking up the belt, held her breath and waited.

Father Dominic was now all brisk efficiency. He gripped the buckle, wrapped the first part round his fist, leaving perhaps half a metre free, moved to her left side, raised his arm and swept the supple length of leather down across the plumpest part of his target.

The effect pleased him. Her bottom quivered in the most appealing way as the *thwack* of the impact rang through the room, he heard a sharp intake of breath and a pink band appeared like magic right where he had aimed. He waited for her to compose herself for the next stroke, the belt dangling down along his leg.

'Father, I hardly felt that one!' Her voice was low and steady and she turned her head towards him, her eyes glinting at him from the shadow of the deep hood. 'I do not think that it should count towards my dozen.'

He gaped at her, totally taken aback. As far as he could see it had been a perfectly good stroke, which had left a clear welt across the white skin. He gathered his wits. 'It is not my intention to flog you, my daughter. Just to remind you of the error of your ways.'

'I understand, Father. But I am not a tender maiden and, though my flesh may look as soft as a child's, I assure you that it is well hardened. I have sinned, and therefore my punishment has to be severe enough to make me truly repentant. Otherwise it would be a waste of your time and effort.'

Father Dominic smiled to himself. It suddenly occurred to him that if woman could withstand the agonies of childbirth, then perhaps twelve slaps with a belt were of little account. Especially when the belt had been softened by age and hard use. He stood back a little, raised his arm right to his shoulder so that his implement hung down his back, then drove it onto the patiently waiting buttocks with almost full force, accelerating the sweep of his arm at the end, so that the leather sank deeply into her flesh.

That was much better. Her bottom wobbled, she lurched against the edge of the table, her head jerked upwards and she wiggled her hips, shaking the flesh around so that the wobbles continued for some time after the belt had fallen away. She gave out a little cry and this time the stripe was a bright red.

'Yes, Father, that was much more effective. Oooh, it burns like the fires of hell.' Then, amazingly, she settled back down and lifted her bottom up, as though welcoming another fiery swathe of pain. In a clear voice, she called out, 'Forgive my sins, oh Lord. First stroke.'

He took careful aim at the first, discounted weal and laid in with aplomb. Again the reaction was all that he could have wished for, even though she had obviously steeled herself to the extent that she did not cry out. But she could not stop her breath hissing through her teeth. Wiggling her hips around briskly, she resumed her position and repeated her little formula.

'Forgive my sins, oh Lord. Second stroke.'

59

The third landed above the red band, leaving room for just one more before the top of her cleft indicated the upper limit of the target. Then there was room for two more below, though the sixth landed half on bottom, half on thighs. At each, her reactions hardly changed. Except that she could no longer resist crying out. Otherwise, he grew increasingly impressed with the way she was taking what was quite a severe beating.

'Would you like a short rest, my daughter?' he asked kindly.

'Oh thank you, Father.'

With a loud sigh, she straightened up and rubbed frantically at her injured rear, her hands shaking it about like a huge red blancmange. Embarrassed, he looked away. Intrigued, he looked back again. After a minute or two, she sighed and bent over again, carefully adjusting the position of her feet to maintain some semblance of modesty. He could not resist a closer inspection of his handiwork. Both buttocks were a bright, glowing red and, where the weals overlapped, almost crimson. He noticed that the flesh on her right flank was slightly puffy, indicating that the very end of the belt was the most effective part.

He then did something which changed his life. Only a small thing and one which took quite a long time to have any effect – he rested his hand on the right cheek of her bottom and then ran it gently over the cleft and onto the left one. He then smoothed that side from top to bottom and did the same to the other. At the time, he was left with little more than a fleeting impression of softness and warmth, but as the days passed, the memory of the feel of the first female behind he had ever touched kept returning to haunt him. For the moment, his thoughts were only concerned with the second part.

'I am ready, Father.' *Thwack!* 'Aaahhh! Forgive my sins, oh Lord. Seventh stroke. Oh, I certainly felt that one. You are re-visiting parts which have already tasted the belt, Father.'

Thwack! 'Owwww. Forgive my sins, oh Lord. Eighth stroke.' Her feet eased further forward, her bottom

rounded and the long cleft widened. He aimed at the base.
Thwack!

'Owwwww, *aahhh*. Oh Mary Mother of God, forgive me
my sins. Stroke number ten. Please, Father, let me catch
my breath.' She gasped, panted and wriggled for several
minutes before sticking her bottom out again.

Thwack! Right across the middle. Her hands flew behind
her, kneading and rubbing as she tried to choke back her
sobs.

'Forgive my sins, oh Lord. Last stroke.'

Crying softly, she leaned forward to grip the edge of the
table and then painfully presented herself for the final
smack, which snaked across the upper parts. She burst into
tears and flopped over the table, her hips bucking and
weaving unashamedly.

Father Dominic, breathing heavily, tossed the belt onto
the table and left the room, but not before he had had a final,
lingering look at her beetroot-coloured posterior. Nor could
he resist another touch, marvelling at the heat of her skin.

She heard the door close behind her, straightened up
painfully, untied the sash, squealing as the coarse material
slithered down over her buttocks. She heaved it back up
over her head and thankfully replaced it with the silk of
her shift.

There was a wash-stand in the corner of the room and
she splashed her face, then with sudden inspiration, filled
the basin, placed it on the floor, bared her bottom again
and lowered it into the cold water, groaning with relief.
Then she dried herself, finished dressing and walked slowly
home, where the obvious course of action was to slip up to
her bedroom, strip naked and lie down on her face with a
wet cloth draped comfortably over her throbbing bottom.

She slept like a log that night and the next day, threw
herself into her normal life with renewed energy and purpose. It was quite a long time before the impure thoughts
started to nag her again.

Sherrie focused on Sir James' face. He was staring out of
the window at the clouds below, looking a little tense but

totally involved in her story. When she stopped, his eyes swivelled round and locked onto hers.

'Interesting . . .' he said thoughtfully. 'One thing that I'm not totally clear about is whether she got a sexual kick from being strapped. It's pretty obvious that she did when her husband spanked her in bed, but that was a sort of foreplay.'

'Yes, she did. Indirectly. She was fairly well conditioned, of course. As you said, he used to warm her bare bottom up for her before making love from time to time, and, as she said in the Confessional, he used to take his belt to her occasionally. That would be frowned on now, but in those days, a wife who was given a dozen moderate strokes on her backside would have counted herself well-loved compared to the majority, who were literally beaten up. And had no one to turn to for help.'

'That I do not approve of!'

'I'm delighted to hear it, Sir James. But going back to Madame Lefarge's feelings, don't forget that she had been without her very loving husband for several months and was pretty frustrated. Her main motivation was a genuine need to pay for her sins but it was this frustration which made her blurt out the fact that she was used to having her bum smacked when she had strayed from the straight and narrow. And I mentioned in the last story that the female bottom is a key element. We are used to having our behinds treated as objects of sexual desire. Sometimes we are very happy with the attention, at other times far from it. But in her case, she instinctively knew that she was quite safe with Father Dominic. Apart from the disciplines of his calling, he was a good man and had never taken advantage of anyone. But he was also young and handsome enough to make exposing herself to him quite exciting.'

'Yes, it does make sense, I suppose. What doesn't, to me, is that he didn't get turned on . . .' Sir James closed his eyes, obviously conjuring up a vision of the events seen through the Father's eyes. 'I mean, she was obviously lovely . . . and the contrast between the rough old robe and her bare bottom and legs must have been incredibly sexy. I'm sure it would have blown my socks off!'

Sherrie laughed. 'As I said, he was a good man with deep convictions. He could see her as something very beautiful and be sympathetic to her desires to suffer physical pain – don't forget that corporal punishment was very common and considered very beneficial – but his training and nature had sublimated his desires almost completely.'

'But you said that when he touched her bottom, it changed his life. How?'

'I'll carry on.' Sherrie replied.

Madame Lefarge was not the only grass widow. With hardly an able-bodied man in the village, most wives were in the same boat, not forgetting that there were several widows – those whose husbands had already been killed in the war.

Some weeks after her beating, Madame Lefarge was having supper with one of her few close friends, a Madame Neige, whose husband was the local apothecary. With great daring, they had opened two bottles of Monsieur Lefarge's best wine and so, with their tongues loosened, they exchanged confidences. Claire Neige did not share her friend's beauty, but nevertheless was a very striking woman, with golden hair and a lovely pale complexion. She had been born and raised in Normandy, which accounted for her colouring – all the other women in the village were local and so typically Mediterranean in appearance.

'I do not know whether it is right to confide in you, Madame Lefarge, because you seem to bear the absence of your husband with great courage and your moods seem to be as cheerful as they ever were. I, by contrast, seem to be in a permanent ill-humour. And my thoughts stray during the lonely nights . . .'

'My dear Madame,' replied Madame Lefarge, 'if you think that I do not miss my beloved husband, then you are very much mistaken. I suggest that you confess fully to Father Dominic the next time you go to Confessional – he was of great assistance to me when I was as troubled as you are.'

And so Madame Neige duly confessed and Father Dominic understood. Five minutes later, she was bending over the table, her nice big bottom as bare as Madame Lefarge's had been and almost as tempting.

Once again, the good Father was stopped in his tracks at the sight awaiting him. His second victim was considerably broader in the beam than the first, but her skin was even paler and she had braced herself by placing her legs some distance apart, so that a few little golden curls of pubic hair peeped out from the junction of her sturdy thighs.

Her buttocks wobbled even more, but she was less accustomed to being spanked and was crying pitifully after the sixth stroke, although she kept her position bravely until the end. Once again, Father Dominic stroked her red flesh at the end and for the second time marvelled at the quality of it.

Madame Neige had recovered by the following morning and, like her predecessor, found that her punishment had given her a new zest for life. The blood fizzed through her veins and there was a determined spring in her step. A day or so later, she hinted to the schoolmistress that she should go to confession: she did, and Father Dominic was treated to the sight of a third female bottom all out on display, this one slender but with a charming chubbiness to it.

A month after her first visit, Madame Lefarge felt the need for a second, by which time Father Dominic had come to the obvious conclusion that there was hardly a single member of his depleted flock who would not benefit from a dose of the belt. In no time at all, he had intimate knowledge of nearly every bottom in the village. Only those under eighteen and over sixty were spared. The former were told to go to their mothers for a sound spanking and the latter that they were too close to the time when they would be meeting their Maker to behave badly. Both approaches proved successful.

In fact one of the mothers had been so impressed by the improvement in her daughter's attitude that she had asked the Father to give her the same treatment, thus furthering his education considerably. Ignoring his muttered protests, she had led him to a suitable chair in the Vestry, made him sit down, plonked herself over his knees and hauled up her skirt and shift to present him with a plump and comely bottom. After the first feel of its yielding softness under his nervous palm, his initial misgivings had evaporated and he had whaled away at her quivering cheeks with great enthusiasm and growing expertise.

From that moment, minor sins were inevitably atoned for by a good spanking on the sinner's bare bottom. The belt was kept in reserve for more serious ones – and for Madame Lefarge, to whom a simple spanking was far too much of a reminder of her husband. Only the belt could make her feel that she had paid for her misdemeanours and she began to call on the Father once a week. Every time, as she bared her backside and slowly bent across the table, she swore that it would be the last occasion that she would submit to the stinging bite of the supple length of leather. But every time she walked home, with her buttocks throbbing hotly behind her, she rejoiced in the release of tension. With the blood sparkling through her veins, she knew that she would be back.

Once again Sherrie paused. Sir James stared out of the window.

'Nice job, the Priesthood,' he said. 'Rotten pay, of course, but excellent perks!' He turned to look at Sherrie and they grinned at each other.

'There's more, Sir James.'

'Good. Please carry on.'

Well, every few months, Father Dominic visited a nearby Convent to assist in the spiritual needs of the nuns. It was an enjoyable duty, as the Mother Superior was an intellectually challenging woman and he had always found their discussions highly stimulating. It had also done his soul good to be at one with the simple devoutness of the Sisters, to concentrate wholly on religious essentials, away from the distractions of his flock.

However, on his next visit, he strode through the fields and up the hill to the Convent with less than his usual enthusiasm. His unusual methods were showing every sign of working and he was loath to leave his congregation even for a few days, just in case his absence led to a slide back to the bad old ways. Plus, with his normal honesty, he acknowledged that he had grown to enjoy the punishments.

He had never spanked or beaten a woman against her will and therefore his conscience was quite clear. On the other hand, he always felt a strange and pleasant excitement whenever he led an erring female into that dusty room. And again, as he strode up the last hill to the lonely, grey stone Convent, he honestly acknowledged that he would miss the sight of his flock's naked bottoms, the ringing sound of his hand on their flesh and, most of all, the wonderful softness of their buttocks.

Later that evening, he and the Mother Superior were discussing the knotty problem of how many angels could fit onto the head of a pin, when he noticed that she lacked her usual concentration.

'I have a problem which is vexing me more than somewhat, Father,' she admitted eventually. 'Some of our novices are showing signs of a lack of devotion to their calling – sometimes I despair of the young. In my day ... well, be that as it may, but – and I hope that what I am about to confide in you will not destress you too much, Father – I know that several of them are seeking non-spiritual comfort from each other.'

Father Dominic blinked at the troubled woman opposite. 'How do you know?'

'Yesterday, I went into one of the cells to see why the occupant had not attended Matins and found two of them curled up in each other's arms.'

'Oh dear, oh dear. And what action have you taken?'

'I have – after a severe reprimand – put them in solitary confinement on a bread and water diet.'

'I see.' Father Dominic stared thoughtfully at the far wall. 'I assume that you have doubts as to the effectiveness of the measures you have taken, Mother Superior.'

'Yes, Father. I cannot help but feel that they will not pass their solitary hours in proper contemplation.'

'I agree.' He silently thanked Madame Lefarge for having provided him with knowledge of a way of dealing with the problem. If this had arisen during a previous visit, he knew he would have felt totally lost. 'Their sins are of the flesh and therefore punishment should be addressed to the flesh as well as to the mind.'

He turned and met the Mother Superior's eyes as he spoke. Her lovely, calm face broke into a relieved smile as his full meaning struck her and her wide brown eyes gleamed in the flickering light of the taper on her desk.

'You are right, Father. I was scourged as a novice – not for any particular sin, simply to remind me of the weakness of the flesh and to improve the strength of my devotion. I feel that perhaps I owe my present position to that early training. Alas, we seem to have lost that sense of discipline. Yes, Father, we shall re-introduce it and I have every confidence that we shall reach new heights of spiritual devotion. Now, should the discipline be superior or inferior?'

'Ah, the upper or lower back. Let me consider the matter properly. I am tired and I would like to pray for guidance.'

'Of course, Father. Let me accompany you to your cell. Would you like some food?'

'That would be most kind.'

And so Father Dominic considered the matter while he ate his simple supper of bread, cheese and fruit and, after Matins the following morning, he and the Mother Superior met again in her room.

'I have decided that in view of their youthfulness and of the particular sin, that inferior discipline would have a greater effect.' He did not see her smile, nor the gleam in her eyes.

'And with what implement, Father?'

'What would you suggest?'

'I was beaten with a seven-tailed whip – a version of the scourge used in the time of our Lord.'

'I see. And do you have such an instrument to hand?'

'No, Father, but I am sure that Sister Francesca, who is in charge of the stables, would be able to fashion one.'

67

'Excellent. But tell her not to make it too severe. She must soften the leather strips. Nor must she make them too long.'

'I understand, Father.'

And so, after Mass the next morning, the two miscreants were punished. As the choir sang the 'Misère', the first one was led slowly down the aisle to the table placed in front of the altar. Her moist eyes were raised heavenwards, her face pale but composed under the shadow of her cowl, her hands clasped in front of her in prayer. The candles flickered and the early morning sun sent beams of multi-coloured light through the stained-glass windows. The novice came to a halt in front of the table and her eyes fell on the sinister whip draped threateningly across the top. She shuddered visibly and then raised her head again. Her quavering voice could be heard joining the choir in her own supplication. Silence fell.

'Raise your habit to above your waist, my child.' The Mother Superior's voice was firm and severe. The novice looked at her in horror and the gasp of surprise from the congregation echoed through the chapel. But that was the limit of her protest at the appalling indignity of her fate. Her trembling hands gripped her skirts and began to haul them up as all eyes were glued on the sight of the slow exposure of her legs, thighs and finally her buttocks.

They were quite gorgeous. Plump, firm, round, divided by a deep and tight cleft, they caused several hearts to flutter and even Father Dominic held his breath while he made a rapid mental comparison with Madame Lefarge's more mature but equally splendid bottom.

Then they changed shape as the girl bent over the table, growing rounder and broader as she stretched out to grip the further edge. Her legs were straight, so that her body formed a perfect right angle and she was ready. The choir gave voice again as the Mother Superior picked up the whip, moved into position, raised it until the thongs hung down her back and then swept them down firmly right across the full spread of naked flesh, leaving a clear pattern of thin pink lines across the whiteness of her skin.

The girl's howl cut through the clear harmony and she

rolled her buttocks around with almost sensual slowness as the sting bit deep. The voices in the choir soared in a lovely descant as the Mother Superior continued in a slow, methodical rhythm and, as the novice grew used to the pain, her wails changed to a brave attempt to join in the 'Ave Maria' and she pressed her bosom to the table, pushing her blushing bottom upwards to meet the whip as it fell across it.

The other nuns and novices began to sing but the punished girl's voice could be heard clearly lamenting her sins and begging forgiveness as her plump cheeks grew steadily redder and redder. Then she began to churn her hips almost frantically and her pleas became shrill and hysterical. Finally, she slumped, her knees relaxed and fell apart. The choir came to the end of their passage and the sounds of the final few strokes were greeted in silence. The girl was moaning quietly, but not purely in pain. Each *thwack* of leather on naked flesh was greeted with an ecstatic wail and a heartfelt 'mea culpa'.

Eventually the Mother Superior's voice rang clearly through the chapel. 'You may rise, my child.'

The young girl struggled to her feet, then turned and sank to her knees, kissing the older woman's boots, wriggling as her robes rubbed against her sore bottom. She stood up again and they could see that the tears pouring down her face were in complete contrast to the fulfilled smile and the shining eyes. With a firm step and with her mouth moving to the words of her silent prayer, she walked back down the aisle and sat down firmly in her normal place.

The second sinner had not had the best view of the proceedings but had been able to see the initial white gleam of her colleague's bare bottom being turned scarlet and had been terrified out of her wits to begin with. But then she had heard her friend's cries as they changed from pain and fear to something else and her resolve had grown. By the time her turn came she was determined to be equally capable of taking her medicine, if not more so. Before the Mother Superior could signal her, she heaved up the back of her habit and tucked it into the sash, revelling in the feel of the cool air on her naked skin.

With her head held high, she strode up the aisle to the waiting table, the twinkling sway of her naked rear holding the full attention of the congregation, and when she came up to the Mother Superior, she knelt at her feet.

'Mother, I have sinned and welcome the scourging I am about to receive. Please whip the evil from my flesh with the full force of your arm.'

She stood up, moved to the table and bent gracefully forward, displaying a slimmer bottom than her predecessor's, but one which was just as white and soft. The choir gave voice, a bright ray of sunshine bathed the rounded and well-divided cheeks and then the whip whistled down and she cried out as though welcoming the sting. Encouraged and inspired by the example of her friend, she was even braver. Her voice was stronger, not faltering until the second dozen had been delivered, and then it broke. But again, there was no despair in her. And, at the end, she too kissed the Mother Superior's feet and returned proudly to her seat.

Father Dominic had watched all this with growing satisfaction. The scourging may have been rather more severe than he would have dished out, but then these were novice nuns who had already shown a spiritual strength and therefore needed a sharper lesson than a distracted housewife.

He was not altogether surprised that, when he took Confession, several of the sisters led him to sentencing them to a similar form of repentance.

So, after every Mass for the remainder of his stay, as many as half a dozen of them followed the example set by the second of the novices and walked bare-bottomed up the aisle to the waiting table and offered themselves to the whip.

He strode back to his village after a longer than usual stay, confident that the Convent would now reach new heights of devotion. He was looking forward to renewing his assault on the varied bottoms of his flock.

Sir James looked hard at Sherrie. 'That was incredible, it really was. But did any of them get sexually turned on? Did they come?'

'Not properly. But a woman's sexuality is very different to a man's, don't forget. The atmosphere, the music, the sense of guilt at being caught with another girl, the rare sight of prominently displayed – and very pretty – bare bottoms, all combined to produce a surge of sensuality. In Madame Lefarge's case, her thoughts were turned to memories of her husband, whereas with the nuns it was all about spiritual rather than sexual ecstasy.'

'I see. Oh God, my ears have just popped. We can't be there already! Yes, damn it, we are. Sherrie, I can't wait another two days. I've got to see your bare bottom now. Otherwise I'll bloody well burst.'

'Well, I'm not sure, Sir James . . . it's a lot to ask of an innocent young girl . . . all right, all right, stay where you are – there isn't time to spank me anyway. There, I'll hold my skirt up and you can pull my knickers down . . .' She paused as he did as she had asked, 'Do you like it?'

'Very, very much.'

Chapter 4

'Before you ask, Sherrie, the meetings went extremely well, we've done even more to increase our liquidity and cut our borrowings and everything is going swimmingly. Now we've got a nice long flight to Hawaii and I'm hungry and thirsty, so as soon as we've taken off, I want you to take all your clothes off and bring me – or rather bring us – a bottle of that excellent Krug and a light lunch. You will not overload the tray, because I want to see you walk back up to the galley as often as possible. And unless I am totally satisfied with the amount of wiggle you put into your walk, I shall certainly spank you.'

'Yes SIR!' Sherrie replied with a happy grin. 'And will you want another story?'

'Of course. I can hardly wait. You are well named, aren't you, Scherezade? Wasn't she the wife of an Arabian prince, who fended off her husband's death sentence by keeping him amused for a thousand and one nights?'

'That's right. And as a little girl I was always spinning yarns so my parents started calling me that. Then it was Sherrie for short.'

'What's your real name?'

'Cheryl.'

'Quite close, then. Not that it matters – I like Sherrie.' He smiled. 'Now, while we're taking off, belt yourself in and start your story. Get me in the mood. Or to be more accurate, get me even more in the mood!'

'Right, Sir James . . . any thoughts on the theme?'

'Not really. As long as female bottoms feature – and punishment.'

72

'Well, let's see. We've covered formal CP but with erotic undertones . . .'

We'll move on a year or so. To 1814. After he had been beaten in Russia and with Wellington going great guns in the south, Napoleon surrendered and was exiled to Elba. The victorious allies celebrated the restitution of the monarchy in Paris and then gathered in Vienna for the Congress which was, everyone hoped, to decide the destiny of the world. It was both socially and politically a glittering occasion.

A member of the British delegation was a certain Lady Harpwell, the wife of a successful Frigate Captain in the Royal Navy, who was still serving with the Mediterranean fleet. Her elder brother was a Colonel on the Duke of Wellington's staff – he had been appointed Britain's principal representative at the Congress – and her Ladyship was asked along to act as an extra hostess. Of high birth, incredibly beautiful and wealthy enough from both her own inheritance and her husband's prize money to hold her head up even in that amazing gathering, she soon created quite an impact.

So much so that there was some unwelcome gossip about her relationship with a rather dashing Hungarian Cavalry Colonel and, as her brother was away in London, an old family friend was summoned by the Duke to give her a stern lecture. The great man could not have chosen a better lecturer.

General Bracegirdle was another cavalryman, noted for his dash and courage in battle but less well-known for his similar qualities in the boudoir. Discretion in all things had been his motto – except when fighting the French! So when the Duke had a quiet word with him, his frown of disapproval was very convincing and nobody guessed that he had been planning Lady Harpwell's downfall for some time.

He waited for the right moment, which came a week or so later at a Ball at the Palace. He led her firmly off for a dance and, after they had finally swirled to a laughing halt,

73

took her off to a quiet corner of one of the refreshment rooms, where he gave her a brief outline of the situation.

She looked up at him and there was a gleam in her dark green eyes which belied her pale face and tightened lips.

'So I have been a wicked girl, have I General Brace-girdle? Am I to be chided and made to stand in a corner? Or am I to be treated as a responsible and grown woman and trusted to entertain our colleagues and allies in a due and proper manner?'

She had completely forgotten, but when she was eight or nine – some twenty years before – the then Major Brace-girdle had been given very good cause to turn her over his knee and dust the seat of her skirts for splashing him with water in the garden. He had not forgotten and her comments sealed her fate. Having said that, she would have probably ended up with a well smacked bottom anyway, because the General was an enthusiast of long standing. He stared down at her, his face grim but, like her, with a twinkle in his eyes.

'I shall call my carriage, we shall make our farewells and retire to my office where we can discuss the matter without interruption. I suggest that you give orders for your own carriage to be outside the Embassy doors in – let us say two hours. You have a quarter of an hour, Madam.'

Thirty minutes later they were facing each other again, this time in the quiet elegance of the General's office. The sentry at the end of the corridor, who was quite used to this sort of activity, had been ordered to allow no one to pass and, as soon as the last of the city's clocks had chimed twelve, the General began.

'To continue our conversation, Antonia, you know as well as I that your behaviour is beginning to set tongues wagging and that we can ill afford even the slightest scandal . . . do not interrupt, Madam. I accept that you have not overstepped the bounds of decency. Yet. Even so, I feel honour-bound to inform you that His Grace himself has noted your activities and it was he who asked me to speak to you. Now, in the beginning, your response to my comments was distinctly flippant. You asked me if I planned to

74

make you stand in a corner, suitably chided. Yes, I shall indeed make you stand in a corner. That one.'

The beautiful face in front of him paled and the generous mouth compressed with irritation. 'General Bracegirdle, will you please do me the honour of treating me like an adult. I totally refute your accusations and I have no intention of altering my behaviour. Do I make myself clear?'

'You do indeed, Madam.'

They looked steadily at each other. The tall, handsome cavalryman had a tight little smile and the lovely young woman was trembling visibly, pale and tense as she began to regret her various outbursts. His calmness was far more threatening than any show of temper.

Without another word he unbuckled his sword belt, letting it clatter to the floor. Slowly unbuttoning his uniform jacket, he took it off and hung it carefully on the back of a convenient chair. Still staring at her, still smiling, he began to roll up his sleeves.

Lady Harpwell knew what was about to happen to her. Her plea to be treated as an adult was going to be totally ignored and her earlier remarks about being ticked off like a little girl were about to rebound on her with a vengeance. She was going to have her bottom smacked! Her first reaction was, naturally, to protest. Violently. But then she realised that her behaviour had been thoroughly reprehensible and maybe she did deserve to be punished. On top of that, General Bracegirdle was extremely handsome, with thighs sturdy enough to make an exciting platform and a muscular right arm which would produce the sort of effect on her flesh which she secretly desired. Her bottom began to tingle and her heart thudded in her chest. For the first time since they left the Palace, her face softened into a smile and she reached behind her and began to pull up her gown.

The General had been prepared for an undignified struggle and a certain amount of earthy language which most would have considered very unseemly from the full lips of such a lovely lady. He had known her for a long time and was very aware that her temperament matched the fiery colour of her hair. He was, therefore, taken aback when he saw the temper fade from her expression and noticed that her hands were busying themselves with her clothing. This was indeed a promising start, he said to himself, and stood silently gazing into her eyes until she stopped fidgeting. He then looked down. Her skirts were bunched up round her waist and were held in place by the pressure of her arms. She had been careful not to pull up the front any further than she had to, though. Her shapely calves, plump knees and the tops of her stockings were exposed and an inch or so of white thigh gleamed in the candlelight. That was all. But then, it was the back aspects which mattered, so, without a word, he moved slowly round to view them.

Her naked buttocks were everything a red-blooded man could wish for. As he paused at her side, he noted the outward curve from her loins, the smoothness of the skin on her flanks and the way her cheek slanted inwards to the top of her thigh; then he moved a bit further and could see the long cleft in the middle. Finally he stood directly behind her and sighed audibly at the full view. He saw that although she was firm enough, the softness of her flesh was evident from the little quivers as she shifted her weight uneasily. Her skin was flawlessly white and looked as if it was as soft as silk.

He reached down and cupped her right cheek and it was as yieldingly firm as he had thought; and smooth; and warm. He sighed again and she must have heard him, because he felt her press herself against his palm.

'Strewth, what an image!' Sir James remarked. 'Right, Sherrie, we must have reached cruising altitude now, so we'll have a little break, I think. If I remember correctly, you were going to strip naked and go and get lunch!'

Sherrie stood up, bent down to give him a quick kiss and then straightened up and began to undo the buttons of her crisp, white blouse, deliberately avoiding his eye as her hands moved downwards, not wanting to distract him.

It would have taken quite a lot to have distracted Sir James, although to begin with he felt strangely uneasy. Was she angry or resentful at being ordered to take her clothes off? Then he saw the happy little smile on her face, relaxed and settled down to enjoy what was happening.

The blouse was unbuttoned, taken off and folded carefully over the back of the nearest seat. Her bra was small, white and looked expensive, even to his untutored eye, moulding her breasts into a curving cleavage. Various impressions flashed through his mind as she dropped her hands to her sides and slowly swayed the upper half of her body to and fro, giving him ample time to take in the detail as well as an overall impression.

She was in terrific shape, he noticed with a pang of envy. Slim, but not skinny. Her upper arms were round and firm, he could only just make out the ridges of her ribs and there was only a slight bulge of flesh above the waistband of her skirt. Her skin had a tint of olive and was lovely and smooth. Her breasts were full. And paler than the rest of her.

He leaned further forward as her hand came up to the side of her skirt and undid the button before easing down the zip. She then started to slide it down over her hips and legs before stepping gracefully out of it and straightening up again. He let out his breath and sat back in his seat for a better, full-length, view.

Her knickers and suspenders were also white, obviously matching her bra, her stockings were a light tan. He saw that her waist was narrower and her hips even rounder than he had thought. Her thighs were long and lovely. There was a little indentation in the lower part of the 'V' of her knickers where the material clung to the cleft. His eyes swept up and down her body, then to her face. She was looking at him solemnly, neither flirtatious nor embarrassed.

'You are much, much lovelier than I even thought possible.' His softly spoken compliment was received with a shy smile and then Sherrie's hands moved up to her back and her bra was suddenly loose, her breasts quivering firmly.

She moved her left hand to the front, holding the wisp of white to her, hiding her nipples for another moment or so. She let the right side slip and bared that breast completely. It was bigger than he had expected and the nipple smaller. Pink against creamy white. And beautiful. As was the left one when she bared that and tossed the bra onto the chair with the rest of her clothes.

Again she stood still for several minutes, letting him study her properly. There was a pink flush on her face, which charmed him. Then she gently swung her torso from side to side and her breasts swayed with independent softness.

Once again he ran his eyes down the full length of her, pausing at her nice little tummy-button. Then he spotted a tiny moist patch on her knickers and caught his breath again as he realised that she was as turned on as he was. He sat back in an attempt to relax a little. Until she turned round to present her rear view and he found himself leaning forward again.

Her knickers were not only on the brief side but her various movements had drawn them up into her bottom-cleft, so that the lower bulges were bare, as were the twin folds where buttocks met thighs. Sir James stared. Once again he felt a bit uneasy at the thought of this exceptionally attractive and highly intelligent woman posing in front of him like a stripper. He cleared his throat and she immediately reassured him by reaching for the waistband of her knickers and easing them slowly down. She paused when they were just clear of her bottom, then pulled them right down to her ankles, bending slowly, allowing him to savour the gradual broadening and tightening of her cheeks to the full. She held her fully-bent position for quite a time and Sir James began to appreciate what he had been missing in life.

Her bottom was so firm that the length of the cleft hardly altered and only a slight widening of the gap near the base hinted at the position of her anus. An inch or so below that point, at the junction of bottom and legs, her sex lips peeped through, diamond shaped, the dark hair obviously trimmed, as the tight line of her slit was clearly visible.

His prick was straining against his trousers and his hands itched for the feel of her. From her attitude right from the beginning, he knew that for some inexplicable reason, she would do anything he wanted, but she had already got so far under his skin and her honest and relaxed attitude to sex was so refreshing that any form of compulsion was unthinkable. It would be far better to take things in easy stages and to move to her rhythm. He leaned right forward and kissed her gently on the tight crown of each cheek. Her skin was as silky as he had hoped. His nostrils flared as her scent reached them.

She slipped her knickers off her feet and stood upright again, making him contemplate the difficult problem of whether her bottom was nicer bent or in its normal position.

'Shall I take my stockings off, Sir James?'

'No, I don't think so. If you don't mind leaving them on, that is,' he added hastily.

'Whatever you like. Actually, I think a girl looks sexier with something on – and I've made sure that the back suspenders are round to the side so that they don't cover up any of my bottom.'

'Yes, so I see . . . Sherrie, you are seriously beautiful.'

'Thank you, Sir James.'

'The pleasure is all mine! Now would you like some help with the lunch?'

'Certainly not. You sit and relax. I'll be as quick as I can.'

She set off up the aisle to the galley and Sir James learned that watching a bare-bottomed girl walking away is one of nature's greatest sights! He sighed deeply and sat gazing out at the clouds, then remembered that she had set off for the galley before he had had time to examine her from the front. With another sigh, he anticipated that pleasure and then began to work out how he was going to broach the subject of spanking her. That thought reminded him of the sight of her jiggling bottom as she walked away and his erection started to feel very constricted. By the time he had made the necessary adjustments,

Sherrie had appeared at the forward part of the cabin, smiling happily – and carrying a solitary glass!

The following few moments taught Sir James that more often than not, the simple pleasures are the best. She walked towards him, her firm breasts swaying and bouncing delightfully and the movement of her thighs drawing his eyes to the neat triangle of dark hair where they joined.

She turned her back on him, bent down to put the glass on the table and walked back up to the galley. It may have taken an extraordinarily long time to fetch everything required for the lunch but, for once, Sir James was more than happy about the slow service and when she finally sat down opposite him, he felt that he had begun to know her body quite well.

The food and drink provided a perfect distraction and in no time he was completely at ease. Her nudity did not seem to bother her one iota and therefore he was soon able to look at her breasts and legs quite unselfconsciously. They talked normally.

'I've been thinking about my country house, Sherrie. I hardly ever use it – in fact I bought it as much for the investment as anything and, remembering what you said earlier about the UK housing market, I'm beginning to think that it would be a good time to sell. I'd make a good profit on it.'

'A good idea. And it might also pay you to go as liquid as possible. Personally, I mean. If you . . .'

So by the time that they had finished, Sir James was switched on and ready for the second instalment of her story. He was even more ready after Sherrie had cleared away, treating him not only to splendid views of her comings and goings, but having also dropped the empty champagne bottle. This had then conveniently rolled under her seat and she had then had to kneel down to find it. He saw her anus for the first time, had initially looked away but had very quickly fixed his eyes on it again and had found it surprisingly appealing.

At last she was back in her seat.

'Now if I remember rightly, the General was stroking her Ladyship's bare bottom,' Sir James prompted her.

That's right. And, as I said, it was an exceptionally lovely one. He knelt behind her, examining it thoroughly, a process which she enjoyed nearly as much as he did, apart from anything else because she had so much confidence in her attractiveness that she was convinced that the sight of her like that would soon distract him from the punishment. Like most women of those days, she had tasted the normal variety of spanking implements in her life, up to and including the birch from her Governess, so had not faced the prospect of discipline with the dread which might have afflicted a complete novice. On the other hand, she had no desire to submit to the humiliation and pain unless there was no alternative. In this case, she hoped that the nakedness of the lower part of her body would suggest a very obvious – and much nicer – alternative to the General. Little did she know that there was little he liked better than a plump bare bottom at his mercy.

So, when he finally stood up and began to carry an armless chair into the centre of the room, she wondered if her charms were beginning to fade.

'Are you truly going to chastise me, General Bracegirdle?'

'I am.'

Holding her breath, she raised the front of her gown, blushing as he stared stonily at the rich red triangle of hair. 'Can you not consider another use for your right hand?'

'Perhaps.' His cold eyes met hers again as he sat down. 'But later. Place yourself across my knees. At once, Madam.'

His parade-ground bark rocked her back on her heels, she let her skirts fall to the ground and, with all the dignity she could muster, she obeyed him, hoping that he would not consider raising her skirts again, then realising that her hopes were completely futile as she felt his hands carefully begin the laborious process of hauling skirt and undergarments up her legs, over her bottom and onto the small of

81

her back. With her weight evenly distributed between hands, middle and feet, she found her position rather more comfortable than she expected and when the raising of her shift finally exposed her, she was reasonably relaxed.

Which was rather more than could be said of General Bracegirdle. If his first view of her bottom had excited him, the gradual undressing had left him seething with impatience as he reached down for the final garment. Her shift was of the same high quality as the rest of her clothes and therefore of much finer material than he was used to. He could clearly see a shadowy line bisecting the target area and it was only the sensual instincts of an experienced lecher which stopped him ripping it upwards.

Instead, he curbed his impatience and inched her last defence upwards with great care, his eyes gleaming wickedly as the first inches of white skin appeared. He paused when her rounded thighs were half bare, and again when the base of her bottom peeped out – two clean-cut folds, twin chubby crescents of white flesh and an inch or so of her deep cleft curving down to disappear between her legs. He ran the tip of his forefinger down the bared part of cleft and along each fold. She hissed and wriggled on his lap. He bared some more and pinched and prodded the crowns of each cheek. He was ready.

Poor Lady Harpwell was in a turmoil. The memories of her previous spankings were vague and consisted mainly of a flurry of activity, which ended with her closely studying the floor and feeling temporarily cool and very vulnerable, immediately followed by a more or less prolonged assault which had always been noisy and painful.

This time the baring had been as prolonged as her previous spankings and while part of her longed for the preparations to continue, she was also horribly aware that his deliberate approach would probably be applied to the actual punishment and therefore she was in for a very sore bottom indeed. In a last-ditch attempt to soften his resolve, she tried the obvious ploy of using her bare bottom to seduce him, weaving it slowly around on his lap, clenching and relaxing the broadened cheeks, rubbing her tummy against his legs and smiling in triumph when she felt a lump under her left hip.

General Bracegirdle watched her oscillating rump and also smiled. She was proving even more rewarding than he had thought possible! He stroked and paddled her buttocks; he prised them apart and openly studied her neat little bottom-hole, making her gasp, first with outrage, then with pleasure as she found the sensation unexpectedly pleasant. At last, he carefully put his left arm across the small of her back, gripped her left hipbone tightly and administered the first spank. It landed crisply right across both sides; her bottom quivered delightfully and a pink, hand-shaped patch sprung up almost at once. She jerked and squeaked. The second landed in exactly the same place and got a similar reaction. As did the first dozen, after which he paused to admire the bright red patch.

With the methodical approach of the successful military man, seasoned with a cavalryman's flair and the creativity of a true sensualist, he continued in the same vein. A hand-sized area of her bottom was carefully selected and treated to a rhythmic dozen until her entire rump shone like a beacon in the subdued light.

The first phase of the assault successfully accomplished, it was time for the second. Using just his fingertips, he flicked away at the few pale bits he could see until her whole behind was more or less the same colour. Then he leaned back, studied the target area with some satisfaction and devoted a little of his attention to her Ladyship. He had been vaguely aware of a certain amount of kicking and wriggling; of the occasional gasp and several fairly loud 'ow's and 'ouch's from over to his left but he felt that she had, on the whole, behaved with the sort of decorum one would expect from a lady of her station in life, and he was impressed by the way she was now lying reasonably still and completely silently over his legs. As a reward, he ran his hand gently over her hot, soft skin.

'Oh, General, that is delightfully soothing.'

Her voice was higher-pitched than normal, but she was clearly keeping herself under control and his respect grew.

This, coupled with the feel of her naked flesh revived his erection until he began to feel a little uncomfortable and this inspired him to begin Phase Three. He tightened the grip of his left hand and set about her again, this time with sharp little spanks which danced all over both sides, in a rapid, staccato rhythm which soon had her bobbing, weaving and kicking her legs in dismay.

The combination of his smacks and her movements set her fat bottom wobbling like a great jelly – one which was quickly changing from raspberry to cherry! She was also much more vocal and by the time he finished and slumped breathless against the back of his chair, she was sobbing like a child. He waited until her wrigglings died down.

'You may rub your bottom, Antonia.'

'Oh, thank you, Sir!' Her hands flew back and desperately clawed away at her blazing rear end, shifting the ample flesh in every direction, obviously not aware that her actions frequently exposed both the lower part of her sex and her anus.

Showing the sort of consideration which made him so popular, General Bracegirdle reached down with his left hand, placed it on her bosom and supported the upper part of her body, making it far easier for her to rub and sooth her bottom. He was slightly surprised that she did not thank him for his gesture but forgave her on the grounds that she was clearly pre-occupied with her bottom.

To her surprise, Lady Harpwell had found the whole experience quite exciting. Possibly the memory of the little spanking he had given her as a young girl had lingered in her subconscious, but whether it had or not, the moment her hands had extinguished the main fires in her bottom, she realised that some of the warmth had spread down to even more sensitive regions, and the firm grip of his hand on her breasts wasn't helping in the least! Nor was the lump once again digging into her left hip. Her bare bottom felt as nice to her hands as her hands did to her burning rump. She deliberately moved her legs apart, pushed her middle further into the air and began to caress her glowing flesh with unmistakable sensuality.

The sight of long, elegant fingers digging into soft redness; the occasional glimpse of glistening sex lips and pretty pink anus caused a slight conflict of interest in General Bracegirdle. The yielding redness made him want to continue the spanking while the glistening holes represented a much more conventional temptation. He was also aware that he had been ordered to bring her back into line and he was not really supposed to roger her. On the other hand, she was so beautiful and he was so frustrated that he didn't think that he could possibly hold back. Fortunately, a combination of experience and unusual sensitivity showed him the way.

He helped her to her feet, stripped her naked, put her back across his knee, placed his left hand on her dangling breasts and set to work with his right. Sharp spanks alternated with squeezes and strokes. Every so often he tickled her slippery sex or tight little anus with a gentle fingertip. He ended up with one finger up her vagina, another up her bottom and a third rubbing her clitty until she was bucking, weaving and whooping as her orgasm convulsed her.

As soon as she had recovered from that, it was time to renew her punishment. He made her bend naked over his desk, her trembling hands gripping the further edge. He moved her legs a long way apart, exposing her glistening orifices and the shining softness of the inside of her thighs. Looking wildly around for a suitable weapon, he spotted his sword. Removing the belt and tossing the hard steel back onto the desk, he gripped the empty scabbard and whacked it down onto her taut buttocks, making her howl in pain.

Finally, he made her get up, kneel down in front of him, loosen his breeches and use her mouth on him.

When they parted by the waiting carriages, he kissed her on the cheek. 'I do not think that our Hungarian Hussar will be of much interest to you now, Madam,' he whispered in her ear. 'We shall, of course, be watching your behaviour, but I think that a review in, let me think, er . . . three days from now – after the Reception at the Belgian embassy – would be appropriate. Meet me here at midnight.'

'Yes, General. And . . . thank you.'

* * *

'And did she turn over a new leaf?' asked Sir James.

'Very much so, Sir James. What I didn't make clear was that her husband was a bit of a dead loss as far as sex was concerned, so she was basically very frustrated. General Bracegirdle's appearance into her life was a godsend. He was handsome, strong, very masculine and, above all, safe, in that as an old family friend – and therefore quite a bit older – he was more or less above suspicion.'

'And they carried on seeing each other?'

'Oh yes. But always discreetly. In fact even the sentries began to believe that it was all above board.'

'Wasn't it?'

'Well, yes and no. They never went all the way, but she always got a well-smacked bottom and afterwards he brought her off with his hands, before she did the same to him. Or she lay down on her tummy and he put his penis in the cleft of her bottom and came that way.'

'You mean he buggered her?' Sir James sounded shocked.

'No, no. Not up her anus. Just between the cheeks.'

'Ummm ... sounds different ... So, she enjoyed being spanked.'

'Yes, very much. Don't forget, she hadn't behaved well, so was feeling guilty enough to accept that she deserved it; then there was the thrill of having a man she secretly fancied staring at her bare bottom, then fondling it; feeling his erection when he put her across his lap. He was, don't forget, a highly experienced womaniser, and he played her like an expert violinist with a Stradivarius. Just as it was beginning to really hurt, he let her rub her bottom. And made sure that her breasts weren't left out! So that when he started again, she was in a very different frame of mind.'

'It wasn't a punishment any longer?'

'That's it. And once she was feeling that way, the pain turned to pleasure, especially under the hand of an expert.'

'How do you mean?'

'Well, don't forget that a girl's bottom and sex are all sort of joined together! So when you smack her cheeks, the wobble affects both her orifices. And a spank all on one buttock moves it apart from the other one and so the flesh shifts around; that also sends a little wave down below. An expert, wanting to turn a girl on – provided, of course, that she is in the right frame of mind – will smack with a curved hand, so that it doesn't sting too much, but will make her bottom shift and wobble around like a jelly. She won't necessarily feel an actual thrill, but it will be very different to a punishment spanking ... Look, I'll show you ... I'll kneel up on my seat, stick my bottom out and give myself a slow-motion spank ... If I hold my hand there, can you see how my right cheek has been pushed up and to one side? Hang on, I'll spread my legs and do it again. There, can you see the shift in my sex?'

'Yes ... I can.'

Sherrie peered over her shoulder and saw that Sir James' eyes were absolutely riveted to her bottom. His mouth was slightly open, his eyes wide and his breathing was hoarse and ragged. It was time to calm him down for a while, before the next build up. She ran both hands over her taut buttocks briefly, then twirled round and sat down.

'Is it beginning to make a bit of sense now, Sir James?'

'Yes, it is.' He sat back, expression and breathing returning to normal. He stared thoughtfully out of the window, then turned his head to look straight into her eyes. 'You know, Sherrie, in just a few days you have taught me so much. For example, I was sorely tempted to reach out and grope you just now and if you hadn't sat down, I certainly would have. But I've learned patience and so I wasn't even slightly annoyed when you thwarted my evil intentions! But, my dear, your time for a spanking is not very far off.'

'Good!'

Their eyes met and her respect for his self-control was clear in her look. So was her eager anticipation.

'I know. I want to savour the waiting. Why don't you fetch another bottle. I take it we have ample supplies? Excellent. And another snack?'

He watched the twinkling sway of her naked behind as she trotted up the aisle again and a warm glow spread through him as he waited patiently for her return. When she appeared again, he looked at her breasts and sex quite openly, revelling in the sense of total and free intimacy which had grown up between them. Similarly, with a satisfying helping of caviare on a deliciously crisp biscuit inside him and the second glass of champagne waiting to be tasted, he closed his eyes and marvelled at the way that they could maintain a companionable silence without any awkwardness. She broke it in the end.

'Be honest, Sir James, from what you've seen of it so far, do you like my bottom?'

'Silly question! I've already told you that I do. I must confess that I haven't seen that many. Bare, that is. But I've had to endure the odd beach holiday and, especially in the South of France, you see a lot which are as good as bare, so I do have some basis for judging it among the very best. And, you're confident enough in yourself to know that.' She blushed and he grinned at her. 'But the thing which is giving me the most pleasure is the way that you are quite happy to show it to me. Most girls that I've known have either been shy or flirtatious. You've made it all seen utterly natural.'

'Well, isn't it? Natural, I mean.'

He laughed. 'I suppose that if you think about it, sex and nudity are about as natural as you can get ... As I said, Sherrie, I've already learned a great deal from you. And I've got a lovely feeling that I'm going to learn a great deal more before we get back to London. I think that it's time that my education took a big step forward. Could I have some more bubbly please ... and do help yourself.'

They looked at each other as they drank and Sir James noticed with a flare of excitement that she was squirming in her seat, wriggling in expectation. He drained his glass. She rose to her feet and stood right in front of him, her hands by her side, patiently waiting for his instructions, not flaunting herself but very desirable. He swept his eyes over her body while he remembered some of the aspects of her stories which had held his attention, looking for clues which would guide him in his attempts to make what was to follow both memorable and enjoyable for all concerned. He made up his mind on the first step.

'Would you like to get dressed again?' It was more of an order than a request but that had always been his approach. She smiled her acceptance and again, he detected a gleam of approval in her eye as his intention to bare her with proper ceremony was made clear.

Soon she was standing before him, again a neat and efficient hostess, but far more enticing now that he knew what lay beneath her clothes.

Then he faced the problem of how to position her and his smoothly masterful approach stuttered as he realised that the cabin seats may have been the last word in executive comfort but left something to be desired when used to place a girl comfortably across one's knees. The prominent arms got in the way! Further evidence of her co-operation came when she showed him how they could be folded down out of the way. So there he was with an extremely comfortable seat which supported his legs as far as his knees and, with the backrest almost vertical, moulded his back equally well.

He took her hand and guided her to his right side and with a little pull, encouraged her to bend over. This she did with all her usual grace, resting her spare hand on his further knee, then dipping her middle until her tummy rested on his thigh, placing both hands on the thickly carpeted floor, shifting her weight forward a little and finally settling down with a soft heaviness which took his breath away. Her dark skirt moulded itself to the roundness of her bottom to the extent that it dipped noticeably into the cleft and between her thighs.

The Sir James of a week or so before would have wrenched her skirt up and knickers down with unseemly haste but, as he had admitted to her, he now knew better. He smoothed his right hand over her legs and bottom, absorbing the feel of her flesh. Her skirt was inched upwards, slowly revealing her stockinged legs, the bare tops of her thighs, the chubby little crescents of naked buttock peeping out from her knickers. He stroked up, enjoying the contrasts between the different materials and bare skin in between. He tucked one side of her silk knickers into her cleft, exposing just the one cheek and tested the difference in feel between the naked and the covered. He repeated the process with the other side. He stroked the small of her back and inched his fingers down towards the waistband of her knickers. They were both holding their breath as their downward journey began.

The top of her cleft appeared, clean-cut and soft-skinned. Then the top of her knickers caught up with the part tucked into the division and they turned themselves inside-out as he pulled them down remorselessly, past her gluteal folds and all the way to her knees.

He smoothed his right hand up her thigh until it reached the top of her stocking, where he paused and enjoyed a lengthy manual assessment of the silk-skinned firmness of both legs. Then, with an audible sigh, he moved onto her bare bottom and uninhibitedly explored the entire area with both hands, up to and including holding the chubby buttocks wide apart to examine the pinky-brown anus buried in the depths of her cleft. After a few moments, he felt her stir on his lap and knew that she wanted the spanking to start, so he pressed his left hand on the smoothness of her loins and raised his right arm.

'Sir James, why don't you roll up your sleeves and rest your arm against my back, gripping my hip. Like General Bracegirdle did to Lady Harpwell. I think you'll find it quite pleasant.'

He did, and yet again she was right. The feel of her skin against the inside of his arm was very nice indeed. He raised his right arm again and administered his first ever spank, which proved to be far more satisfying than he could possibly have imagined. The ringing noise, the unexpected impression of the softness of her skin, the yielding quality of her flesh and the way it quivered under the impact, the little jerk of her body on his legs, her muted gasp, the pink patch rising dramatically on the cream-coloured background, all combined to make him realise that he had been living a far too sheltered life. With a spreading grin, he continued.

Sherrie was of course used to being punished by a real

expert but she was quite happy to lie there and let Sir James learn as he went along. Sure enough, after a few minutes of delivering uneven spanks randomly all over her bottom, he paused to take stock and then set about her much more methodically. He settled into a steady rhythm and worked steadily down from top to base and from side to side and she was soon reacting in her normal manner, bobbing her hips up and down so that she was actually pushing up to meet his hand. She began to gasp and pant as the welcome pain washed through her and realised that his ability to grasp the essentials of a new experience was a contributory factor in his success!

Not surprisingly, he stopped periodically as though checking to see how close she was to her limits, obviously not aware that they were extremely high. Again, Sherrie forgave him for letting her fall away from the peak of pleasure which she was gradually climbing. 'He'll learn,' she muttered to herself as his hand explored her warm curves, 'and very quickly at this rate!' as another ringing spank echoed through the cabin to indicate the start of another round.

Just as she was beginning to feel that she was going to have to summon up some of her deeper reserves – and as her sex was beginning to tingle insistently, he came to a halt, breathing heavily. Remembering the look on his face when she had described the sight of Lady Harpwell rubbing her bottom, she followed suit and was not in the least surprised when his left hand whipped round to support her bosom and she could massage away with revealing enthusiasm.

She was pleased when, after he had helped her to her feet, he took charge. He made her take all her clothes off and walk up and down the aisle, blatantly admitting that if watching her walk away from him with her bottom all bare was one of the most exciting things he had ever seen, repeating the exercise with her bottom bright red was extra special. It was his idea to kiss her better; hers to kneel up on one of the seats with her rear end sticking out high, wide and very handsome; his to reach out and stroke her dangling boobs; hers to transfer one of his hands to her sex. Just before she came, he showed that he was now on more familiar territory and, with some skill, slipped down his trousers while at the same time maintaining his delightful attentions to her clitty and then slipped into her from behind. The combination of his cock and finger sent her into a rather noisy and obviously highly satisfying climax.

Sir James once again proved his gentlemanly qualities by lifting her up, sitting down and holding her on his knee until she had recovered before taking his own clothes off and making love with her on the floor.

They lay there for quite a long time afterwards. There was no need to say anything and she lay in happy comfort on top of him, her head pillowed on his chest, while he stroked her hair with one hand and her tingling bottom with the other.

He was distinctly disappointed when a change in the note of the engines warned them that they were starting the descent into Hawaii and it was time to rejoin the outside world.

Chapter 5

Sherrie had enjoyed Hawaii rather more than she had expected. High-rise tourist traps were not usually her first-choice holiday spots but there was an atmosphere about the place which was contagious and the beach was fantastic. She had managed to get away into the interior of the island for a morning and had found the change stimulating. She had also exchanged meaningful glances across a crowded bar with a dishy blonde and the glances had encouraged her to move across and make her acquaintance. Betty was a corporate lawyer from New York and the spark had been obvious to them both from the beginning. After a long lunch, they had gone back to the beach for a short tanning session, which had quite naturally begun with a mutual rubbing-in of sunblock, during which the touch of Betty's hands on her back and thighs had confirmed Sherrie's expectations. And then the feel of Betty's skin had aroused her desires even more, especially when she had smoothed the lotion up the backs of her thighs, trailing her fingertips into the deep folds at the top, where her nice round buttocks curved up into the bikini.

They had talked easily for an hour or so before they started to burn in the afternoon sun, by which time Sherrie's hotel room was a mutually agreeable destination. Betty had taken up the running from the beginning and Sherrie found that being expertly pampered made a lovely change, especially as the young American was eloquently complimentary. It also helped that she was just as keen on bottoms, and Sherrie lay happily on her tummy, her skin tingling from the sun and sea, her bikini bottom neatly rolled down to her knees, while soft hands stroked and kneaded her bare buttocks.

'Sherrie, you have got the most gorgeous ass I've ever seen.'

Betty's voice was breathless, husky. Thrilling. Her hands pressed into the relaxed mounds and shifted them around, kneading them apart and squeezing them together. Then Sherrie felt her thumbs digging in, the cleft opening until a breath of conditioned air on her most intimate orifice made her shudder. She was not disappointed. Soft, slightly damp hair tickled her; she felt warm breath on sensitive skin; her eyes screwed shut and her own breath whistled out of her lungs and the moist heat of Betty's tongue touched her hypersensitive little anus.

The subsequent love-making had been energetic and diverting and, as she waited for Sir James, the memories of the feel and scents of Betty's femininity lingered. All in all, it had been a perfect little break and Sherrie was looking forward to the next stage in their journey with renewed enthusiasm.

He arrived eventually. And she noticed at once that he was looking haggard and careworn.

'Let's get the hell out of here,' he muttered as he flung his briefcase and jacket onto a spare seat and slumped down into his usual place.

Sherrie picked up the intercom, had a quick word with the pilot and, to her relief, the engines started up almost immediately. They taxied quickly to the end of the runway. As soon as the aircraft had eased out of its noisy climb and was ascending normally, she undid her belt, slipped into the galley and opened a bottle of non-vintage champagne. Putting it, a bottle of brandy, two glasses and an ice bucket onto a tray, she rejoined Sir James.

'Would a champagne cocktail hit the right spot?'

'Sherrie, what a brilliant idea!'

He watched her mix the drinks, pleased that she felt that she no longer had to ask whether he wanted her to join him – and admiring the deftness of her hands. The slim length of her fingers round the neck of one of the bottles suddenly struck him as very suggestive indeed! Some of the tension left him as a familiar tingle in his groin provided a forceful reminder of pleasures past and hope for more to come. The cocktail was cold, sharp, smooth and warming. Perfect.

'Problems?' She asked him.

'Oh nothing serious. The air conditioning in the Boardroom broke, which didn't help much, but the main problem is that I seem to spend more and more time listening to earnest young executives droning on and on about what they plan to do. And trying to keep awake for long enough to see the one flaw.'

'Which flaw?'

'Oh it varies, but there's always one. The secret is to spot it, draw attention to it in a way which makes them think (a) that I'm a genius and (b) that there may be other things wrong with their proposals. Sometimes all I have to do is glare at them with a raised eyebrow. Occasionally I have to spell it out but that's usually with the more stupid and less experienced ones. Anyway. We've made a lot of progress.'

'Good. Would you like some lunch? I cook a mean Beef Stroganoff.'

'Fantastic. Now I come to think of it, I haven't had a thing to eat since breakfast.'

'Coming up. Now what would you like to drink with it. We've got some excellent Burgundies – and some even better Bordeaux. How about a '73 Mouton?'

'Perfect,' he sighed wearily.

'I'll get it open right away. And what would you like to do while I'm in the galley? Music? A video?'

'Oh Lord ... some Mozart perhaps? Don Giovanni? Figaro? Or failing that, a video of a pretty girl getting a sound spanking would do nicely!'

'I'll see what I can do, Sir James,' Sherrie replied with a very convincing expression of prim disapproval on her face. He grinned at her as she flounced up the aisle, and again when she flipped up the back of her skirt and waggled her rear at him. He took a long swig from his glass, realised that his nagging headache was all but gone, then took off his tie and closed his eyes, waiting for the music to continue the soothing process.

A humming sound made him open them again. A section of the bulkhead opposite him was moving to the side and a blank screen came slowly into view. He felt a surge of lust at the wild thought that he was going to see a spanking video and then he came to his senses and realised that even if there were such things, a respectable aircraft rental company would hardly have them on board.

The screen flickered into life. Then went dark. He stared, puzzled and then jumped as a hand appeared, almost filling the screen. A feminine hand. With long, slender fingers and manicured nails. The fingers sank appreciably into whatever they were resting on and he frowned. The disembodied hand moved to the top, the fingers curled and slipped underneath something right at the very edge of the screen. It moved slowly down and white replaced the black. White with a tint of pink. The hand moved from side to side, tugging and there was a break in the whiteness. A thin, relatively dark line.

Suddenly it dawned on him that he was watching a bottom being bared. In close up. His jaw dropped and his prick rose. Breathing unevenly, he gaped at the slow and steady unveiling of an outstandingly pretty rump, the exposed flesh bulging firmly over the stretched waistband of what he could now see was a pair of tight black ski-pants. The gluteal folds popped into view, the whiteness replaced the black completely and the disembodied hand began to caress the equally disembodied, and now totally bare, bottom.

He craned forward, elbows on his knees and his chin cupped in his hands, eyes glinting and a disbelieving smile on his face. To his delight, if no longer to his surprise, the hand disappeared and then blurred across his vision until it met the flesh with a crack loud enough to make him jump again.

By the time a grinning Sherrie emerged from the galley, pushing a trolley from which a heavenly-scented steam rose, the hand was still beating down, but the buttocks were a dramatic scarlet. Far redder than hers had been after his attentions.

He dragged his gaze from the screen, sniffed appreciatively, tasted the wine, murmured his approval and looked back up at the screen. Somehow Sherrie had paused the video, and had done so on a perfect frame. The punishing hand had just smacked into the left buttock, sinking into the relaxed flesh, pulling it away from the other cheek and forcing the lower part of the cleft open. The tiny pink anus was clearly visible. Sir James gaped, remembering Sherrie's little demonstration of the effect of a smack on the more sensitive areas of a girl's body and seeing the proof clear in front of him.

'Would you like me to take my clothes off?'

He forced his reeling brain to concentrate on the immediate matter of lunch. 'No, no. It would only distract me . . . from the food.'

She bent forward, gave him a quick kiss and served him with the deftness which was such an integral part of her. He watched her fill his glass and suddenly realised that it had been her hand in the video. He looked at her with renewed interest, stared at her right hand and envied it for its prolonged contact with that lovely bottom.

She rewound the film and they ate and watched in silence and when they had finished the Stroganoff and the claret, she asked him if he would like a sorbet and coffee.

'Yes please, Sherrie. And this time I *would* like you to take your clothes off please. All of them. I want you absolutely, stark, naked!'

Grinning at him, she complied and took the plates and so on back to the galley. One item at a time!

By the time they had drained their coffee cups, he was feeling even better than usual and followed the movements of her bare bottom up the aisle with another erection having to be eased into a comfortable position. She returned and stood before him, happily letting his eyes sweep up and down the full length of her body.

He looked at her breasts, tummy, sex and legs, marvelling first at her incredible beauty and second at his amazing good fortune. He leaned forward and gently kissed the neat triangle of dark hair, breathing her scent – expensive soap and excited woman – deep into his lungs. He wanted to make love to her; he wanted to spank her again; he wanted to talk to her; he wanted another story. He stared at her middle and decided that another story should be the first item on the agenda.

'Right, Sir James. Let's think.'

We'll move to more modern times. The early thirties in the States – somewhere in the mid-West, like Kansas. Jed Forrest and Lou, his wife, owned a small but reasonably fertile farm. They had just survived the Depression and were fairly content with their general lot, or rather they had been until his niece, Virginia arrived. She was the step-daughter of his brother, Esau, who had found farm life much too demanding and run off to Chicago where he had happily stayed.

He had drifted into one of the gangs during Prohibition, had spent some time in gaol before double-crossing his colleagues and fleeing to New York, leaving Virginia directions to the farm and with just enough money for the bus fare to the nearest town, from where she had managed to get a lift from a friendly neighbour. At the time she was nineteen, extremely attractive to look at but showing all the signs of having a rather unattractive personality.

Jed and Lou had never managed to produce a family and so welcomed Virginia far more generously than she deserved. She hated the heat, the dust, the silence, the farmyard smells, the lack of boys, the fact that she was expected to earn her keep by helping her aunt, the fact that her clothes were getting shabby and there were no decent shops where she could go to replace them, the fact that she had no money and Uncle Jed showed no sign of offering her any. All in all she was miserable and made no effort to put a brave face on things.

Quite understandably, her relatives soon lost patience with her. Aunt Lou was the first to crack. She had asked her to feed the chickens three times without any result;

finally she lost her temper and hauled the squawking girl onto the verandah by the ear. Ignoring the general caterwauling and the screeched excuses on the lines that the foul birds had already pecked two of her last pairs of stockings to pieces, she plonked herself down on a sturdy, upright chair and heaved the struggling little minx over her equally sturdy knees. She aimed a good swipe in the general direction of the seat of her skirt and landed plumb in the centre, at which point both participants in the drama froze into immobility. Aunt Lou had never spanked anyone and Virginia had never been spanked, so there was this short period while they assessed the situation.

Lou's feelings were inevitably a little more complex than her niece's. She was basically a very good-natured woman and by the time she had pinned the young girl across her lap, her bad temper had begun to evaporate. She was sympathetic enough to appreciate that Virginia had not had an easy time and a cruel beating was the last thing she needed. On the other hand, she was finding the process strangely enjoyable. Virginia's body felt soft and heavy on her thighs; her rounded bottom moulded itself attractively to the seat of her thin skirt and, above all, she was relishing the sense of power, having been in a similar position over Jed's lap often enough to give her an underlying curiosity about the active role. She stared down at the girl's behind, pondering her next move.

Virginia was merely nervous. Several friends of hers had been paddled by their parents and had treated her to lurid descriptions of the agonies involved – which, of course, they had endured with amazing courage – and she had no desire to try it out for herself. And yet, she had begun to like her aunt and uncle and was guiltily aware that she had been a pain. She felt her eyes fill with tears of remorse, mixed with bitterness and humiliation.

Sir James broke in. 'Sorry, Sherrie, but what exactly does "paddled" mean?'

'It's a very American form of punishment. It's basically a wooden or leather implement. Some of them are roughly the same size and shape as a table tennis bat, others more like a cricket bat. Only much thinner, of course. Most kids of Virginia's age would have faced one. At home or at school.'

'Thank you. Please, carry on.'

Well, Lou took several minutes over her decision on how best to deal with the errant girl and, while she was thinking about it, Jed had come back to the farmhouse to wash and bandage a cut hand. Approaching the house from the side, he was abruptly faced with the arresting view of Virginia's legs leading steeply up under her skirt to her upthrust seat. His wife was absently tucking a loose strand of dark blonde hair back behind her ear while she studied her target. It made an arresting little tableau and Jed eased himself down into a squat to make himself less conspicuous.

Just then Lou had decided to compromise. As this was the girl's initiation at their hands, she would raise her skirt but respect her modesty by leaving her panties in place, certain that they would be as skimpy as the rest of her clothes. She reached down with both hands and started to tug upwards. There was an immediate wail from her niece.

'No, Auntie Lou, please don't . . . please . . . oh nooooo!'

The older woman had been a little surprised at the intensity of the protests, until she had whisked the skirt firmly over the rounded humps. She was shocked to be confronted by a totally bare bottom. It was white, womanly, divided by a nice long and deep cleft, trembling and very spankable, but the unexpected revelation temporarily blinded her to its beauty.

'It just ain't decent to go round with no panties on, Virginia,' she chided.

There was no anger in her voice and this somehow made Virginia feel all the more ashamed of herself. Tears poured down her face and she could feel her bottom shake and quiver as sobs racked her body. But then her aunt's hand was stroking and kneading and soothing and squeezing, which was so nice that her fears subsided and she stopped crying. Then she felt a strong left arm pin her down on the big thighs, the other hand left her right cheek and she knew that she was about to face the unknown.

Auntie Lou was a plump, strong woman. She wasn't fat, and beneath her home-made and rather shapeless dress, there was a fine figure, if not exactly fashion model material. Constant hard work had made her strong enough to redden a pumpkin-sized bottom in no time. Luckily for Virginia, she was also unusually sensitive and there was something so appealing about the soft whiteness spread out in front of her which restrained her natural desire to try and drive her hand right into the plump target. It may have been no more than a reasonably firm spank but it was still more than adequate. Virginia's bottom wobbled like a blancmange, she pressed herself hard into the supporting lap, her loud 'Oowwww' rang out as clear as a coyote's howl and a nice pink patch flared into view right in the middle of the left buttock.

Auntie Lou now understood why her husband was so keen on spanking her, especially as she realised that her bottom was considerably bigger and plumper than Virginia's, so presumably would be even more satisfying to smack. She sighed, deeply enough to make her big bosom heave dramatically. She ran her hand over the pink blotch, and although all the scrubbing, sweeping, hoeing and so on had hardened her palm, she could still feel the difference in temperature between the spanked and unspanked skin.

'You really have got a cute bottom, 'Ginia honey. Real pretty. Lovely soft skin.'

'Sure do seem a shame to spoil it by spanking it some more, don't it, Auntie Lou?'

Lou glanced to her left, just as her niece craned her head round. Her wide blue eyes met Virginia's tear-filled, darker blue ones. An impish smile curved Lou's neat mouth and suddenly she felt a bubble of laughter well up inside her. She put her head back and roared.

Jed pushed back his battered and sweat-stained stetson and scratched his head.

'What the tarnation is so funny?' he wondered to himself. 'Never will understand women.'

Lou wiped her eyes and re-focused on Virginia's bottom. 'Now don't you be so sassy, young lady. You've earned yourself a good spanking and that's what you're gonna get. And it's your fault that it's on your bare bottom. Mind you, I can't say I'm not happy that you forgot your panties. As I said, it sure is cute. But it'll look a darn sight cuter when it's nice and red. But first I'm gonna give it a good feel.'

Suddenly Virginia was beginning to feel a great deal better. It was as if most of her frustrations had seeped away with her tears and as she turned her head back to stare at the well-swept wooden floor, she could feel Auntie Lou's body still shaking with laughter. It had been affectionate rather than scornful and, for the first time since her arrival, she started to feel part of the family. The complimentary remarks about her bottom helped. She had had it groped by one or two of the many boys who had swarmed around her in the city, although most of them had locked straight onto her tits and so she had never really considered that her rear end was anything more than something comfortable to sit on – as often as possible.

Now that the stroking right palm was shifting her relaxed flesh around and sending most unexpected little thrills into all the right places, her heart began to thud in her chest and as a set of questing fingertips traced the line of her cleft and began to probe between her thighs, she slumped against the softness of the motherly thighs and her legs eased apart of their own accord.

Lou was enjoying herself nearly as much as Virginia. Her upbringing – on a similar farm – had given her an earthiness typical of country folk and Jed was quite a sensual man in his quiet way. He had been very taken with her bottom on their wedding night and she had no inhibitions in taking open pleasure in the sight and feel of Virginia's. Apart from that, it was a rare opportunity to take the weight off her feet.

By this time the pink mark left by her first spank was fading and Lou realised that there was too much to do to let her sit around for the whole morning, so she pressed down on the small of Virginia's back with her left hand, extracted her right from the excitingly soft and warm burrow between her thighs and carried on spanking.

Virginia tensed as she felt the re-arrangement of her punisher's hands and screwed her pretty little face up at the imminent prospect of pain. She heard the sound of the hand smacking her left cheek, felt her flesh quiver and absorbed the hot waves surging through her bottom. But to her surprise, it didn't really hurt. It was as if the interval between the two smacks had anaesthetised her, which in effect, is what had happened, because the rapport which had sprung up between them had relaxed her mind and her aunt's stroking hand had done the same to her body. She started to find her position almost exciting, especially the intimate contact between her tummy and the broad thighs. Being bare-bottomed was giving her a thrill.

Auntie Lou was not nearly sophisticated enough to realise what was happening to Virginia, and was in any case far too wrapped up in her own pleasure to care whether the girl was enjoying it or not. Their combined weight was squashing her ample rump against the hard wooden seat of the chair, the girl's body felt softly heavy on her thighs, her blotched bottom filled her vision most prettily. It felt delightfully soft under her palm and the quivers and wobbles were highly entertaining.

She took her time. Resting her business hand on the relatively cool flesh of the nearer thigh, she surveyed the target area carefully, selected the area for the next slap, moved her hand to that spot to get the range, and then smacked. Quite hard but not viciously. Then her hand slipped back onto the thigh while she watched the reddening of the smacked area, before giving the whole surface of the bottom a thorough rub, realising that the movements caused by rubbing were nearly as pleasing as those resulting from the spank. The hand returned to the thigh, fingertips idly stroking the particularly soft skin on the inside and the process was repeated.

Jed shook his head in amazement. If a girl needed spanking, then one got on with it. This drawn-out approach seemed to him to be a waste of time and, however nice it was to look at Virginia's bottom, he had the fencing to get back to. He sneaked out of sight, washed his injured hand in a bucket of water by the tank, tied his handkerchief round it and loped back to work.

In the meantime, Virginia was suffering from a mixture of emotions. Auntie Lou was getting the hang of it by now and there was a distinctly sharper ring to the impacts of flesh on flesh, each one making her jerk and gasp before she could steady herself for the fondling which followed. That was real nice and seemed to spread the throbbing heat deeper into her flesh as much as it soothed the skin. But nothing could disguise the basic fact that her bottom was very sore – and she was getting the distinct impression that her aunt was beginning to enjoy administering the punishment rather more than was necessary.

The waves of heat seemed to spread out from Virginia's bottom and into her pussy. All her senses sharpened. She could smell the hot, dusty earth, with the occasional waft of farmyard, and Auntie Lou's perfume. She was fully aware of the comforting pressure of the left hand on her back; she could feel every waft of breeze on her skin; she sensed that those blue eyes were fixed on her bare flesh.

Auntie Lou was gloating over the younger girl's bare bottom. And the yielding weight of her was bringing a nice tingle to her own pussy, just as her nostrils flared at the musky scent from Virginia's. She trailed a finger down the cleft, stroked her buttocks, then steadied herself with a spell of deep breathing before settling down to a more scientific spanking, covering the whole bottom with a flurry of sharp smacks, pausing, then laying on a dozen harder ones to the lower curves.

'Let's really redden the bit you sit on, 'Ginia. Not that you're going to do much sitting this morning.' *Smack*. 'There's the chickens to feed,' *smack* 'the kitchen floor to sweep', *smack* 'the bread to be made,' *smack* 'and ... er ... and ...' *smack* 'and ...' *smack* 'I'll soon think of all the other chores that need doing!' *Smack – smack – smack!*

She rested her hand on the coolness of the top of Virginia's thigh, sat back and took stock. Her niece was panting and wailing; the lower area of her bottom was a rich red in colour and her right hand was stinging quite noticeably. On the other hand, once the assault had stopped and the immediate burning had presumably died down a little, the girl had settled back across her knees as though expecting more. Again, Lou idly traced the length of the cleft with the tip of her forefinger, tickled the base just where the twin thigh-folds curved in to meet it. The girl wriggled with pleasure and gave a faint 'Ooooh!' Lou smiled and let her hand roam at will.

Lou was not a woman given to self-analysis. Perhaps if Virginia had been a blood relative rather than the unknown step-daughter of a brother-in-law she had only met at her wedding, she may have behaved differently, but there were no feelings of kinship to soften her attitude. Similarly, if Virginia had behaved as one would have expected from an eighteen-year-old having her bare bottom spanked for the first time and struggled and roared in protest, Auntie Lou would have used her superior strength to overwhelm her while she whacked away at the errant behind until both parties had had enough. As it was, she sensed that the spanking was fulfilling for them both.

Even though she couldn't see the girl's face, she suddenly appreciated how very pretty she was, with her wavy golden hair, full lips, smooth fair skin, straight back and splendid curves both fore and aft. Hopefully her spanking would remove her habitually surly expression and encourage her to get up off her backside and join in properly. And if it didn't, it was proving such a satisfying experience that she would be more than happy to find excuses to do it again. With a warm glow spreading through her middle, Lou finished the punishment with another, prolonged flurry of crisp little smacks. Helping the wailing girl to her feet, she watched in fascination as Virginia turned her back and rubbed heartily away, before sending her about her business.

The transformation was marked. Supper that evening was the happiest meal they had had since Virginia's arrival and, for some reason, Jed had been especially vigorous in bed, with his horny hands gripping Lou's big buttocks with great enthusiasm. He had decided not to breathe a word about what he had witnessed and had also made up his mind that Virginia's bottom was certainly not going to be Lou's sole preserve. He was a patient man and quite happy to bide his time. In the meantime, he found renewed pleasure in his wife's ample rump.

A week later, Jed decided that it would not be natural if he pretended that he hadn't noticed the change and broached the subject one evening.

'Oh, I give her a good spanking. A few days ago, now. Did her no end of good.'

'It sure has. Where is she now?'

'Gone for a walk. Down to the creek, I think. She likes it there.'

'Good. Now, d'you remember what I said to you about fixing the chicken run?'

'Oh, Jed, I plumb forgot. I'm really sorry and I'll fix it first thing tomorrow.'

''Course you will. But it's clearly far too long since I've given you a spanking. Get yourself ready and come here.'

'Oh Jed . . .'

He had always made her bare her own bottom for punishment, claiming that he didn't see why he should do all the work. Lou hiked up her skirts, tucked them carefully into her belt, walked up to his chair and stood in front of him, letting him study the tight seat of her cotton panties. Back to the old routine, she thought to herself. And her heart thudded and her deep, uneven breathing made her breasts heave under her loose blouse. She moved her hands to her hips, tucked her thumbs into the waistband and began to inch her panties downwards, slowly exposing herself to him, smiling at the heaviness of his breathing. When her arms were at full stretch, she let go and shuddered as the panties slithered down her legs to her ankles. She stood still. Her bottom tingled under the intensity of his gaze and she couldn't prevent it from clenching, horribly aware that the muscular spasm made her buttocks dimple. She forced them to relax.

She couldn't remember when she had last felt as wound up before a spanking. Dealing with Virginia must have had something to do with it. Just as her nerves were at breaking point, Jed patted her and, with a sob of relief, she turned and flung herself across his legs, whimpering her longing for the splatting hand on her bare flesh.

Jed made her wait for a while. Inspired by the happy expression he had seen on her face while she was playing with Virginia, he re-acquainted himself with her bottom before setting it into almost liquid motion as he spanked her hard and fast.

Her skin reddened even more rapidly than her niece's and as he was spanking her a great deal harder, it was only a couple of minutes before she was a bright scarlet and howling like a banshee. He eased up a little to spin it out a bit longer, but soon the sight of her big red bottom inspired other thoughts. In a trice, he had whisked her panties right off, led her into the kitchen, where she happily bent over the table, while he undid his jeans and then, holding her hot cheeks apart, he drove his prick into her wet and willing sex from behind.

From that moment, life was much more agreeable for all three. Virginia soon forgot the pain, but always remembered both the peculiar sense of intimacy with Auntie Lou and the period after her punishment when she had wandered down to the creek and stripped off for a swim. The cool water had soothed her beautifully, but it had been the feeling that all her frustrations had been washed away which was most satisfying. She and her aunt began to work cheerfully together and what had been boring chores suddenly became almost fulfilling.

Lou probably gained the most. She had been lonely but now she had a companion and daughter all rolled into one. She listened, deliciously appalled, to the girl's stories of life in the big city; her flashy mother and her many 'friends', almost all male; her father's gambling cronies, with their wandering hands and generous presents to the pretty young girl. She loved having someone with whom she could discuss all the feminine things which were a completely closed book to Jed. In return, Virginia showed an increasing interest in the farm and, in short, began to grow up.

Even Jed mellowed towards her. She was prettier than ever, which helped. Her hair lightened in the sun and fresh air, her complexion cleared, her aunt's cooking filled out the hollows and the healthy life kept her trim and fit-looking. He was sensitive enough to appreciate what she was doing for Lou, and found simple pleasure in watching them together, their laughter like a tonic. He noticed the young girl's influence on his wife too – her hair looked far less like a crow's nest, her dresses began to fit properly, showing off her curves, and their love life improved dramatically.

Hardly surprisingly, after a month or so, Lou began to find that her eyes wandered to the seat of her niece's skirt and she summoned up memories of the spanking and lingered over them. Then one very hot day, the two of them were fixing the gutters, with Virginia up the ladder and Lou holding it and giving generally superfluous advice. A gust of hot wind blew both skirts up to their owners' waists. Lou was able to spare a hand to put herself in order but poor Virginia couldn't. Neither was she wearing any panties, so Lou was treated to the splendid sight of her bare legs sweeping upwards to a completely naked bottom.

Seen from directly below, it looked bigger and even more enticing than in any other position and Virginia's immediate fate was sealed.

'Shame on you, 'Ginia! You ain't wearing no panties again.'

'Oh Gawd! It's so hot, Auntie Lou, and I . . . Are you gonna spank me again?'

'Yup.'

'Oh cripes . . . shall I just finish this bit?'

'Yup.'

And so, not caring that her skirts were still up, Virginia carried on, her feelings distinctly mixed. On the one hand, she felt a bit ashamed of herself and rather dreaded being put across her aunt's knee with her bare bottom so prominently positioned; nor was she looking forward to the pain. On the other, she remembered feeling so calm and at peace once the burning throb had subsided and turned into a lovely glow. She screwed in the final screw, put the tools into the bag, covered herself and climbed down. They looked at each other and with sudden insight, she saw the desire on her aunt's pretty face.

Lou was churning away inside. The odd but exciting view of Virginia's bare bottom had made her feel all hot and bothered and she was dying to get her over her knee; to see and feel her flesh; to turn her skin red. To dominate, for only the second time in her life.

'Auntie Lou, would you like me to put some panties on? Or do you want my bottom all bare?'

'Definitely bare, honey.'

'The same chair?'

'Yup.'

Hand in hand, they walked slowly up the verandah steps and up to the solid wooden seat. Lou plonked herself down, her heart pounding as Virginia rested her hands on her further thigh, smiled nervously and then lowered herself until hands and feet were resting securely on the wooden floor. Then she reached back and tugged up her dress until it was up to her waist, settled down again and drew her legs in a little, cocking her bottom up as if to say, 'There you are, Auntie Lou, it's all yours'. So Lou helped herself. She stroked and tickled and squeezed and rubbed. She spanked. Hard and fast. She revelled in the wobbles and gasps and cries. She soothed the heated flesh until it was ready for more spanks. Which were then delivered with furious energy until poor Virginia was howling in genuine distress. Then she soothed her – and the cycle could start all over again.

At last, Lou was too tired to continue and her niece was sobbing her heart out, so she hoisted her up and sat her on her lap, her left hand rubbing the crimson cheeks of her bottom and her right holding the quaking girl to her big breasts, rocking her like a baby.

A good spanking became a regular part of their lives and

was always followed by a pretty intimate cuddle. Perhaps surprisingly – at least to those who have to put things into compartments – there was never any sex between them. Lou's enjoyment of the intimacy of a spanking without inhibition and holding the sobbing girl in her arms afterwards was no more than tender loving care. In fact, every time she smacked Virginia, her main desire was to offer her own bottom to her husband, for she was now far more sympathetic to the pleasure he clearly derived from spanking her! Besides, it always ended up with her bending over the nearest piece of suitable furniture while he reamed her.

By contrast, Virginia was increasingly hot and bothered by it all. She 'asked for' a spanking more and more frequently and inevitably trotted down to the creek for a cooling swim afterwards. And after her swim, she would find her favourite rock and dry off in the sun, her right hand busy on her neat little sex. At first, the memories of her recent spanking were enough to get her going, but after a while, she began to fantasise about being put across Jed's lean thighs while his horny farmer's hand walloped her bare bottom.

Inevitably, she got what she had been looking for. She aggravated him once too often. It's more than possible that if he hadn't witnessed her first spanking, he would have done no more than tear a strip off her, but the memory of her chubby little cheeks thrust up in the air was firmly etched in his mind and he seized the opportunity to get in on the act. He sent her to her room – where she lay on her bed in an ecstasy of fear – while he discussed the matter with his wife.

Slightly to his surprise, Lou seemed less than enthusiastic about the prospect of him punishing their 'niece'. He stared at her red face and then understood – she was worried that he might be tempted to finish Virginia off in the way he did her. Smiling inwardly, he reassured her and suggested that a few good licks with a hickory switch would do the trick. Lou's troubled face cleared and she agreed wholeheartedly.

Jed and Lou settled on the punishment, their excitement unspoken but understood by both. The preparations were made. The sawhorse moved from the shed to the middle of the courtyard and a folded blanket draped over the crossbar to protect the delicate skin of Virginia's stomach. A suitable switch was cut and peeled. The erring girl was brought out and calmly advised first of her shortcomings and then her sentence.

Her pretty face set and pale, she tucked her skirt into her belt, slipped her panties down and off and bent over the bench, hands on the warm dust, legs straight out behind with toes digging in for maximum support. The midday sun was hot on her naked skin, her breathing was uneven, her heart pounded in her chest. Sweat trickled down the inside of her arms and she gritted her teeth in expectation. She knew that she was about to move into an unknown and very painful territory but, for some reason, she felt a strange exhilaration. Her bottom felt incredibly exposed and she knew that her uncle and aunt were staring at her. She peered back between her legs and could see their parted lips and gleaming eyes. Facing front again, she felt all the nerve-ends in her buttocks began to tingle insistently. The look on her uncle's face as he stared at her had been exciting enough to reduce her fear a little. Auntie Lou's eyes and hands on her ass had been nice, but with a man, it was even nicer. She thought of the way he was always reaching across to squeeze and pat his wife's bottom and suddenly she understood why it always produced a soft smile.

Jed swallowed hard. Virginia's bottom was narrower than Lou's, which he had seen in a smaller pose on several occasions, with a more pronounced pout, but the whiteness of the skin, the soft look of the cleft and the tuft of hair peeping out from between the thighs, were all fundamentally similar and well worth a lingering look. Clearing his throat, he moved into position. Naturally, he had to make sure that his niece's buttocks were properly positioned and, equally naturally, the best way to check that they were neither too loose or too tense was to feel them. This he did, and they were so soft and smooth that it wasn't until Lou coughed pointedly that he addressed himself to the business in hand.

He stood back, rested the switch across the centre of the target and whisked it down. It was not a hard stroke, more of a wristy flick than full sweep of his muscular arm, but a thin line leapt into view right across the centre, bright red against the whiteness and 'Ginia cried out at the biting smart and jerked. Jed waited for her to settle, then brought the pale switch whistling down to land half an inch above the first one, producing a similar but more pronounced reaction from the girl. The third was noticeably harder and made her straighten up, her buttocks clamped together so tightly that they dimpled. She was panting loudly and moaned as she bent over again and her striped bottom slowly rose up for the fourth stroke. He hit the base of her quivering cheeks and then stood back to take stock.

Lou let out her breath. She could see that Jed was being as restrained as she had expected but the effects of the switch had surprised her. It had never occurred to her to examine her rump after one of her whippings. The weals were turning darker and a pink stain between them was ample evidence of the pain they were causing. Lou felt a surge of concern for the youngster.

Virginia was awash with agony. Her whole bottom blazed and throbbed away behind her and she seriously doubted whether she could take many more without making a silly spectacle of herself. Luckily, her instincts came to her rescue. Instead of fighting, she found that drawing the waves of pain inside herself and savouring them made it far easier, while the unexpected interval gave the pain time to ebb a little.

Jed saw the gradual change in her position as she relaxed and administered the next three strokes in rapid succession, making her throw herself around on the sawhorse and kick her legs frantically in the air. Years of wielding axes, hoes, spades and horsewhips had made him uncannily accurate and these three lines were as even and as well-spaced as the first. He let Virginia settle down again and then moved forward to examine his handiwork. The sight of his rapt expression as he peered closely at the quivering cheeks inspired his wife to join him. Side by side, they stared. Then they had to feel, to assess the heat properly.

'I reckon another three should do her, Lou.'

'Yup,' replied Lou.

'Just three more, 'Ginia honey. Brace yourself. And you've taken your punishment like a man.'

Virginia stifled a wild desire to giggle at the incongruous compliment and braced herself, sliding her upper body a little further forwards, bending her knees inward and arching her back down. The result was that her bottom loomed up in blatant invitation, slightly disturbing Lou, who was still standing directly behind her and therefore had a clear view of the lower part of her niece's neat little pussy. By the time she had decided to suggest a reversion to the original position, Jed was resting the hickory between two of the long, mauve weals.

Staying close, she watched the fraying switch whistle through the air and sink into the plumpest part of Virginia's bottom. The girl cried out and humped up and down, making her parted buttocks shake and quiver. But they were soon thrust up again and Lou realised that her worries were groundless. Virginia was just like her.

The last two were the hardest of all and brought floods of tears and anguished sobs. Even so, there was no attempt to get up after the last one and the vivid bottom settled back on the horse, as though willingly submitting to a final examination.

She moved opposite her husband and, heads touching, they admired his handiwork, until he rather brusquely told Virginia she could go, suggesting that the creek would be an ideal destination. She staggered to her feet and, with her skirt tucked well up and out of the way, set off, her dark-red bottom moving with none of her normal smooth coordination as she hobbled stiffly along. Lou's own bottom began to tingle and she looked hard at Jed. He just stared back, saying nothing. Knowing that he would hardly walk away, Lou turned to the horse, tucked her skirt into her belt, lowered her panties, bending right down to work them clear of her feet, and bent over, her broad cheeks a stark contrast to Virginia's pertness.

In the meantime, Virginia had reached the creek, stripped and waded in up to her knees. Slowly and with several heartfelt groans, she lowered her rump into the water and squatted there, letting the coolness get to work on her burning buttocks. After some five minutes, she straightened up and peered over her shoulder to inspect the damage.

'Virginia,' she said aloud, 'you deserved that whipping. But I reckon it'll be a long time before you ask for another one.'

Hiding behind a tree, a minstrel watched the tableau with bated breath. The girl's beauty was striking by any standards but as she stood there, slim and pale, the rippling water up to her knees and with the stripes drawing his eye to her lovely, pert bottom, he was stunned. Then she turned and waded back, treating her unseen admirer to a view of her breasts, thighs and the dark triangle at their join, put her dress on and disappeared.

He whistled to himself, stood up and went about his business. As he did so, a song came to mind: 'In the Blue Ridge Mountains of Virginia.'

Sir James laughed aloud, then stared out of the window, lost in his thoughts.

'Sherrie, that was great. Tell me, did they ever meet? The musician and Virginia, I mean?'

'Oh yes, he was a local lad and they met at a Barn Dance soon afterwards. They got married and moved in with Jed and Lou. And very soon after they did so, Jed had had one glass of whiskey too many, slightly over-reacted to one of Lou's minor misdemeanours and spanked her bare bottom in front of the other two. Her howls of embarrassment were drowned by Jed's shouted instructions to the minstrel to do the same to Virginia, but her calm voice cut through the racket: 'Wait till Uncle Jed's finished. I want to watch and I'm sure Auntie Lou'll want to watch me getting it. Besides, ain't she got the plumpest, juiciest bottom you ever did see?'

114

And from that moment, the girls happily bared and bent at regular and frequent intervals.

'Excellent. Now, Sherrie my dear, it's time that you bared and bent,' Sir James told her. 'Hang on, how do you let down these arms? Oh yes . . . there we are. Now, over you go . . . and we'll have this up . . . and these down, if you don't mind. Not that I would take any notice if you did. Let's hope that you enjoy this as much as I'm going to . . . take *that*!'

Chapter 6

Sherrie made sure that Sir James had a decent sleep and when he awoke, they were on the last part of their flight to Sydney, still with four hours flying time still ahead of them. She showed him the bathroom, told him how to operate the shower, and when he professed to be totally incompetent at handling such complex technology, stripped off to help him. He found that being carefully soaped by a naked girl an interesting experience which promised greater things for a future occasion when the cubicle was big enough to fit two bodies.

After a breakfast of smoked salmon and scrambled eggs, Blue Mountain coffee and Buck's Fizz, he gave serious thought to the rest of the morning.

'Sherrie, I must do a little work. Can you give me half an hour? Then I'd love another story.'

'Of course, Sir James,' she agreed, 'just press the button when you're ready.'

To his surprise, it only took him twenty minutes to do his summary of the key points of the trip so far and to write a message to his London headquarters. He stabbed at the button.

'Could you get this sent off please? And then we'll get down to enjoying ourselves!'

Sherrie returned and was immediately asked to strip.

'Completely, or would you like me to keep my stockings on?'

'Yes, that would be nice ... could you come closer, so that I can touch the nice bits as they come into view? That's better.'

'What do you mean, "the nice bits"?' she said laughing, 'I'm nice all over.'

'I know, but I mean those bits which you usually keep hidden.'

'Oh, you mean my ruder parts, Sir James. Why didn't you say so?'

Laughing, he watched her take off her skirt and blouse, then raised a hand in an unmistakable gesture to hold it right there. Reaching up, he ran the tip of his forefinger along the line of her collarbone, down her cleavage, down the flat stomach to her tummy-button, where he lingered.

'I've learned a hell of a lot from you already, Sherrie.' His voice was low and thoughtful. 'For example, before I met you, it would never have occurred to me that looking at and touching a girl whose ruder parts are still covered up could possibly be this exciting. Yet I've already got a hard-on ... You've got a lovely belly-button ... a perfect circle ... and so deep. And I love the way your thighs bulge a little over the tops of your stockings. I'm not suggesting that they're fat, far from it. It's just very, very feminine.'

'Well, not many editors of Women's magazines would agree with me,' Sherrie said, 'but I think that it is perfectly natural – and healthy – for girls to have fatter thighs and buttocks than men. I'm not too keen on the fashion model shape.'

'Neither am I. Could you turn round please? God, your back view is gorgeous, Sherrie, it really is. I know a bit about keeping fit – I used to play rugby for Leicester and once had an England trial. This is the place to look for surplus fat.' He took a generous pinch of flesh by her ribs and there was less than half an inch between his finger and thumb. 'You're seriously fit ...' He slipped her knickers down. 'And yet your bottom's so plump ... can you feel how far my finger sinks in?'

'Yesss, Sir James,' she sighed.

He leaned forward and kissed the roundest part of her left cheek.

'That was fantastic! I suppose that I've often kissed a

girl's breasts – they're so lovely and soft – but I never realised that kissing her bottom could be as nice. I can't believe how my mouth kept on sinking into your flesh. And yet it looks so firm . . . almost solid. Did you know that you've got two big dimples . . . just here, above your bottom?'

'Of course I know.'

'How?' he asked, intrigued.

'Videos.'

'Eh?'

'I've seen videos of my back view,' she explained patiently.

'Ah. I'm not sure that I want to know more. Not at this stage, anyway. I might get jealous . . . Did these videos include your bottom?'

'Yes.'

'Then I definitely *would* get jealous.' He kissed her other cheek and then tugged her black knickers up again. 'You can take them off now.'

She did so in her own inimitable way. Having tucked her thumbs into the waistband, she combined the downward movement with a gradual bending, until she was holding the rumpled garment by her feet with her knees bent inward and her bare bottom jutting into his face. She paused then, presumably sensing that he was enjoying the view and made herself more comfortable by shuffling her feet further apart and bending a bit more at the knees.

Sir James was concerned for his blood pressure. Her buttocks showed no signs of the spanking he had given her the night before. They were creamy-white, smooth and well separated. At the base of her open cleft, at least two inches of her sparsely-haired cunt held his eye, before it travelled two inches up, where a patch of darker pink revealed the position of her anus. He kissed the crown of both cheeks and then, with some trepidation, he placed a hand on each half and eased them apart, exposing the rudest of her 'ruder parts'.

To his surprise, he found it beautiful. Hairless, a lovely pinky-brown in colour, slightly wrinkled round the edges and with a fascinating, tight, pouting, little sphincter in the middle. He also found it incredibly sexy, but initially put that thought down to the fact that he was examining the most private and secret part of her body. He let go, thoughtfully.

'Did you like looking at my bottom-hole?' Her voice seemed to come from a long way away.

'Yes. Very much.'

'Have you ever looked at one before?'

'I don't think I've ever seen one – before yours, I mean, let alone looked at one.'

'I really have got a lot to teach you . . .' she said softly.

'That's nice to know. Sherrie, once again I'm torn between carrying on with this and hearing another story. Let's go for the story – I'm definitely learning the benefits of patience!'

Sherrie stepped out of her knickers, took off her bra, sat down and executed a slow, '*Basic Instinct*' style leg-cross. She stared out to some distant horizon as she collected her thoughts, forcing her mind to ignore the feeling of the luxurious upholstery on her bare bottom and the tingle his inspection had induced in her anus.

Let's stay in the States. Our heroine is another young girl with an unhappy past. Like Virginia, she was the victim of a broken marriage, although her circumstances were completely different. For a start, she was half English. Her father was a relatively unknown writer who had met an American chorus girl in London, married her when she got pregnant and had managed to get a lucrative job churning out B-movie scripts in Hollywood in 1925, where he stayed, in spite of the inevitable divorce. Susan, their offspring, turned out to be a quiet beauty. But one who always seemed to be in some sort of trouble. We'll join her in 1940, she is twenty-two and has just been sent to a special penitentiary situated in the eastern part of California, totally isolated and with a farm attached where the girls spend most of the days working their little tails off.

As I said, Susan was gorgeous. Quite tall – about five

foot five – with long, dark hair, an elfin face, big brown eyes and a rather English figure; small boobs and biggish hips, although, like her American mother, she had lovely long legs. Her normal expression was a sort of wide-eyed innocence, a look which had led several policemen to let her off with a caution on the grounds that no one who looked that sweet could possibly have done whatever it was she was accused of.

Unfortunately, her looks did not save her from the charge of being drunk in charge of a car and reckless driving, which was why she was in the clink.

Sure enough, she was soon in trouble. Warden McCluskey, who was in charge of her dormitory and also helped supervise the work parties, was not the sort of woman to be taken in by a pair of big eyes, even when they filled with what seemed to be tears of remorse and confusion. She had seen it all before. At thirty-five, she was shortish, a bit on the stocky side, with big firm boobs and a tightly rounded, bustling bottom. Years of authority and an unfulfilled sex life had hardened her face, although in repose her basic prettiness was still visible.

Susan's mother had never nagged her about her untidiness, so it came as a rude shock when Warden McCluskey made her make her bed and tidy her locker again and again until it would have passed muster in a Marine Corps barracks. She had never had to do any proper physical work, so she couldn't understand why they all made such a fuss about her frequent rests. She had pretended to faint, but all the Warden in charge had done was to throw a bucket of water over her. In all, prison was far worse than she had feared.

By the end of Susan's second week, McClusky felt that it was high time that she had a quiet talk with her. On the next Sunday afternoon, there was a nervous tap on her office door – fifteen minutes later than ordered.

'Come in . . . you're late. I said two o'clock,' the Warden snapped.

'Sorry Ma'am . . . I sort of forgot. About the time, I mean,' Susan explained, smiling prettily.

'OK, we'll come back to that later. Now listen here, young lady, I have had just about enough of you ...' Susan's failings were listed in considerable detail. 'I reckon I'm going to do you a favour by bringing you up short, because if you carry on the way you are, you're never going to be out of trouble. So, Susan, I'm gonna offer you a choice. This is unofficial, by the way, so it won't appear on your record. This time.'

'Thank you, Ma'am ... what's the choice, Ma'am?'

Hard blue eyes locked onto the moist brown ones. Warden McCluskey took a deep breath. 'Either I paddle your butt for you or you eat my pussy!'

Susan gasped and blushed. She gazed unseeingly at the wall as various memories raced through her brain.

She thought of her friend Betsy, who had won a scholarship to one of the top East Coast Universities and had been accepted into one of the Sororities. She had told the open-mouthed Susan about the initiation ceremonies with great relish, lingering on the humiliation of having to lift her nightie and bend over for a dozen with the paddle. For no reason. Then she had found a hairbrush and demonstrated on Susan. Even through her panties it had hurt like hell. But the afterglow had been something else and, when she got back home, she had fingered herself for the first time.

A beach party, at midnight. Two of the girls had gone skinny-dipping and their white, bobbing bottoms as they ran into the ocean had fascinated her.

Shower time in the penitentiary. En masse. Naked bodies everywhere. Pink, white, brown. The amazing variety in the colour of the girls' pussy hair and in the size of their boobs. Feeling hot eyes on her own nakedness. A hand patting her bare rump and a soft voice in her ear –'That's one cute ass you've got there, honey.' She had whirled round, flaming with embarrassment but there were too many girls around to be sure of who had done it. But the impression had lingered until after lights out and her hand had stolen between her thighs again. Again in the shower, accidentally bumping bottoms with a girl and the way the

121

impression of firm softness had stayed. The image of a tall, blonde girl, dreamily soaping her pussy, then turning to do her bottom, rubbing the bar of soap up and down her cleft, the gleaming cheeks quivering. Glistening.

The only pleasures there at the penitentiary seemed to involve bare bottoms.

Susan's eyes focused on the Warden's. 'That's some choice, Ma'am ... Can't I have both?' She smiled her soft, shy smile and Warden McCluskey thought that Christmas, Thanksgiving, Independence Day and her birthday had all come at once.

'Sure you can, honey ... the paddling first.'

She reached into her desk drawer and slowly took out her favourite paddle and put it down in front of her wide-eyed victim.

Susan almost changed her mind. The weapon looked horribly effective – some eighteen inches long, six wide, made from highly polished wood, with rounded corners and a thick, leather-bound handle.

On the upper side she could clearly see a drawing of a girl bending over and gripping her ankles, thrusting her pantied bottom up in the air. She was looking back and her mouth was wide open in an 'O' of pain.

'Did you draw this, Ma'am,' she asked.

'Yes.'

'It's real good.'

'Thank you.' The Warden smiled coolly. 'Hand it to me, please.'

It was lighter than she had expected and Susan felt reassured. 'How would you like me, Ma'am?'

'Lay your belly on the top of the desk and reach out to hold on to the far side ... legs straight down ... further apart ... more ... that's it.'

The anonymous girl in the shower room had been spot on in her assessment of Susan's bottom. The central seam of her jeans pressed into the division, slightly separating the cheeks and making their shape very clear. Even though Warden McCluskey already knew from careful observation in the shower room that Susan was especially well endowed, she bent down until her face was only inches away from the main point of her interest and felt away to her heart's content. Already turned on by the prospect of paddling her, the combination of Susan's submissiveness and the tightly packed seat of her jeans made it all even more promising.

Susan was equally hyped up. She was scared, but finding pleasure in her fear. The roaming palm on her bottom concentrated her feelings in that part of her, but not exclusively. There was a nice hollowness in her tummy; her chest was all tight and constricted; her nipples were sort of tingling and aching. Not as much as her rear end though, especially when the hand wandered downwards and pressed briefly against her pussy, but enough to notice. And there was the pussy-eating to look forward to. Her own body felt so nice under her hands – surely another girl's would feel even nicer? There was just the minor matter of the spanking. She remembered that her mother had sometimes threatened to spank her. Never had done, but one time, when she was about fifteen or sixteen, when she had wriggled out of her punishment with her usual skill, she had wondered what it would have felt like. Oh well, she would soon find out – and that paddle was too light to hurt that much.

Warden McCluskey was ready. She hefted the paddle, laid it against the upper part of the girl's bottom and let fly, revelling in the sound of the impact, which was the aspect of a good paddling she loved most. A sort of hollow 'thwack', nicer than any music. Especially when there was a good, high-pitched howl to accompany it. There wasn't one forthcoming from Susan, which disappointed her a little, but it was only the first stroke after all, and there was plenty of time. She drove the second one in a little bit harder. The sound was even nicer, she clearly saw the girl's bottom quiver but that was all. She didn't even wriggle or jerk. The third one thudded into the base. Ah, a jerk that time. And a little wriggle. She glanced to her left and was surprised to see that Susan had her head turned towards her, obviously following the movements of the paddle. Her eyes were shining, but not with the first sign of tears – and she was *smiling*. Warden McCluskey was puzzled and she frowned at her victim.

Susan stood up and slowly massaged her rump. 'Ma'am, you sure do know how to spank a girl's bottom. But these jeans are awful thick. Why don't I take them down?' She hesitated and then her eyes widened. 'That is, as long as you don't mind?'

There was another pause. Warden McCluskey cleared her throat and tried to regain the initiative.

'Yeah. Drop 'em.'

Susan turned her back and tugged away until the jeans could slither down her legs. Her plain white panties had been drawn up into her cleft and two nice crescents of bare, pink buttock-flesh peeped out.

'How about my panties, Ma'am?'

Warden McCluskey looked up at the innocent expression and then back at the pert cheeks and heaved a silent sigh. Normally it took about two spankings before she got around to lowering a girl's jeans but Susan was clearly a special case. She held the girl's eyes and played for time.

'What about them?'

'Shall I take them down, Ma'am? I'll feel the spanking much more and I've been a very naughty girl so it's right that I feel it. I don't think my bottom will offend you. One of the girls said it was real nice. In the showers, so she could see it, you know, she wasn't guessing or anything.'

The Warden's habitually stern expression softened slowly as she smiled. A smile of complete fulfilment.

'Fine, Susan. Take your panties down. To your knees. We'll have your pretty ass as bare as it was the day you were born.'

'Yes Ma'am . . . is that OK? Shall I bend over again?'

'No, stand there. Let me have a look . . . Mmmm, I haven't done much damage – it's just a little pink, that's all.'

'Oooh Ma'am, you've got nice hands . . . 'specially when you touch me there. Is my bottom nice?'

'Sure is. But it'll look even nicer when it's all red. Bend over the desk again. Legs apart. Back down, bottom up. Good.'

Thwack!

'Ow!' Susan howled.

Thwack!

'Oooh. It does sting more on my bare bottom, Ma'am.' *Thwack!* 'Oh God, I really felt that one. Seems to hurt a bit more low down. Near my pussy.' *Thwack!* 'Ouch!' *Thwack!*

'Was that one just on my left cheek, Ma'am? My bottom's so hot, it's hard to tell.' *Thwack!* 'Aaaah!! Oh, can I give it a rub, Ma'am? Please Ma'am. Thank you . . . That's better. It'll help me take the rest . . . Oohh . . . I can feel my bottom wobble like a jello when you hit it, Ma'am. Does it?' She paused, waiting for the Warden to respond. When she didn't Susan carried on talking. 'Is it nice? If it is, would you like me to put my feet further back? It'll make it softer – not so tight – and it should wobble even more. Shall I try? Like this?'

Thwack! 'Wowwww!' *Thwack!* 'Owwww!' *Thwack!*

'Oh my! I'm hotter than a pepper sprout, Ma'am. Can I have another rest. Oh, Ma'am, I'll rub it if you prefer. No, your hands are great . . . just great, honest . . . Ma'am, just a thought. Would you like me to kiss your bottom before I lick your pussy? I'd like to.'

'Maybe,' the Warden replied with a slight tremor in her voice, 'but you've got a heap of spanking to get through first. I want you properly red. And crying. Now bend over again and this time tuck your knees right under the desk and tighten your bottom up. That's real nice. I'm going to give you – let's think – another twelve like this and then we'll see. Grip the edge hard, cos I don't want your hands anywhere near your bottom. Press your tits right down on the desk. Good.'

Susan obeyed and held her breath. It was all proving more exciting than she had thought possible. Her bottom was throbbing and sizzling behind her and her new position was the best yet. She could feel cool air in her open cleft and between her thighs, convincing her that her pussy must have been visible. She wondered what she looked like – and whether Warden McCluskey was enjoying herself.

She seemed to be. The tingling spread out from between her legs into her tummy.

Warden McCluskey was still crouched down behind the bending girl. Susan would have been very reassured had she been able to see the lustful expression on her punisher's face, although she would have been amazed at the startling redness of her buttocks, highlighted by the white slash of the widened cleft. The Warden stared at the tuft of dark hair at the base of the cleft, breathed in the musky scent and felt a surge of lust when she saw a little bead of moisture at the top of the slit.

She moved back to the side and swept the paddle upwards, right across the base, bringing Susan up onto tiptoe and making her squawk. The next two strokes landed on the same place and it was time for another inspection, which revealed a charmingly duotone bottom, with the lower half a rich crimson in contrast to the bright red of the top. Grunting her satisfaction, she moved back and delivered the next three on the centre, smiling with grim satisfaction when, after each one, Susan half straightened to rub her backside, her anguished face turned pleadingly towards her before finding no mercy, she bent over again. But each time she did so, her bottom protruded just a little bit more.

After another examination, numbers seven, eight and nine added their contribution to the upper slopes of Susan's bottom, each stroke administered in quick succession, so that Susan had no time to react in between them. As the paddle fell away after the third of the series, she stood bolt upright, wailing and clutching her injured rear.

Pretending to be seriously angry, Warden McCluskey squatted down behind her, looked hard and long and knew that the girl had taken just about enough. But there was plenty of time. The girl had quite the sexiest and prettiest bottom she could remember paddling and was such a willing victim that she couldn't bear to finish just yet.

Irritated by her snivelling, she dug a handkerchief out of her pocket, passed it up to her, waited until she had blown her nose and wiped her eyes, then put it back and pondered.

'Well, Susan, your butt's really red. No bruises, though – that's why I like to use a light, shiny paddle. Stings like hell, but doesn't do any real damage. Not like the Governor's, that's made out of heavy leather. With holes in it. Leaves big blisters all over a naughty girl's bottom. And she always does it on the bare.'

'Oh. Don't think I like the sound of that.'

'Well be a good girl, then.'

'I will . . . Would you like me to kiss your bottom and eat your pussy now?'

Warden McCluskey, with her vision filled with Susan's bare bottom was almost tempted to kiss it before answering the girl's question but that would be bad for discipline. Maybe some other time.

'OK. I may not have finished with you but while you're kissing my ass, yours will be cooling off a bit. Up you get. And leave your jeans . . . no, take 'em right off.' As soon as this had been done, she gripped the girl under the chin and held her face close to hers. The brown eyes were red and moist, the full mouth slack and her cheeks flushed and tear-stained. Gorgeous. 'OK, Susan, this is what you're gonna do. Get down on your knees behind me, tuck the back of my skirt up, slip my panties down and kiss every inch of my ass. Slowly. If you do it good, I might let you go round again. And I hope you realise that you're a helluva lucky girl. Not many of you get to see what you're gonna see and even fewer kiss it. Now move.'

'Yes, ma'am.'

Susan fell onto her knees, took two handfuls of skirt hem and began to heave upwards, her eyes fixed on the tight seat. The stinging in her own bottom had settled to a throbbing warmth which reminded her strongly of the afterglow left by Betsy's hairbrush. The prospect of getting a really good look at a bare female bottom added a lot to her already high level of excitement. And from what she could tell from the bulging khaki, the bottom she was about to see was nice, plump and firmly rounded. She got the skirt up to waist level with a little difficulty and stared at the panties, which were regulation khaki, long-legged and singularly unattractive. Holding her breath yet again, she fumbled for the waistband and whisked them firmly down, exhaling gustily as the twin cheeks quivered into the open.

Bare, Warden McCluskey's bottom looked even bigger than it did all covered up and was a great deal more attractive. It was creamy-white, with very curvy cheeks, a particularly tight cleft and wide folds at the top of each thigh. Sighing again, Susan rested her hands on the hips, bent forward and applied pursed lips to the crown of the left buttock.

She had suggested doing this in an instinctive attempt to distract the Warden from spanking her too hard and for too long. It hadn't worked, as the pain in her own bottom made clear but, now that she had taken the plunge, she was loving it. The bare skin was so soft, smooth and warm under her lips. The cheeks may have looked as solid as stone but the flesh yielded under the slightest pressure of her mouth. As she brushed across the cleft, the extra warmth and softness of the skin there was noticeable. She grew bolder. She opened her mouth and flicked the tip of her tongue over a little bulge of flesh trapped between her lips; she moved her hands down, placed her thumbs alongside the top of the cleft and, easing it open, kissed and licked the little lump where Warden McCluskey's spine ended; she craned her head back and did the same along each gluteal fold. She heard the sighs of pleasure from above and bent to her task with renewed enthusiasm, moving her hands round to the front so that they gripped the tops of the thighs and she could pull the bottom into her face.

She became aware of a rather nice feeling invading her own rear and realised that she was resting on her heels. She had cocked her bottom far enough back to press her pussy against them and the waves of pleasure made her quite keen to get on with eating pussy. In the meantime, kissing bare bottom was fine to be getting on with, so she got on with it. After another circuit or two, she coughed.

'Am I doing alright, Ma'am?'

'Just fine, Susan, just fine. Keep going, my pussy's warming up nicely.'

'Could you just bend forward a little bit, Ma'am?' She ran a fingertip down the cleft. 'Then I can kiss you here.'

The bottom loomed even closer and broadened as her mentor complied. Susan reached up, placed her lips at the start of the division and moved slowly downwards, enjoying the extra intimacy.

'Do the same again – but with your tongue.'

'Yes Ma'am.'

'Aahh, that's real nice. Now pull the cheeks apart. Further. Now kiss my asshole.'

'Oh Ma'am!' Shuddering, she nervously eased the two halves aside. The bottom-hole popped into view, neat and pink. Susan stared at it, strangely fascinated then, taking a deep breath, she rammed her face into the gap and kissed. It was soft and warm in there and there was the scent of turned-on female and scented soap. She stuck her tongue out, tentatively at first, found it all perfectly acceptable and was soon licking away.

If Susan found it pleasant, Warden McCluskey could hardly contain herself. It was sheer bliss. Her bottom wriggled and she grabbed one of Susan's hands and pushed it down onto her pussy, where it began to diddle away with a natural skill.

Half an hour later, the cries from the Warden's third climax faded. She was on her back, knees up to her chest, bare from the waist down and Susan's head was buried between her thighs, her soft hair tickling them as her stiffened tongue stabbed at the sensitive clitoris.

'Was I really good, Ma'am?' Susan asked nervously a bit later.

'The best, honey.' She stood up and held the girl close, reaching down to stroke a rounded and still very warm cheek.

'Can I maybe . . . sometime . . . come back again? I will try to be good, honest . . . but maybe another paddling will help . . . you know, Ma'am . . . sort of remind me. And I'd love to kiss and eat you again afterwards. I loved your bottom, I really did. And your pussy tasted so nice. I'll kiss your tits as well. If you want me to, that is.'

The arms tightened. 'I think we'll keep the paddle for when you're naughty, but the rest sounds like a great idea!'

'Oh. What'll you do if I'm only a bit naughty?'

'Give you a nice little spanking. Across my knee.' The Warden smiled.

'Oh thank you, Ma'am. On my bare bottom?'

'You bet!'

'That would be nice. Next Sunday?'

'We'll see. Now dress me and then pull your clothes back up and get back to your dorm. That's fine. Feel a bit tight, do they?'

'Yes, they do. Bye Ma'am ... and ... thank you.'

'See you, Susan. Hey, don't I get a goodbye kiss?'

'Wow.' Sir James stared at Sherrie in amazement. 'That was your best tale yet.' He looked out of the window, obviously reliving it. 'The paddle sounds quite entertaining ... And I liked the fact that it was mainly sexy fun, rather than pure punishment.'

'I agree. But it's best if there is a fair amount of pain.'

'Yes I suppose so. You like being spanked – would you have enjoyed being paddled like Susan?'

'Very much, as long as Warden McCluskey turned me on. Which I think she would have.'

'Why?'

'A good question. She was authoritative, pretty, expert – she was clever in the way she kept giving Susan time to recover before carrying on – and possibly most important of all, keen on bottoms.'

'That's interesting. You wouldn't be so keen if the person beating you was just treating your buttocks as a target. As opposed to your back. Or legs. Or even hands, I suppose.'

'That's right. I love showing off my bottom. I get a kick out of walking up and down a beach in just a thong, so that the cheeks are completely bare. I add a lot to my natural wiggle and love imagining the wide eyes following me. I got serious pleasure when you made me walk up and down the aisle, knowing that watching was exciting you. It was, wasn't it?'

'Er, since you ask, it blew my socks off.'

'I love that expression. Where was I? Oh yes, presenting my derrière for a spanking or a beating is very important. In the beginning, anyway. After a bit, the pain takes over. Well, not completely. I'm always conscious of my bottom.'

'What is it about the pain that excites you?' he asked, curious.

'It's very difficult to explain. It obviously starts in my bottom. But after a bit, the waves spread and warm me up right through my middle. Then there comes a point when it seriously hurts and I want it to stop. And I feel the after-glow which Susan felt after Betsy's hairbrush. But every so often, especially when I'm in the right mood, and/or I'm being thrashed by a real expert, it washes right through me and ends up in my brain. I see flashes of bright light at every stroke. It takes me over and I'm like putty in his – or her – hands. I *have* to withstand it. To conquer it. When I do, it's a bit like a monster orgasm. And afterwards, the blood sings through my veins and I feel physically and mentally refreshed.'

'I see. Would you have enjoyed licking Warden McCluskey's anus?'

'Yes.'

'The ultimate submission?'

'Only partly. Assuming it's all nice and kosher, it's also a nice feeling, doing it to someone you're fond of. Or in thrall to. Especially if you have to hold the cheeks apart and burrow in between them. And bottom-holes can be quite pretty – I don't remember you throwing up when you looked at mine!'

'Far from it.' Sir James laughed, then looked at her seriously. 'Sherrie, will you please kneel up on your seat and stick your bottom up. I'd like to find out what it's like for myself.'

'With pleasure!' Once again, he looked avidly on as she

turned her back on him and slowly thrust her rump upwards and outwards, the cleft gradually opening up like an
exotic flower until her anus was visible between the tight
cheeks. Sir James followed Susan's example and, like her,
found that the process was far from distasteful. He then
slid his hand between Sherrie's thighs, found her clitoris
and, very shortly, the combined stimulation brought her
off.

He helped her to her feet and held her tight until her
breathing had steadied.

'Shall we have a coffee break, Sir James?' she suggested.

'Good idea.'

Once again he watched the steady sway of her rear as she
went to the galley and then sat back and decided that it
was high time he gave her another spanking. But before he
broached the subject, there were two cups of her excellent
coffee to drink and further questions.

'Sherrie, how many different implements have we
covered in your stories? The birch, the paddle, the belt, the
thonged whip in the convent, a switch . . . what else?'

'The General's scabbard.'

'Oh yes. But that was extempore. What others are there?
The cane, obviously . . . do you have a favourite?'

'To answer your last question first, not really. I quite like
the riding crop . . . but there isn't really a set rule. As you
said, the General used his scabbard when he couldn't lay
his hands on anything else, so one could use anything. It
could be flat, like a hairbrush or a slipper. Or long and thin
like the scabbard. Whippy and flexible like a length of flex.
Or rubber hose. They will all hurt, some much more than
others, of course. In the end, the effect all depends on the
person wielding the implement.'

'Yes, I imagine it does. Why the crop?' he asked, intrigued, 'what's special about it?'

'It doesn't bite quite as maddeningly as the cane, so it's
just a bit easier to take and you know the little leather tab
on the end? Well you can feel that – most of the time, anyway – and the very different feel adds something special to
a stroke. But, as I said, I see the implement more as the

medium, not the message. In other words, the important thing is the communication between me, my bare bottom and my punisher.'

'Do you prefer it on your bare bottom?'

'Definitely. Tell you what, Sir James, I've got some implements with me. We've got plenty of time, so why don't you try them out on me?'

'Er . . . yes,' he said uncertainly, 'but won't your bottom get marked?'

'Not too badly. And don't forget that you've got the best part of a week in Australia, so it will be back to pure white by the time you return!'

'It's a deal. Go get 'em.'

She was back in a trice, carrying a large sports bag, which she dumped on one of the seats and they bent to the task of examining the contents. A couple of canes, a tawse, a large leather paddle, a hairbrush, a leather-soled slipper and a martinet.

'No riding crop, I see.'

'Oh hell, I must have left it behind. I'll try and get one in Australia.'

'Good. OK, now let me think. Actually, I think I'd like to start with my hand – if that's all right with you.'

'Of course it is. Can I make a suggestion, Sir James? I'd like to put some clothes on. It's that bit sexier – for me, anyway – to have my bottom peeping out from between raised skirt and lowered knickers.'

'Fine, go ahead.'

He watched as she quickly slipped on her blouse, knickers and skirt and then turned back to face him, her expression calm, her eyes steadily looking into his, a little smile turning up the corners of her full mouth. It occurred to him that this was one of those moments he would remember for the rest of his life and determined to savour it to the full. Stepping back so that he could take in the full length of her, he looked at her as though for the first time and she reacted perfectly, pulling her shoulders back and standing to attention, focusing on some distant point.

Her blouse was tight across her breasts and thin enough

to reveal the dark circles of her nipples. Under his scrutiny, they puckered and the centres pressed against the silk. Her neat skirt was too thick to mould itself to her thighs but could disguise neither the basic flatness of her tummy nor the curves of her hips. His eyes travelled down and lingered on the shapeliness of her legs before sweeping up to her face.

He now knew her more intimately than anyone in his life so far. Or did he? With the insight of the seriously turned on, he sensed that he had not touched her soul. Her body, perhaps, her mind certainly. But he had probably already reached the limit of her need for him. For a moment he felt incredibly sad but then gave himself a mental kick up the backside. 'For Christ's sake, count your lucky stars, James. She's amazing. Just enjoy everything she offers you for as long as you can.'

He remembered something she had said recently, the importance of which had escaped him at the time. 'Communication between me, my bare bottom and my punisher.' That was what it was all about. Even if he couldn't understand how or why she wanted pain, he could still communicate his affection, desire and respect for her. Through her bottom. Her bare bottom. And with all the implements at his disposal.

Stepping up to her, he cupped the firm smoothness of her cheek in his palm and ran his thumb across her soft mouth.

'Sherrie, my dear, I am going to spank, paddle, strap and cane you. On your naked buttocks.' Her mouth pouted on the ball of his thumb and the slight suction of her kiss sent a tingle right down to the end of his prick. 'I shall love every minute, every second. You've got the most beautiful and seductive bottom I've ever seen and I am going to relish every quiver, every little wobble, all your cries. By the time I have finished with it, it'll look like a tropical sunset. And when I think that you've had enough – when I feel that you are truly sorry – I'll kiss it better and then bend you right over so that I can see your sweet little anus and bugger you. Do I make myself perfectly clear?'

'Oh yes, Sir James.'

He sat down, guided her across his knees, slowly bared her bottom, stroked it to get her nerve-ends properly tingling and then spanked her, steadily and firmly but with frequent intervals, which he happily used to enjoy the feel of her skin and flesh.

He kept her over his knee while he acquainted himself with slipper and hairbrush.

Her bottom was very red indeed by the time the echo of the last splatting impact of wood against feminine flesh had faded.

'Oh, Sir James, can I have a few minutes to cool off a bit? Oh, that's lovely ... a bit harder, please. Rub the heat into me. Aaahhh!'

'That'll do you. I think this paddle should be next. Up you get and I'll have you lying across the seat of my chair. Not bad, Sherrie, but try moving your feet apart ... a bit further. That's it – I can see your pussy protruding beneath your thighs. Very nice too. Ready?'

The paddle was stiff and shiny. Her relaxed cheeks wobbled beautifully and a dozen strokes made them glow like twin beacons, in spite of the bright sunlight flooding the cabin.

'What's your favourite position for the tawse, Sherrie?'

'Bending over the back of the chair? My bottom will be a little tighter but should still wobble a bit ... you do like seeing it wobble when you smack it, don't you?'

'Very much. OK, over you go.'

The different viewpoint emphasised the sharp curves where her buttocks met in the middle. Out of the corner of his eye, he noticed that her head was turned towards him and he met her eyes.

'You're doing terribly well, Sir James. My whole bottom is burning beautifully.'

'I'm glad to hear it. It's lovely and red.'

'I thought it must be.'

'Six?' he suggested.

'Oh, twelve, please.'

A dozen times the divided tails of the Pride of Lochgelly

sank into her, each one forcing her against the back of the seat and making her churn her hips around. After the last one, Sir James tossed the warm leather aside and squatted behind her, using hands, lips, tongue and words to soothe and praise her.

'I'm ready for the martinet now, Sir James. It's best given on a really tight bottom. Then the middle bits of the thongs can get into my cleft. It's soft and very sensitive in there.'

He followed her round to the front of the seat and held his breath as her bottom tightened and spread open to expose both orifices, and then he kissed the hot skin at the rounded crown of each cheek, picked up the multi-tailed whip and slashed it firmly across the full and generous width before him.

She shrieked. Not that that deterred him, for he knew that she had built herself up to take far more. But, as soon as she had brought herself under control, he moved behind her again and ran his tongue over each mauve line. He did the same after every stroke, so that her cries changed to little mewing sounds of pleasure, especially when he lingered over the raised bumps where the tips had bitten into her flank.

After a dozen strokes from France's contribution to the joys of corporal punishment, he put her back across his knee so that he could stroke and rub her more easily. He parted her buttocks and trailed the tip of his forefinger round the subtle corrugations surrounding her anus and smiled as she wriggled and hissed at his touch. Then she pushed her hips up in the air and spread her thighs, so that he could slide his finger down and into the wet warmth of her sex and she came with happy abandon.

At last it was time for the cane. He chose the lighter one and whisked it around, marvelling at its menacing flexibility. She bent over and took a firm grip of her ankles. Her naked bottom loomed up at him, deep scarlet, beautifully divided and willingly offered.

He had been a county class squash player in his youth and it all came flooding back to him as he used arm and wrist to drive the supple malacca into her yielding flesh. Eighteen strokes later, she turned her face towards him. Tears were pouring down her cheeks, but her eyes shone with desire.

His cock had been at full stretch for ages and he could wait no longer. He tore at zips and buttons in feverish haste and had just tossed away his second sock when she stopped him dead in his tracks. She took a tube of lubricating jelly out of her bag, knelt on his seat, stuck her livid rump into the air, then slowly and lasciviously anointed her own anus in readiness. The sight of her slim, glistening finger sliding into the tight hole until it was buried up to the knuckle was almost too much for him and she only just got her hand out of the way in time before he was pressing the tip of his prick at the entrance.

Her hot, velvety passage enveloped him and it was all he could do to stay on his feet as she milked him dry, using a combination of smooth movements of her hips and expert use of her sphincter muscle.

He felt utterly drained and couldn't manage even a muttered protest as she sponged him down with a nurse's skill, sat him down, moved the seat until it was flat enough to form a bed, wrapped a blanket round him and darkened the cabin.

When she eventually woke him to tell him that they were descending and would be landing at Sydney in twenty minutes, he felt sharper and more clear-headed than he had done for years – and quite prepared to take Australia by storm.

Chapter 7

Sherrie both enjoyed and appreciated the week's break that Sir James' schedule had allowed her. She spent the first few days in a deserted beach-house on the North coast of Queensland, lying around, either in a rather old-fashioned bikini which covered her bottom completely to protect it from the sun, or nothing at all, her favoured costume for the early mornings and late afternoons, when she could meander along the beach and swim in the way she liked best. The chances of her being spotted were remote and she relaxed completely.

When all her marks had faded, she drove back to Sydney and savoured its cosmopolitan flavour to the full. A chance encounter with a strikingly lovely Thai girl led to a satisfying diversion for the last two days and she enjoyed her neat little bottom and hairless fanny to the full.

Almost too soon, she was back on duty, waiting at the open door of the jet as Sir James' car glided to a halt and he emerged, surrounded by a troop of shirt-sleeved young colleagues, all exuding a typically Australian air of brisk, informal efficiency. She studied him carefully as he strode towards her, glad to see him looking fit, tanned and grinning from ear to ear. He sprang up the steps, gave her a smacking kiss, pinched her bottom as she bent forward to close the door and generally made a nuisance of himself.

Scolding him roundly, she pushed him into the main cabin, took his coat and briefcase, sat him down and belted him up. As soon as he had begun to behave himself she stood out of harm's way, turned her back and, baring her bottom, waggled it violently at him.

With a strangled yelp, he tried to undo his belt and jump on her but she forestalled him by covering herself up and telling him that he had to observe take-off procedures and stay seated.

'And no smoking, Sir.' She glared at him with prim disapproval.

'I don't smoke,' he retorted.

'Well no steaming then.'

He laughed and promised to be a good boy, which he was until they had completed their noisy climb and were on course for New Zealand.

'Sherrie, I am sorry about that earlier. I got carried away at seeing you after all this time. Can I undo my belt now?'

'Will you promise to keep your hands to yourself?'

'Certainly not.'

'In that case ... of course you may! I should imagine that it's been a pretty successful week.'

'It has. Tell you what, Sherrie, let's have a bottle of that Krug and I'll tell you about it. I know that it's a bit early but what the hell?'

'As you say, what the hell?' She got up and started up the aisle towards the galley.

'Hang on, Sherrie. Would you strip? Firstly, I love seeing you bare and secondly, I want to see if I marked your bottom.'

She strolled back, smiling. 'With pleasure, Sir James.' Her fingers moved quickly down the row of buttons on the front of her blouse and, in her usual efficient way she soon had everything off except her stockings and knickers. Turning her back on him, she hooked her fingers in the waistband and bent forward, standing still, deliberately teasing him.

Not that he objected. This pair of briefs were white and showed off her lightly suntanned back and legs to perfection. He guessed that they were smaller than the bikini she had worn, because he could see a dividing line between brown and cream skin above and below. They were also almost transparent and her bottom cleft was easily visible; dark, exciting and full of memories!

She slipped them down and stood still, most of her weight on her right leg, so that the cheek above it bulged tightly. She then shifted to the left leg, her bottom changing shape as she did so. He stared and was vastly relieved that it was as flawless as ever, although on very close inspection, he thought that he could see a few faint brown smudges on her right hip, the last traces of the martinet. As he sat back, she slowly bent right over to work her knickers to her feet, her knees tucked well forward so that her rump was pointedly tight and open. She stayed down, the shape of her body like a question mark and he sensed that she was in fact posing a question – 'would you like me to stay like this so that you can help yourself?'

He answered the silent question with an unspoken reply and placed a hand on each cheek, smoothing around the tautness, loving the silkiness of her skin. He ran the tip of his forefinger up and down her cleft and smiled at her muted gasp. Parting her properly, he looked right into her bottom, and trailed a fingertip over the pinky-brown centre.

'No damage here?' he asked softly.

'Of course not.'

'You enjoyed it?'

'Very, very much,' she purred.

'So did I.'

He applied his tongue, gently at first and then as hard as he could and he felt her sway as the strength left her legs. He helped her to kneel up on the seat, where she buried her face in her hands and poked her rear right up at him. Now both her passages were exposed and he took the time to look again before sweeping his tongue up and down the full length of her division until she was moaning softly. Sinking back on his heels, he used his right forefinger to titillate her anus while with the left he played with her sex. Somehow she seemed to draw both fingers inside her and enclose them in her moist warmth. He could feel one against the other through the thin wall separating the two passages and felt a new pleasure in pleasing her.

Slipping his fingers out, he turned her over, eased her

forward until her bottom was off the edge of the seat and then folded her legs right back, again exposing her to the full. With her in this position, though, he was able to concentrate more fully on her sex. He rested his hands on her thighs, extended his thumbs, pressed them into the furred lips and drew them apart, opening up the glistening, coral-pink folds inside. He pushed his tongue into her, then sucked her clitoris into his mouth, nibbling gently until her hands clamped round the back of his head as she came.

The champagne tasted even better than usual, and he raised his glass to her in tribute as she sat opposite him, her legs neatly crossed. Only her breasts and thighs reminding him of her nudity. He was therefore able to give virtually all of his attention to their discussion on the Australian tour and, once again, he appreciated her grasp of the essentials and her informed common sense.

By the time he had finished, so was the bottle. He held it up to the light just in case she hadn't noticed that there was nothing in it and she took the hint, trotting up to the galley to replace it. Once again, the sight of her naked walk was enough to transfer his concentration from business to pleasure. When she had refilled his glass, she looked at her watch.

'It's nearly lunch time, Sir James. Are you hungry?'

'Yes I am. What do you suggest?'

'Well, how about lobster thermidor?'

'Brilliant thinking.'

'Right, I'll get on with it. Are you happy to sit and work while I'm cooking – or would you like to see another video?' she asked him.

'Have you got another spanking one?'

'Of course.' She smiled.

'Then yes please. By the way, was that you doing the dishing out in the last one?'

'Yes.'

'I thought I recognised the hand!'

After a few minutes contentedly watching her setting up the screen and then twinkling up the aisle, he settled back, glass in hand, bottle beside him. The screen flickered into life, informing him that he was about to see '*The Dancing Mistress*'.

The plot proved to be fairly straightforward – a dancing class was being instructed by an energetic teacher, with the only point of real interest in the opening scene being the tiny leotards worn by the whole cast. There were a lot of naked buttocks on view and Sir James looked on with approval. After some five minutes of energetic and highly watchable action, the teacher called a halt.

'OK girls, you can knock off now – except for Anne and Kathy. You two stay behind.' The camera followed the four liberated girls trotting away, cleverly focusing on their backsides, one by one, and then swung back to those belonging to the two detainees, side by side and nervously clenched. 'Right,' the teacher said sternly after the others had left, 'I've warned you often enough and now you're about to find out that I don't make empty threats. As I promised you last time, you're both going to get a good spanking. Now get those bottoms bare.'

The camera zoomed back to show all three participants, two with wide open mouths and nervously fluttering hands.

'But that means taking our cozzies right off, Melissa,' said one to the teacher.

'That's right,' said the other. 'Look, we're as good as bare as it is. Especially if we tuck them up even further. Like this.'

She hitched the back of her leotard right into her cleft and turned to show the result. There was a close-up of Melissa's face – fair-skinned, sensual and very pretty. A pink tongue drifted slowly along her bottom lip as she looked down and then she lifted her eyes to meet the protester's, suddenly cold and hard.

'If I say bare bottom I mean bare bottom. Now get them off!'

Two back views, then one. Shiny lycra sliding down, the camera following only as far as the plump bottom, staying on it as the pink material reluctantly emerged from the enfolding flesh and then recording it bend and contort as the

142

girl stepped out of her costume. The same again – a slimmer rump this time and not so tightly divided.

'Kathy, fetch that chair and bring it over here.' Close-up of Kathy's moving bottom, a pause then her front view as she returned. A well-trimmed blonde bush, the lower part shaved, leaving the plump lips of her cunt bare.

Melissa's scantily-clad buttocks descended, seen from below the seat of the chair, spreading as they came closer and then plumping out as she sat down.

Close-up of Melissa's naked lap, firmly muscled thighs. Her elegant hand patted the right one, making it quiver. 'Come on, Kathy love, over you go.' Zoom back to take in Kathy's nervous approach, the bending and settling, then in again so that the screen was filled with her bouncing cheeks, and Melissa's flashing hand. The camera angle changed every so often keeping Sir James' interest at a high level throughout a very sound spanking, one which only ended when the girl's bottom was the colour of a ripe cherry. Eventually she was allowed to get up and rub herself and Sir James watched the frantic wobbling, amazed that she could take so much without even crying.

Anne's punishment was a duplication of Kathy's, although her much plumper rear made for enough contrast to keep him interested.

After a lingering close up of the two red behinds, the girls were made to go through their routines again. Still naked. A whirling kaleidoscope of bosoms, thighs, fannies and red buttocks.

The last scene had Sir James on the edge of his seat. Back in the changing room, the girls cuddled each other sorrowfully, then kissed each other better. The sight of a screen full of a red bottom being lovingly kissed by a pretty, full and feminine mouth took his breath away. And the finale, with them writhing around on the floor in an energetic *soixante-neuf* almost had him ringing the bell to order Sherrie to give him instant relief. Only the knowledge that no chef appreciates being interrupted in the middle of a masterpiece stayed his hand.

Luckily, the masterpiece arrived very soon after the

screen had gone blank and soon after that, Sir James was taking the first forkful of one of his favourite dishes. With Sherrie watching anxiously, he closed his eyes and slowly chewed. Sheer perfection! There was the thin, cheesy crust; then melted cheese, a strong hint of sherry and the firm white flesh of the lobster, with the fluffy rice setting the whole thing off a treat.

'Sherrie, you are a genius. Absolutely delicious. Now, eat up and I hope that you enjoy yours as much as I am. Hang on, pass your glass. Your health, my dear. And thank you.'

'And yours, Sir James. It really is nice to be appreciated.'

'You are.'

They ate in silence. Sir James often said that the best food deserved a reverential approach and gave his full attention to his plate – and glass. Delicately picking up the last few grains of rice, he speared the last chunk of lobster, ran it round the shell to collect the last of the cheese and popped it into his mouth, then sat back with an eloquent sigh.

'I made a chocolate mousse, Sir James. Would you like some? And perhaps we could share a half bottle of Sauternes – Chateau Yquem?'

'Yes please!'

His prick stiffened as he watched her walk to the galley. The videos had widened his knowledge of the female bottom more than ever but none of the girls could hold a candle to Sherrie.

Half an hour later, he finished the last of his wine, the rich sweetness a perfect accompaniment to the mousse, drained his coffee and looked up at her.

'Can I have another story?' he asked.

'Why not. Let me just clear away ... Right. Let me think. The last one was about punishment and sex, so let's make this one about fun rather than punishment, and with the sex element very much in the background ...'

Imagine, it's 1955, Washington DC and four women have just finished adding up the scores after their regular whist session. They are all comfortably off, enjoying a fairly hectic social life as all their husbands work in various Government departments, although none are politicians. They all enjoy the cut and thrust of whist, finding it a slightly less demanding game than bridge, although just as exciting. Jackie, their hostess, is the oldest at thirty-five, the richest and far and away the best player. Tall, dark, very curvy both fore and aft and with a quiet air of authority, she was sitting back with a slightly smug expression, having won even more easily than usual.

Betty and Louise were evenly matched. The former was the stunner of the group and especially popular at parties, where her lovely red hair, excellent fashion sense and dazzling smile attracted men like bees to a honeypot. Louise, thirty like Betty, was quieter in every sense but capable and very intelligent, popular with men and women.

Lastly came the biggest loser – this time and every time. Heather was short, and at twenty-five she was the youngest, very blonde, plump and a little fluffy, the sort of girl who tends to bring out parental feelings in members of both sexes, which is probably why she was married to a man ten years old than her.

She hands Jackie several dollar bills with a troubled expression.

Our story takes off at this point.

Jackie noticed her discomfiture immediately and before reaching for the martini jug which was the traditional end-of-game treat, quietly asked what was wrong.

'Nothing, honestly, Jackie.'

Betty was less perceptive but more determined and she pressed her.

'Come on, honey. Something's troubling you and if you can't tell your best friends about it, then that's really sad.'

'Well . . . I enjoy our games. Very much, but I keep on losing and Jimmy is starting to question me about my allowance. I never seem to have enough and I daren't tell him about losing so much to you all.'

'That's ridiculous,' Louise chimed in. 'It's only a few dollars a week.'

'I know. But he doesn't give me that much. He pays all the bills anyway.' She looked vacantly out of the window and her eyes were bright with tears. Jackie poured out the Martinis and while three of them savoured that biting first sip, Heather took a big gulp. 'He goes on and on at me. You know, sometimes I wish he'd spank me. I was reading a magazine in the hairdresser the other day and there was a letter from a woman in Des Moines. She said that her husband spanked her regularly and she preferred it that way. He was firm, but quite fair. They discussed it beforehand so that she could defend herself and if she had a good reason, he always let her off. The point was that when she had had her spanking, it was all over. A clean slate. And he cuddled her afterwards and it brought them even closer together.'

There was quite a long silence, with Heather still wrapped up in her troubles and the other three mulling over what she had said. Jackie was distinctly amused at the thought of her husband threatening to smack her; Betty found the idea quite promising and Louise simply couldn't imagine Paul even dreaming of suggesting it. He had far too strong a sense of self-preservation! Then their eyes swivelled to the glum little face of their friend. Jackie was the first to think of a possible solution, although she only just beat Betty to the draw.

'Now listen, the last thing we want is to make trouble for you, Heather. And I'm sure we all agree that the game wouldn't be the same without you. So why don't you pay in spanks rather than dollars?'

Heather looked at her, blinking and open-mouthed. 'But . . .'

Betty waxed enthusiastic. 'I think that's a great idea, Jackie. But it wouldn't be fair if it was only Heather who got spanked. Let's face it, our husbands are much more reasonable than Jimmy, so with us it isn't the money that's important, it's winning and losing. So surely it'll be even more exciting if we all pay, as you said, in spanks not dollars. What do you think, Louise?'

Louise looked thoughtful. If her husband putting her

across his knee was inconceivable, this was different. It was not a case of submission. Just a game between girls. She smiled. 'OK.'

They all turned to Heather, who blushed and lowered her eyes. As the worst player, she would obviously be the main recipient. Her bottom began to tingle and she felt a strange hollowness in her tummy. 'Alright,' she whispered. 'But let's not tell a soul. Our secret.'

'Sure thing,' said Betty promptly. 'And we'll start next week. Now we ought to settle the details. I know, we keep our own scores, just like we do now, and pay all debts at the end. What about the stakes? Six spanks a trick?'

Louise thought that six sounded a bit much and they eventually agreed to start off with one and see how it went.

On the following Wednesday, each followed her normal routine, seeing her husband off to work, having a leisurely breakfast and then dressing in plenty of time for their usual 9.30 a.m. start. It was then that their minds began to concentrate on the new regime. Every one showered or bathed more thoroughly; they all dug out their best stockings and gave considerable thought to their panties. And Heather decided to risk a roll-on girdle.

They went their separate ways to Jackie's home, enjoyed a cup of coffee, made idle talk and moved into the dining room, where the cards, scoring books and pencils had already been laid out.

None of them noticed anything different in the atmosphere for the first few rubbers. Heather was losing as usual, but not by that much and there was little to separate the other three. Then, as they cut for partners, Betty groaned when she drew the fluffy little blonde.

'Hey, Heather, will you try and remember which are trumps this time? If we don't pull our socks up, we're both going to end up with sore buns.'

That did it. There was now a distinct edge to the play and they were all concentrating much harder, with the prospect of a smacked bottom already proving a more effective incentive than they would have thought possible.

'For Heaven's sake, Heather,' cried Betty at the end of

that rubber, 'surely you could have worked out that I held the Queen of Hearts, so why lead with the Ace?'

'I'm sorry,' Heather replied, her voice small.

From that moment, Heather did tighten up her play and, when they added up the final scores, it was far more even than usual. Jackie had won, but not by much and they worked out that she had to give Louise three, Betty eleven and Heather fourteen. The three losers heaved a sigh of relief at the lightness of their sentences and looked expectantly at Jackie, firmly placing the responsibility of organising the finale on her capable shoulders.

'I've just had a thought,' she announced, smiling ominously, 'although I am the overall winner, Louise you beat the other two and you, Betty just scraped ahead of Heather. I don't see why you shouldn't claim some of the spoils of victory. This is what I suggest. Heather, you've got the most coming to you, so what if I spank you first, then I deal with Betty and then Louise. When I've finished, Louise spanks first Heather and then Betty and, last of all, Heather gets hers from Betty. That way, we get a bit of variety and Heather gets a bit of a break between sessions.' There was a murmur of approval. 'Good. Now we don't seem to have given much thought to how and with what. Any suggestions?' They looked from one to the other, frowning.

'Across the knee is usual, isn't it? That's how I used to get spanked by my Momma.'

'OK Betty, we can see how it feels. Happy about that you two?'

'Yeah.' 'Sure.' Everyone seemed to agree.

'Right, that leaves the what with,' Jackie said.

'I used to get the hairbrush,' said Betty with a hint of pride.

'I bet that hurt,' Louise said, frowning.

'It sure did.'

'Hang on, this isn't supposed to be a punishment,' Louise put in, 'just paying our dues. What's wrong with the good old hand?'

'Nothing,' Jackie agreed. 'Yep, let's see how we get on. We can always change things. Right Heather, come here.'

A red-faced Heather got up and nervously slid round the table to stand at her hostess's right side, staring glumly down at the waiting lap. The other two nudged each other.

'Can't see a thing from here. Let's move nearer the action,' whispered Betty. Louise's reply consisted of no more than a little smile and they stood and moved as one. By the time they were a yard or so behind Heather, she had begun the embarrassing process of bending over Jackie's knee, so they were treated to the arresting sight of her ample rump straining the seat of her dress to its limits as she reached down for the carpeted floor on the far side. Half stumbling, she lurched all the way over and somehow ended up more or less in the traditional position, requiring a few little wriggles to get her weight balanced between hands, feet and middle.

The other three stared at her up-thrust rear, slightly suspiciously. They were worldly enough to have some idea what a girl's bottom should look like in that position and the solid globe facing them just didn't look right. There was no sign of the dividing valley between the cheeks. Not surprisingly, Betty was the first to comment.

'Heather, are you wearing a girdle?'

'No I'm not.' Her voice was a little muffled but not muffled enough to hide the note of panic.

'What does it feel like, Jackie?' urged Betty. An elegant and manicured right hand smoothed slowly over the seat of the thin skirt, the fingers probed at the roundest part and then withdrew. Jackie frowned. Then looked up at Betty and Louise.

'A roll-on,' she declared.

'Heather, that's cheating!' exclaimed Betty.

'Naughty girl,' added Louise.

'I'm sorry,' wailed Heather.

Betty's eyes were gleaming. This was proving to be more fun than expected. 'I don't know what you think, Jackie, but I reckon you ought to pull her skirt up.'

This was greeted with a murmur of approval from Louise, a beam from Jackie and a little wail of dismay from Heather. Needless to say, with three against one, the loser was told to stand up and do as she was told. She clambered to her feet, bright red in the face.

'Hey come on, girls. This is seriously embarrassing. It's only a little roll-on, honest. I'll feel it OK, I promise.'

'We're waiting,' was the only response, so with a theatrical sigh, she turned her back on them and dragged her skirt up to her waist, then stood there awkwardly while the two onlookers crouched down on either side of Jackie's chair to get a good look.

It was not exactly an unpleasant sight by any standards. She had nice legs, plump but firm thighs which looked very nice in her dark tan stockings and the roll-on was quite a light one. On the other hand, it definitely compressed her buttocks. Jackie reached out and gave each side a squeeze and then Betty and Louise did the same. The three of them looked at each other as the same thought crossed their minds at the same time. Betty winked at her friends and then turned her attention back to Heather's seat.

'I don't think she will feel anything through that. I think we should make her take it down.'

'Oh no!' screeched Heather as she whirled to face them. 'You can't do that to me.'

'Why not?' asked Betty innocently. 'You're the one that tried to cheat.'

'I agree,' said Jackie finally, 'and as I'm the winner, what I say goes.'

Rather to their surprise, the normally meek Heather didn't cave in immediately but stood in apparent defiance, glaring at each of them in turn.

'Well if I've got to have it on my bare bottom, I don't see why you two shouldn't.'

Louise and Betty stared at each other, eyebrows raised.

'Are you wearing a roll-on, Louise?'

'No, just panties. What about you?'

'Same. Still . . . I guess Heather's got a point, you know. Besides, getting it on the bare would make it more . . . you know . . . more like losing. Jackie, it looks like you'll be doing most of the spanking, what do you feel?'

'Fine by me. And judging from the way you guys have

improved this week, I'll be getting my share of licks and I'm quite happy to grin and bare it! Come on, Heather, let's have that nice bottom of yours all bare.'

Heather turned her back again and began to tug and heave her final protection down, red-faced but with a gleam in her eyes which would probably have puzzled the others had they been able to see it – except Betty, who could pick up sexual vibrations in a crowded room from ten paces. Heather had been resigned to getting the lion's share of the penalties and the prospect of spanks had worried her far less than deceiving her husband. On the other hand, submitting to such a childish ordeal was embarrassing enough to have made her play far better than usual and having to take it on her naked bottom made it far worse. She swallowed convulsively as the slowly expanding bared area bulged over the descending elastic, knowing that she was rounder than normal down there and that women tended to be far more critical of another girl's curves than men. Leaving the rolled-down roll-on half way down her plump thighs, she straightened up and waited for the first derogatory comments. And waited.

Her three best friends were fascinated at the sight she was presenting. There was no denying that she was on the plump side but Heather's bottom was beautifully proportioned, with flawless skin, clean cut folds at the base of each cheek and a nice, tight cleft and what Heather had forgotten was that they were studying it's suitability as a target, not as judges in a Beauty Queen competition. Seen in that light, she looked so tempting, so sweet and so adorable that all three rubbed their hands in anticipation.

'Come here, Heather,' said Jackie eventually and with a loud and eloquent sigh, Heather shuffled round and bent over for the second time, much more gracefully this time.

She looked quite a bit bigger in that position. Her buttocks were broader and the cleft more open. Even more tempting. Jackie gave in immediately, raised her right arm to shoulder level and let fly.

All four were impressed with the result. Heather gave out a loud squeal of dismay and clenched tightly; Louise and Betty whistled at the immediate fleshy ripple as the stiff palm sank in and at the way a bright pink, hand-shaped mark leaped into view. Jackie rubbed her hand on Heather's bare thigh and relived the vivid impression of softness. All four heads rang with the unbelievably loud noise.

Jackie stared down thoughtfully. That first spank had been so satisfying that she had been thrown off balance by the intensity of her feelings. Everything leading up to it had been fairly explicable, from the element of 'naughtiness' in the original idea of spanking the losers to the first sight of Heather's big bare bottom. All that had made her smile. But when she had looked down on that expanse of soft white flesh on her lap, she had felt a most peculiar hollow-ness in her tummy. The curviness of it all; that enticing cleft and the folds at the base of each cheek, had brought about an urgency in her desire to spank her friend. And the feel of her hand flattening that ample buttock had thrilled her to the core.

Breathing deeply in an attempt to steady herself, she idly traced the red outline of her hand with a finger, then raised her hand and lashed an equally powerful spank into the unmarked cheek, paused for a second, then delivered the remaining dozen in a flurry of activity, making Heather's bottom bounce and wobble dramatically.

Louise and Betty had watched the spanking with growing trepidation, both of them naturally thinking of their own behinds as they stared at Heather's. Louise tended to see the indignity rather than the sensuality and was definitely having second thoughts. Betty's nervousness was consider-ably reduced by the pleasure Heather seemed to be getting from Jackie's soothing hand on her red cheeks and the prospect of hers in the same position seemed less awesome.

In the meantime, Heather herself was in a bit of a tur-moil. It had been more painful than she had expected but now it was all settling down to a not unpleasant throb. None of them had made any nasty remarks about her fat bottom, which had helped. And Jackie's hand on it was really very nice indeed! She waited to be told to get up and, when Jackie eventually patted her bottom and helped her to her feet, she was almost disappointed.

She smiled shyly at the others, felt a glow inside her at the warmth of their praise at the way she had taken it and then tucked her dress up at the back, enjoying the coolness of the air on her hot skin and almost looking forward to the next dose!

'Your turn now, Betty,' announced Jackie briskly.

'Shall I get my skirt up out of the way?'

'Yes, might as well.'

Typically, she tucked both front and back well up, apparently more concerned about unnecessary creasing than exposure. Jackie looked at her legs with honest admiration and beamed up at her, already knowing that spanking her would offer very different pleasures. Easily the most sensual of her friends, always wearing clothes which gave a clear impression of her figure and with a mischievous twinkle in her eye, she was bound to be far more brazen then the essentially shy Heather. Returning her smile, the gorgeous redhead turned her back, peered down at her over her shoulder, tucked her thumbs into the waistband of her outrageously diaphanous panties and raised a questioning eyebrow.

'Don't worry, Betty, I'll take them down for you.'

Betty smiled and nodded, stepped up until her knees brushed against the side of Jackie's thigh, bent down, rested her hands on the other thigh and gracefully lowered her middle into position, sliding her feet backwards as she did so, before finally resting her hands on the floor.

As soon as she was still, Jackie whisked her silk knickers down to her knees and gazed at only the second bottom she had seen at such close quarters. A lot smaller than Heather's but with even whiter skin and a looser cleft, it was just as tempting, so after a quick feel, she administered the eleven smacks, this time producing a more even, red stain and making Betty squeal loudly at each one.

She scrambled to her feet, hopped around rubbing vigorously for a minute or so and then gleefully told Louise that it was her turn.

With only three smacks to face, Louise did not have much pain to worry about although, as she shared neither Heather's basic submissiveness nor Betty's sensuality, she could not anticipate any pleasure in lying over anyone's lap with her panties down. Still, she had agreed to the new regime and so there was no way out, although she was damned if she was going to give Jackie the satisfaction of baring her buttocks, so had her skirt and slip up and her knickers down almost before she had arrived at the waiting lap.

The spanks were delivered with long intervals between them. She kept still between the first two, the handprint glowing on her flesh and, remembering that her predecessors had looked more sweet than silly, began to change her mind about the whole thing.

She craned round between the second and third blow and was further reassured to see both Heather and Betty looking at her with serious interest. She looked down at the carpet again and began to realise that her bottom was far more sensitive than she had thought, especially when Jackie was stroking it. The third spank made her wince but then she realised that it was her turn to spank Betty and Heather and she was suddenly much more enthusiastic about the whole thing. She took Jackie's place on the chair and decided to warm up on Betty. Summoning her to her side with an imperious gesture of her forefinger, she was soon faced with a close up view of a saucy pair of tightly-filled panties. These were soon whisked down and her vision was then filled by a very pretty pink bottom.

'Eleven spanks, I think, Betty.'

'No, Louise, it's eleven for Heather and three for me.'

'Oh yes.' With her usual brisk efficiency, Louise delivered the first blow which flattened the crown of her left buttock. The second landed on the same part of the right and the third fell across the middle, so that she had a most attractive dark pink patch across the centre.

'Up you get. Come here, Heather.'

By the time Louise's eleven had added considerably to the redness left by Jackie's original treatment, she, like Jackie, had come to appreciate the peculiar satisfaction in spanking a good meaty pair of buttocks, and she made way for Betty's turn on Heather with the smug air of self-satisfaction common to most new converts. And she watched Heather's pert rump bounce away under the impact of her final eight smacks with much more enjoyment than she had the first time.

They rearranged their clothing where necessary, had one more Martini and went home, each in her own way pleased with the new arrangements.

Sherrie saw that Sir James was as absorbed as ever, staring out of the window as his imagination brought her words to life. She took a deep breath and continued.

The next game went very much as the first had done, with Heather playing with renewed confidence and actually beating Betty, although Louise ended up only a few points behind Jackie. Loser's bottoms were bared and smacked as before and then a fresh jug of Martini made. All four agreed that the game had been as tense and exciting as any they had played.

'But,' said Betty, 'I'm not sure that we've got the stakes right. By my standards I lost quite badly today, yet my ass is only sort of warm and tingling. It should be quite sore. What do you think, Heather?'

'I agree. But what do you suggest? Using something that stings a lot more? Or more spanks? As far as I'm concerned, something like a hairbrush or a paddle will probably leave bruises.'

Jackie smiled enigmatically and looked at the other three in turn. The prospect of slamming something like a hairbrush into her friends' soft buttocks had an immediate appeal but then a tingle in her right palm reminded her of the advantages of actually feeling the softness.

'Oh I don't think we need to use anything more than our hands,' she said. 'Any thoughts, Louise?'

'Fine by me.' Louise had shuddered inwardly at the prospect of anything more demanding than a relatively soft hand.

'So, how about raising the stakes to six spanks a point?' proposed Jackie.

All agreed and they concentrated on the icy bite of the Martinis. Betty broke the silence. 'I don't know about you guys, but I get a bit of a kick out of it all. The spanking, I mean. It reminds me of the games of Doctors and Nurses I used to play when I was a kid. All very innocent really, but there's something just a bit naughty about it and that makes it exciting.'

The others giggled rather self-consciously at the thought but not a voice was raised in protest.

The next week Jackie lost. She came third. Louise had won and, to everyone's surprise, Heather had come second. When she announced the result there was a stunned silence, eventually broken by Betty.

'Oh goody, we get to see your bottom all bare at last!'

She had put her finger on the key element. Being spanked was secondary. The excitement, the shame, the punishment was in lying over someone's lap with one's naked rear on very prominent display, and Louise was far too bright and perceptive not to grasp this. She dragged out the presentation, making Jackie stand with her back to them while her clothing was adjusted and then the finer points of her figure inspected and discussed, while she stood as still as possible, self-conscious, but secretly rather enjoying it, especially when they all openly expressed their admiration of her generously curved behind.

And after the inspection, she was spanked with due ceremony and Louise set the tone of their future sessions by making her take up several positions, ending with her kneeling on a footstool with her bottom up in the air. From that moment on, all the girls took advantage of the increase in the number of spanks to add variety and, as their resistance to the stinging pain increased with practise, they usually ended up with quite red bottoms.

We'll leave the final word to Heather's husband, as he turned out the bedside light, drained and happy after one of the best love sessions ever. 'There must be something about whist — you're always on great form after your game. What is it?'

Heather smiled in the darkness.

'Now that would be telling!'

Sir James sighed deeply. 'I liked that one. As you said, fun. I like the thought of the three of them peering at Jackie's bottom, seeing it for the first time. I can't rationalise why I find the thought of girls being fascinated by another girl's body – and her bottom in particular – so exciting. I just do.'

'Don't worry about it, Sir James. You're by no means the only man who thinks like that, I promise. Just accept it and enjoy the pleasure.'

'I will. Not a bad philosophy, now you come to think about it. Unless, of course, the pleasure comes from something beyond the pale, like rape.'

'True. What would you like to do now, Sir James?'

'What would you like?'

Their eyes met. God, she's lovely, he thought as his eyes swept from her smiling face to her breasts nestling softly in her folded arms, down her stomach to her thighs, where the top part of her triangle was just visible between them. His clothes felt unbearably restrictive and he grinned at her when she seemed to read his thoughts and quietly asked him to strip. He did so, clumsily and eventually stood naked before her, his prick softened by his self-consciousness. She looked down and the pink tip of her tongue slowly ran round her full lips, which then parted as she watched it surge up towards her. She got up, kissed him, then sank to her knees and he felt the wet heat of her mouth enveloping the end of his cock. His knees buckled at her initial touch but he locked his muscles, closed his eyes and cleared his mind of everything bar her. Her hands smoothed over his buttocks, squeezing and probing and the pressure built up inside him.

He was just about to stop her when her face swam before him, her mouth wet and incredibly sexy. He pulled her against his chest, dropped his hands onto the yielding firmness of her marvellous bottom and pressed into it, squashing his prick into her tummy. Warm satin against

157

his whole front. Their mouths clashed, crushing his lower lip against his teeth and the sharp pain made him gasp, sucking her breath deep into his lungs. Their tongues lashed against each other. They parted to draw breath and she craned up and licked his ear, making him gasp in surprise. Her hair tickled his face, soft and scented. Pushing her away, he ran his hands over her breasts, teasing the hard nipples, squeezing them until she hissed at the near-pain.

As one, they sank down onto the rich pile of the carpet, kissing again, four hands roaming frantically. He could take no more and eased round until he was kneeling between her thighs and her hands clawed into his shoulders, pulling him to her as his prick seemed to find its own way into the hot slipperiness of her sex.

They became one flesh, moving in perfect rhythm. Her skin was unbelievably smooth; her mouth as hot, wet and clinging as her cunt and her heels drummed hard on his back.

It was all too much. He felt the pressure mount and with an initial groan of disappointment at what he felt was a premature climax, he let the waves swamp him.

Much later, he rolled over onto his back, using his considerable strength to hold them tightly together, so that his prick stayed in her. He kissed her gently and his hands slipped down the firmness of her back onto the softness of her bottom, rolling the relaxed mounds this way and that, exciting her all over again. Her kisses got harder and more passionate and, rather to his surprise, he felt the walls of her passage tightening round his cock. Then he realised that he was erect again. He supported her while she brought her legs back up, then she straightened her torso so she was squatting on him, bringing different and even more intense pressures to bear. Her breasts bobbed firmly in front of him and the softness of her buttocks on his thighs waxed and waned as she rocked slowly up and down. His left hand reached up for her breast, his right stole behind her, rested on her bottom, the tips of his extended fingers in the open cleft, tickling her anus, then the middle finger wrigged into the tight little orifice and he smilingly watched her climax. From the look on her face, it was as good as his had been. But not as good as his second!

There was ample time for a shower, supper and a nap before they landed at Wellington for the New Zealand tour.

Chapter 8

New Zealand had always been one of Sherrie's favourite places and she made full use of the three days they spent there, seeing old friends, arranging a day walking in the mountains and another getting in some sailing, happy to have a rest from the highly charged sexual atmosphere which had developed so satisfactorily with Sir James.

So she waited for him in the aircraft in an expectant frame of mind. He stepped out of the car, shook hands with the Managing Director of the Group's leading company and strode towards her. Then she noticed that his face was as black as thunder and felt the first little flutter of panic. He brushed rudely past her, flung his briefcase on one of the seats, plonked himself down on another and glared at her. The butterflies in her tummy took flight.

Just as he opened his mouth, she knew what it was about – he had specifically asked her to organise a ticket to the big Rugby match that weekend. She had forgotten. The hot surge of guilt made her head swim and the taste of fear was like acid. He had intrigued her, won her sympathy and admiration for the way he had accepted the strange circumstances of their meeting and for his willingness to listen. But, for all his power and wealth, he had not disturbed her inner self. Until now.

'The rugger match, Sir James. I forgot. Not intentionally, I promise, and there is absolutely no excuse.'

'Fair enough, Sherrie,' he replied calmly, 'but I am going to punish you.'

'Of course, Sir James.'

They both sat silently through the take-off, Sir James

feeling strangely calm and Sherrie still absorbed in her nervousness. Almost too soon for both, the safety belt light went off and her time had come.

She stood up and faced him, hands down by her sides, head up and forcing herself to take deep, even breaths. His stern face loomed into her vision and her pulse began to race.

'There's nothing more to say, Sherrie, is there?'

'No, Sir James,' she replied meekly.

'Right. Take your skirt off and then go and fetch your cane.'

'Yes, sir.'

He sat down again and she turned her back on him, her hands moving to the side of her skirt, her fingers oddly clumsy. The rasp of the zip sliding down was loud in the tense silence. She tugged the tight waistband over the swell of her hips and the friction brought the knickers down with it, so that the first few inches of her cleft caught his eye before she raised her hand and tugged them back into place. Once her skirt had passed her bottom, it slid down easily and she stepped out of it, slowly bent down to pick it up, then folded it carefully and placed it on the opposite seat. Without a word from him, she stood before him for several minutes, giving him time to study her, before setting off to fetch the implement from her bag.

Sir James lingered over the memories of her wondrous bottom, past and present, inwardly debating whether it would be a good idea to warm her up with a sound spanking before giving her the cane. Deciding that it was, he sprang to his feet and folded the armrests down, sitting down again just as she appeared at the top of the aisle, carrying the cane. She walked slowly but steadily back, the slender yellow wand held casually at her side, and he studied her expression, searching for a clue to her feelings. She was totally impassive, which comforted him, as, although he wanted to punish her properly, he did not want her to be terrified out of her wits at the prospect. As it was, her acceptance of her ordeal was perfect.

'I am going to give you a spanking first, Sherrie, then a good, long caning. Come over my knee.'

161

'Yes, Sir James. Shall I bare my bottom?' she asked, turning back to face him and moving slowly round to his right.

He thought about the implications for a moment, then realised that for her to take her own knickers down was that much more submissive.

'Yes.'

She slipped them down, plonked herself across his legs and, holding her firmly down, he got straight on with it, spanking fast and hard, so that her bottom was in perpetual motion, only stopping when it was a rich, even pink all over.

Slightly to his surprise, she had started to wriggle and cry out well before the end and his first thought was that she had been trying to make him ease off. He dismissed that as unworthy of her – it was far more likely that because she was not looking for any pleasure in what he was doing, it hurt much more.

He looked down at her bottom and realised that his feelings were also very different. The anger that had been building up inside him had disappeared with the first spank. He felt calm and relaxed and for a moment was tempted to let her off, knowing that it would not be difficult to bring the atmosphere back to sensual normality and cane her simply for pleasure. But perhaps that would be far more cruel? Besides, he could not imagine that he would get many other chances to punish a girl like this. Suddenly the sense of power dominated all other thoughts. He tapped her shoulder, told her to get up and then stood facing her, feeling tall and strong. Her eyes were bright and steady on his, her mouth tight and her shoulders set back.

He then made her bend over the back of his seat, her head low, her bottom high, her legs apart and her knees bent inwards, so that her buttocks protruded nicely. There was not enough room in the narrow cabin to allow him to take a proper swing at her, but he found that his first wristy flick was effective enough to make her jerk and cry out as it produced a satisfying weal.

He moved steadily up her tight bottom, up to the beginning of the parting, then down again, joining the weals, then adding one to the other and she got steadily redder and redder. He focused almost exclusively on her buttocks, only vaguely aware of the increasing volume of her whimpers and moans, hoping that she could sense his strengthening respect and admiration for her through the vibrant rattan. Suddenly he knew that enough was enough and, tossing the cane aside, lifted her up and drew her into his arms.

Her body felt small and frail, shaking as she at last gave in to the sobs. Moving his hands down onto the corrugated heat of her bottom, he gently suggested that some coffee would be a good idea – and if she would like to bring him a damp cloth, he would see if it helped! She smiled up at him.

'I would love a cup of coffee, Sir James. And perhaps a tot of brandy with it? And I do have some rather special cream – if you wouldn't mind rubbing it into my bottom, it would be even better than a cloth.'

Ten minutes later she was lying over his lap, sipping coffee and groaning softly as he applied the cream and five minutes after that, he had reclined one of the seats and was tucking a blanket round her, telling her that there was time for a good rest before dinner.

'And to hell with the Rugby – I learnt more from that!'

She smiled at him and for the first time, the shutters over her eyes lifted, giving him a glimpse of the warmth behind them.

Sir James sipped his brandy while Sherrie cleared away and began to realise that he felt more content and settled than he could remember. Sherrie had had a profound effect on him. Not only had she asked enough intelligent questions to enable him to handle the tour with a clear mind and clear objectives, she had somehow sensed the nature of the desires he had kept buried deep in his subconscious and had eased them into the open so effectively that they were now a part of him. He was well fed, rested, tingling with energy and very much back on top. Her naked figure loomed before him.

'Another story, Sir James?'
'Please.'

We'll move to the present day, to a fair-sized, isolated house in Hertfordshire, owned by a Fiona Hamilton. Having recently decided that she was fed up with the rat race, she had resigned as Senior Art Director of Smily & Cockburn, the London advertising agency, and had set up on her own, converting one of the outhouses into a studio.

She was soon busy enough to recruit two colleagues; Sophie, a twenty-two-year-old graphic artist and Jenny, thirty-one, to do the general admin. and book-keeping.

It had all worked out very well. Fiona's income may have taken something of a nosedive but with independent means that never was a problem. She had not missed the commuting, the endless meetings and least of all, the inevitable office politics.

Sophie had proved to be a jewel. She was very creative, had the sort of clear mind which could quickly grasp the essentials of a brief. Her copy-writing skills were improving in leaps and bounds, so that their client base – mainly small, local companies – was already healthy and growing rapidly, and Fiona could devote her full attention on the national accounts she had brought with her. So, they were all busy, happy in their work and in each other's company. Fiona's calm maturity was a perfect foil to Sophie's rather puppy-like effervescence, while Jenny's down-to-earth efficiency kept their feet on the ground.

The best part of the week was Friday evening. Unless there was a serious panic on, they would put the answering machine on at half-past five, open a bottle of wine – champagne if business had been good – and have an hour or so to unwind, review work done and in hand, put the world to rights, or whatever. On one such evening, they had been talking about the advantages of being an all-girl team and Fiona had summed up her view.

'To reduce the thing to basics, I like not having to worry about having my bottom pinched.'

The other two looked at her, rather surprised. She was

164

tall, elegant, slim and very self-possessed and not the sort of girl whom one would expect to have that done to her. Sophie then stared dreamily out of the picture window and a smile lit up her impish little face.

'I dunno. I used to quite like having mine pinched. Depended who was doing it, of course. Mostly it was harmless fun.'

That week had been a very good one, they were actually into a second bottle of bubbly, so were even less inhibited than usual.

Jenny stared at her young colleague and felt a bubble of mischief well up inside her. 'Good God, Sophie, why haven't you said so before. I love pinching bottoms – and I bet yours is perfect for it.'

Sophie grinned. 'Catch me and you can find out . . .' and she set off at a good pace, followed by Jenny who had had to put her glass down and so was slightly slower off the mark. Still, for a plumpish girl, she was surprisingly fast and had the giggling Sophie cornered in less than two minutes. She reached out, took a firm grasp of an ear, easily accessible under the short, black hair and led the eloquently protesting artist firmly towards her desk.

Fiona had been watching the horseplay with an enigmatic smile. Part of her was pleased at this evidence of the happy atmosphere she had been so keen to produce in her little company, but there was more to it than that. For all her genuine respect for Sophie's abilities, she had also been attracted to her from the very beginning. Especially to her jutting bottom and had recently found it very hard to stop her eyes straying to the seat of the youngster's short tight skirt – or even tighter jeans. This unexpected turn of events produced a sweet and sour tingle between her legs and she was very tempted to join in at once, but then decided to stay cool and see what happened.

Jenny made Sophie bend over the desk and then addressed herself to her protruding rump, running her hand over it and vainly trying to achieve a satisfactory pinch, shaking her head in mock frustration as the stretched denim defeated her.

'This isn't any good, Sophie. Your skirt's far too tight, so I'd better pull it up.'

'Honestly, everyone else managed all right with it down. Still, who am I to object? I'm only the office junior, that's all!' Muttering away, Sophie stood up and heaved, the hem inching upwards and slowly exposing a pair of bare, slender and shapely thighs. Then Fiona held her breath as the rising skirt revealed twin crescents of pale buttock-flesh, bulging firmly out of the lacy edges of her knickers. She exhaled as the whole bottom popped into view, quivering into normal shape as the tight denim finally relinquished its hold.

While the two participants grinned at each other, Fiona kept as still as she could, content in her spectator's role. Sophie's bottom was gorgeous. Her hips were almost boyishly narrow, but the outward jut of the plump cheeks was anything but and their firmness was evident from the tiny gluteal folds. Her skin was pure white and as smooth as silk. Sophie bent over again, her new posture spreading her rump and making it look even more feminine and mouthwatering!

Fiona tore her eyes away from it and glanced at Jenny, wondering how she would react to the near-naked target, specifically if, as a happily-married woman, she would back off a little. Far from it. With a gleam in her eye and the broadest of grins, she bent to her self-appointed task with obvious enthusiasm, running her hand over every inch before settling on the bare part of the silent girl's left cheek, extending her forefinger and thumb, pressing them in deep and slowly squeezing until the flesh bulged out beneath them.

'Ooooh,' said Sophie breathily, 'that *was* nice. Could you do the other side please, Jenny?'

'Anything to oblige,' she replied and did so, tucking the knickers even further into the depths of the central divide.

Sophie gave a little wriggle, then craned her head round to catch the Boss's eye.

'Would you like a go, Fiona?'

'Why not.' She stood up and moved to Sophie's other

166

side, next to Jenny. The two heads almost touched as they bent down for the best possible view, one with blonde and immaculately styled hair, the other's brown and shoulder length.

'Hasn't she got a sweet little bottom?' Jenny broke the silence and Fiona nodded in agreement, stroking the naked part.

While all this was going on, Sophie was beginning to enjoy herself. She had always liked having her behind touched but few of her boyfriends seemed to share her enthusiasm and none had given her this funny feeling in her tummy. As her colleagues studied her, she tried to identify the reason for the difference. Part of it was that putting her bottom on display for a mock-formal pinching was the basic object of the exercise and she was not having to anticipate the clumsy and impatient groping which boys were prone to subject her to. Then there was her position. Being bent over the desk really concentrated the mind! The only irritant was that her knickers were in a rather uncomfortable position, something that Fiona apparently sympathised with.

'The trouble is, Jenny, that you've pinched the bare bits and that doesn't leave an awful lot for me. Hang on, I'll try pulling her knickers up a bit further ... umm, that's better – several fingerfuls there now.' She gave them another tug, which made Sophie squeak.

'Oh Fiona, that's very uncomfortable. Couldn't you pull them down? I don't mind.'

'Anything to oblige,' was the immediate reply and Sophie felt two fingers sliding under the waistband. Not aware that the others were doing exactly the same, she held her breath as her knickers slid slowly down over her protruding rump and were then left to slither down her legs. She had never felt so naked. It gave her second thoughts to begin with but after a while she relaxed. After all, she told herself firmly, it was all girls together and if they didn't want to see her with her knickers down, they wouldn't have pulled them down. She rested her chin on her hands and began to enjoy having her bare bottom studied so closely.

167

After a prolonged look, Fiona carefully selected her spot and applied forefinger and thumb in the approved manner, squeezing longer and harder than Jenny had done and obviously enjoying it even more. She moved to the other side, repeated the movement and then stood back.

'Can I have another go?' asked Jenny.

'All right,' replied Sophie, sticking her rump out again.

Quite understandably, Fiona helped herself to the lower curves before Sophie was allowed up. Grinning impishly, she adjusted her clothing, flounced back to her desk and finished her champagne. Fiona replenished their glasses, they picked up the conversation roughly at the point where they had left it and eventually went their various ways.

Fiona opened the studio on the following Monday morning, feeling just a little worried that she had revealed rather more of her true feelings about Sophie in general and her bottom in particular than she wanted. The happy atmosphere was far more important than her dreams and she wouldn't want to jeopardise it. So she was very relieved when Sophie bounded in, late as usual, gave her a smacking kiss on the cheek and immediately launched into a blow-by-blow description of an horrendously boring weekend spent with some dreadful relatives. She made coffee, asked where Jenny was, remembered that she had a dental appointment and then settled down to finish the artwork for a brochure. When she had done it and got Fiona's approval, it was time for more coffee, which they took out to the patio.

'Fiona, look . . . I hope you don't feel that Jenny and I went over the top on Friday.'

'Course not, silly. Dash it, I joined in, didn't I?'

'Yes . . . but I feel that I shouldn't have asked you to take my knickers down.'

Fiona saw her chance and went for it. 'Why not? You've got a gorgeous little bottom and, well, if thy knickers offend thee, pluck them off and cast them from thee!'

'Only you could bring religion into it!' Sophie said, laughing. 'Seriously, do you mean it? That my bottom's nice?'

'I wouldn't have said it if I didn't.'

'I suppose not. Mind you, Jenny started it . . . I bet she's got a nice one too.'

'Er . . . yes, she probably has.'

'Well, I'm sure that she'll give us an excuse to pinch it before long and then we can see for ourselves.'

Fiona laughed and they got back to work. Jenny arrived after lunch and her swollen face was the main topic of non-business conversation for the next couple of days, which was perhaps fortunate, because they were suddenly flooded with work and couldn't relax until the following Friday. At midday the last piece of artwork went off to the printers, Jenny finished the invoices and three clients passed proofs of their brochures without wanting a single alteration.

They sat back and Fiona suggested a salad lunch on the patio.

'And a long one, we deserve it! I'll get it ready.' She went off to the house.

Stretching and yawning, the other two girls ambled across to the house and walked round to the patio, complaining half-heartedly about the heat. As they came round the corner, they stopped dead.

'Jenny, do you see what I see?' Sophie said.

'The paddling pool, you mean?'

'Yes, you silly girl. And it's full of lovely cool water. Come on. Let's get in.'

'But I haven't got anything to wear!' Jenny protested.

'Well, don't wear anything then. Come on, I'm sure that Fiona won't mind. Last one in is a fat blob of lard.'

'Right.'

It was effectively a draw, and both naked girls stepped in and sat down, their faces screwed up as the cold water enveloped their middles.

'Ahhh, that's lovely. You're not as silly as you look, Sophie. No, NO! Don't you *dare* splash me.'

'All right. It's too hot anyway. Oh look, I can just stretch out. That's better. You try . . . you've got lovely boobs, Jenny. Mine are far too small.'

'Don't worry about it – your nice bottom makes up for it.'

Strangely pleased at the compliment and enjoying the innocent intimacy of mutual nudity, Sophie held her face up to the sun and sighed in deep contentment.

'I wish it was a bit deeper,' Jenny said after a while. 'My boobs are getting hot.'

'I know, kneel up and stick them in the water. Like this.'

She demonstrated, sleek and shining and as graceful as a young seal, ending up with her face and chest immersed and her rounded rump thrust high in the air. Blushing and grinning, Jenny followed suit, staying under until she had to surface for air, then going down again.

Just then Fiona came through the sitting room, and as she got as far as the patio doors, was faced with a sight she would not forget in a hurry. Two very attractive and completely bare bottoms loomed up over the edge of the pool, glistening in the bright sunshine and below each one, there were diamond-shaped patches of dripping dark hair. She managed to put the tray down on a convenient table before she dropped it and looked on open-mouthed. Luckily perhaps, they soon swivelled back to a sitting position, so that she could calm herself, open the door and pour out the champagne as though the whole thing was utterly normal.

She could sit opposite them while they basked in the sun, openly looking at their very different bosoms without suffering the same pangs of lust which their bottoms had produced and enjoying their childlike attitude to their nudity, especially when they had finished eating and Sophie insisted that she and Jenny should clear up. They both leapt out of the pool and bustled around without a trace of self-consciousness and when they trotted through the door with their last load, Fiona had already reached the conclusion that watching a naked girl walking away was a delightful sight. In their absence, she reflected over the differences in the two bodies. Jenny's was more womanly, with lovely plump breasts, a nicely rounded tummy and much broader hips and buttocks. But there was something especially appealing about Sophie's long and narrow bum.

The way it jostled and twinkled when she walked. She tore her mind away, looked at the clear water and was tempted. Irresistibly. So, by the time they giggled their way back into view, she was sitting in the pool, naked and loving it.

She stood up, ready to get out.

'You have got a nice figure, Boss. Don't you agree, Sophie?'

'Terrific . . . I wonder what sort of bottom she's got?'

'Bit of a skinny one I should think.'

That was too much! 'No it bloody well isn't skinny!'

'Prove it,' they chorused.

Fiona stood in the pool scowling at them ferociously, hands on her hips, quite happy for them to take a fresh look at her breasts and a new one at her neat blonde bush – and even happier to keep the little minxes waiting. Eventually she grinned back, turned round, twirled this way and that, finally bending over to touch her toes. She emerged to a round of applause and a series of genuine compliments.

It was then time to dress, clear up the final bits and pieces in the office and break off early.

The weather broke and the paddling pool was put away, but the next step forward came soon afterwards.

Sophie had made an uncharacteristic cock-up, pasting down the wrong copy onto a vital piece of artwork and the ensuing confusion caused some major headaches and a lot of ducking and diving, plus a big overtime bill from the printers. When the dust had settled, they were quietly eating lunch, with a shame-faced Sophie chewing listlessly away, when she broke the silence.

'Fiona, Jenny . . . I don't know what to say . . . other than I really am sorry to have caused so much extra work for you both. I feel such an idiot. Honestly, Fiona, I ought to have my bottom smacked.'

Fiona looked up at her, startled and for some reason, remembering an incident from the far-off past. She had been on holiday near Newquay in Cornwall with a crowd of university friends and, wanting a bit of solitude had slipped away to sunbathe in the dunes, finding a perfect ridge, high up and with large tussocks to give her even more privacy. She had been woken from a nice doze by a young female voice, squealing in mock terror, had peered down and seen a very pretty girl being chased by her boyfriend. She had let him catch her as soon as they were in the secluded hollow below her and, to her obvious pleasure, he had dumped her across his knee, delicately tucked her bikini into the groove between her chubby buttocks and started to spank her, gently but firmly enough to make her quiver nicely. She had been facing away from her, so Fiona couldn't see her face at all, but her body language had left her in no doubt that she was loving it. Even when he pulled her pants down to her knees and finished her off with a quick volley on her completely bare bottom, she had hardly protested. After a quick kiss and cuddle, she had covered herself and they had walked back to the beach, laughing happily.

She had forgotten all about it, but the memory produced the same flutter in her groin. There was no way she was going to let Sophie back out now! 'Fair enough, love. It probably is the best way to deal with it. Get it over and done with and then that'll be it. It needn't be mentioned again – wipe the slate clean.'

'Yes, Fiona, that's exactly it.'

'Right, let's get started. Jenny, can I borrow your chair?'

'Yes of course. Hang on, I'll move it into the middle. Give you some room.'

'Thanks ... Um, Jenny you don't have to watch. Not if you don't want to.'

Jenny blushed and looked at Sophie, uncertain.

'I'd like her to watch, Fiona. I put her to quite a bit of trouble as well. Do you mind, Jenny?'

' 'Course not.'

By this time Fiona was sitting down and ready, trying hard to control the fluttering in her fanny – and failing dismally. 'Come here, Sophie.' The young girl sidled towards her, her woebegone little face touching her deeply. She came round to her right side and was about to bend over when Fiona took her moist hand and stopped her, then guided her round between her spread knees and undid the top button of her jeans. She looked up into the troubled brown eyes. 'I'm going to do it properly, Sophie. On your bare bottom. And hard. Otherwise it would be a waste of time.'

'Yes, Fiona.'

With the blood racing through her veins, Fiona pulled the zip down, eased the tight jeans all the way to her ankles, turned her round and slipped the plain white bikini briefs down to her knees. She had every intention of being business-like about the whole process, but Sophie's bare bottom was enough to lead a saint astray. The jutting, plump buttocks, the unbelievably tight and deep cleft, the tiny folds and the flawless skin, held her widened eyes for several minutes before she guided the erring girl across her knees.

Fiona knew that the only honourable course was to start the spanking immediately, but could not resist a lingering feel. Oh God, so firm and smooth, and yet so soft! She had to break the spell and the only way was to start spanking this bewitching girl. Hard and often. For everyone's sake.

The ringing sound of her hand on Sophie's bare bottom rang in her ears. Her right palm was stinging; her eyes saw nothing but firmly rippling and reddening flesh; her thighs ached under the weight. But it was the most fulfilling thing she had done in her whole life and the only niggle was a background worry that it would put Sophie off bottoms!

Had she been able to read Sophie's mind, she would have been far more relaxed about it. As she lay comfortably over her boss's lap, sensing that she was enjoying the close-up view of her bottom and feeling it wobble and catch fire under the fusillade of searing smacks, she felt such a surge of affection for Fiona that her heart felt fit to burst. 'God it hurts,' she said to herself. 'And it is exactly what I've been needing for so long.' Tears poured down her cheeks and her sobs racked her slim frame – but she dug her toes into the carpet and kept her receptive bottom as still as possible.

A wide-eyed Jenny watched, spellbound. Each vicious

crack as flesh slammed into flesh made her blink in sympathy and she could not believe how much Sophie's bottom wobbled as it was smacked. The young girl's stoicism amazed her. Then she began to understand Sophie's need for atonement and her breathing settled down to near-normal. As a long-standing bottom lover, she concentrated on the vision before her, and suddenly it was one of the most exciting sights she had ever seen. She envied Fiona, remembering the pinching. Then she was wondering what it would be like to be on the receiving end.

Jenny concentrated on the action, trying to lock the many impressions in her mind, before having one of her relatively few inspirations. She slipped to her desk, got the company instant camera out of one of the drawers, checked that there was a film in it, aimed and fired.

The flash startled Fiona and she whipped her head round, saw what had caused it, frowned at Jenny, looked down at Sophie's bottom, looked back up and nodded her approval before raising her arm again. Relieved, Jenny reloaded, moved around to get a different angle and took another one.

Sophie had been vaguely aware of the first flash but had been far too wrapped up in her sore bottom to give it more than a fleeting thought. Not that she was seriously regretting having asked for a spanking. The pain seemed to have washed away all her frustrations and not even the sound of the smacks registered with her. She seemed to consist of little more than a big soft bottom. One that she sensed attracted Fiona and therefore her one conscious thought was to hold it still so that it could be smacked with minimum effort and maximum effect.

She gradually realised that everything was a lot quieter. She could hear someone sobbing noisily, then realised that it was her. The carpet beneath her swam into focus through her tears, she shook her head and knew for certain that it was all over. At that stage, the pain really struck home and she began to writhe around, moaning, longing to reach back and clutch her stinging cheeks but knowing that she would only fall off if she tried. Then Fiona's hands roamed all over the afflicted area and the relief was immediate. She bent her elbows, tucked her knees in and cocked her bottom up.

Jenny finished the film and, seeing how pre-occupied the two main participants were, slipped back to her desk and gloated over the results.

Rubbing Sophie better was almost as satisfying as spanking her, Fiona decided as she shifted the pliant cheeks around. Then she felt a new tension under her hand and guessed the recovery process was virtually complete. Sighing, she patted each cheek a couple of times and helped her to her feet, standing up and impulsively folding the bare-bottomed girl in her arms. She had stopped crying, and only the occasional little shudder and the dampness of the face against her cheek made it different from any other cuddle. Unable to think of anything to say, she kept quiet.

'You haven't finished with me, have you Fiona?'

Jerking her head back, she stared in amazement at the solemn little face. 'Well, I . . . Do you think you deserve some more?'

'Yes.'

With a one hundred per cent increase in her pulse rate, Fiona kissed her on the lips. 'All right. It was a silly mistake after all. Bending over the desk? Like when we pinched you?'

'OK.'

Fiona thought she saw a promising gleam in the youngster's eyes as she turned away, but then was distracted when Sophie nearly tripped over her dangling jeans and bent down to remove them, her pouting bottom stretched and open. She watched open-mouthed as the process was repeated with the knickers before she trotted freely over to the desk and bent over it, tucking her legs under so that the two pink and jutting halves were nicely separated by a line of white.

She moved up beside her willing victim, risked a quick stroke or two while she enjoyed the different point of view, then raised her hand for the first smack of Phase Two.

Jenny in the meantime was feeling a bit superfluous. Happily married, she was not in the least jealous of the obvious rapport between her colleagues – on the contrary, she was broad-minded enough to feel happy for them. But Sophie's bare bottom could still attract her more than somewhat so, risking Fiona's wrath, she reloaded the camera and managed to catch the last two spanks. Then she sat down again. And found herself hoping that her husband would be in the mood later on! Sophie and Fiona were in each other's arms again now, so Jenny slipped out to make some coffee.

'Gosh, Fiona, if I'd known you had such a hard hand, I'd have kept my mouth shut.'

'I'm glad you didn't, Sophie. Is it really sore?'

'It still feels as though someone has dipped it in boiling oil.'

Jenny dumped the tray down and came over to inspect the damage. 'Gosh, Sophie, you are red! Like me to get a mirror so you can have a look?'

'Yes please.' The mirror was fetched and positioned. 'Oh my God,' Sophie exclaimed when her naked rump swam into focus. 'You've cracked it!'

It wasn't exactly the funniest joke but more than enough to get rid of the inevitable tension. When they had pulled themselves together, Fiona found some handcream and suggested that as Jenny had missed out on the spanking, she might like to apply it. Jenny, unusually sensitive, said that if Sophie lay full-length across the spare desk, they could both do it. With full agreement from all concerned, Sophie heaved herself up, turned over and lay down, sighing with pleasure as the cooling balm was lovingly spread over her bottom, which, by now, was no longer stinging but glowing with a very sexy warmth. When they finished, she insisted on staying bare from the waist down. 'I'm far too sore to put my jeans back on and I hope that you'll both feel terribly guilty every time you see my bottom.'

She spent the rest of the afternoon standing up at her drawing board, distracting the other two unashamedly.

A few days later, Fiona was away all day and Jenny confessed to taking the photos. Sophie squawked indignantly and demanded to see them. 'Gosh Jenny, look at the way her hand's sinking into my bottom in this one. And don't I look red here? My bum looks awfully big.'

'It isn't, Sophie, honestly. Stand up – look, it curves out beautifully this way, but it's lovely and firm. And it's got the most gorgeous crack down the middle.

'Has it? It's funny looking at pictures of it like this. I suppose it is quite sexy. Some of my boyfriends have liked it, anyway.'

'I bet,' Jenny said with feeling.

'Can I look at yours, Jenny?'

'But you've already seen it. When we were in the pool.'

'I know, but I didn't look at it. Not properly.'

'I see what you mean. All right. How would you like me?'

'Across my lap? Yes, like this.' Sophie pointed at one of the early photos. 'And I'll take your knickers down. That's really nice, Jenny . . . lovely and soft . . . and your crack's very nice. Is it nice when I tickle it, like that? I loved it when Fiona did it to me. Now Jenny, about those photos . . . you did not ask my permission, and that was naughty of you. Very naughty.'

'Oh no! Now listen Sophie, I don't want to be spanked . . . please!'

'Too bad, Jenny. I've got you over my lap, your nice fat bottom all bare . . .'

'It isn't fat. Well all right, it is a bit, but there's no need to rub it in.'

'Don't interrupt! Where was I? Oh yes, your nice fat bottom bare, so it would be a waste of time not to smack it for you. Take that!'

For the next week or so, life went on much as before. Sophie and Jenny teased each other a bit more; Sophie was a little quieter and she and Fiona worked even better together. Then on another baking hot Friday, they managed to clear their desks before lunch, so the patio and paddling pool beckoned. Without a trace of self-consciousness, they stripped off, had a dip, ate lunch and sunbathed on a large rug. Sophie was on her back, knees up and parted, with the sun warming up her sex. She felt very aroused, and being Sophie, did not see why she should keep her feelings to herself.

She sat up and looked to her left. Jenny was on her tummy, eyes closed blissfully and her softly relaxed bottom swelling up from the small of her back. To her right, Fiona's smaller and tighter bum looked even more appetising. They also looked rather hot. Spotting a couple of little plastic buckets, Sophie got up slowly, quietly retrieved them, filled them from the pool, tip-toed back to her dozing colleagues and tipped the contents steadily over their naked bottoms.

They woke up with a chorus of shrieks, looked at each other, looked up at Sophie's triumphant grin, gave chase, caught her and led her back to the patio.

'Oh no, it was only a joke, girls, I didn't mean to scare you. Please don't spank my poor little bottom!' She was forced down onto the rug, still protesting. Then she felt a soft, squashy weight on her shoulders and realised that Jenny was sitting on her to hold her down. A similar feeling on the backs of her knees told her that Fiona had done the same. Her nerves in her bottom flared into life as she anticipated the inevitable.

With four hands on one bare bottom, it was no contest. In no time at all, it had shuddered its way to a rich, red glow and its owner was pleading for mercy. She did not get it. Fiona, remembering how she had looked when she had taken off her jeans, made her repeat the position and Sophie found the knowledge that they could see her sex oddly exciting. As was the feel of the tips of their fingers flicking into her open cleft.

They rubbed her better and watched her sit in the cooling water, her sweet little face screwed up in ecstasy. Lying down on the rug again, they had a second bottle of wine. The effect of the heat, the spanking and the drink had got rid of any lingering inhibitions.

'Sophie, do you mind if I ask you a personal question?'

'Fire away, Jenny.'

'Do you like being spanked?'

'Yes, I suppose I do. I must have a sensitive bottom. And it's lovely afterwards. It sort of glows. Like now. How about you? Does Bill spank you?'

'He does, but only in fun,' Jenny admitted. 'And yes, I love it.'

'I know what you mean!' Sophie said with feeling. 'But what about a serious spanking? Like my first one? How would you feel about offering Fiona your bottom if you made a stupid mistake?'

'The same as you, I think. That it was a good punishment.'

'Ah. Well, you remember that Credit Note you were going to send off to RKL before the end of the month? You haven't, have you?' Sophie said triumphantly.

'Oh my God!'

Sophie grinned and turned to their boss who had been following their conversation with interest. 'Back to the studio, Fiona?'

They made Jenny lead the way, and she felt horribly conscious of the way her big, bare bottom wobbled as she walked. Then there was the slightly embarrassing feel of Fiona's naked thighs under her as she went over her lap. She saw the flare of the camera and groaned. Then squealed as her left cheek burned. She gritted her teeth and took it, eventually agreeing with Sophie that this was a good way to pay for one's mistakes. It did hurt, though. But afterwards, she felt that the slight barrier which had grown between her and the other two had disappeared.

They solved all their disagreements in the same way. Every Friday, one or both of them bared and bent for swift and effective retribution. Even Fiona succumbed when she had erred. Less happily than the other two – although she did admit that the afterglow was 'very nice'.

One day, Jenny was on holiday and Fiona and Sophie had both made mistakes and agreed to spank each other. After her turn on the receiving end, Sophie suggested that she should lay at full length on one of the desks, so that Fiona could apply the cream. This was followed by a trail of soft kisses, covering every inch of buttock. Then a hot, wet tongue.

'Is that nice, Fiona?' Sophie's voice was low and hoarse.

'Blissful. Especially there! Sophie! That's very rude. But fabulous. Whatever you're doing, don't stop . . .'

It was the start of a long and beautiful relationship.

Sir James sat up straight. 'Sherrie, that was great, it really was . . . I loved Sophie. And I can so easily imagine that sort of office atmosphere.' He gazed out of the window, lost in thought and then he focused on her again. 'You know, I think my PA, Carol, would have enjoyed that.'

'What makes you say that, Sir James?'

'I'm not sure. She would certainly agree with me that the intimate atmosphere of Fiona's little company is like our office. It may sound odd to you, but she and I work in a separate building, with my Managing Director running our Head Office. It means I don't get distracted so much.'

'Have you spanked her?' Sherrie had a mischievous glint in her eye and Sir James was sorely tempted to bring the conversation to a halt as quickly as possible and put her across his knee.

'No I have not. Not company policy!'

'Maybe you should. But after office hours, of course, when company policy wouldn't apply.'

He laughed, then frowned. 'Funny you should say that. I remember one thing – we were in a light-hearted mood and she had forgotten to do something relatively unimportant. I said something like 'smacked bottoms all round' and she blushed, rather prettily. I didn't think anything of it at the time, but knowing what I know now, I wonder.'

'Sounds promising,' Sherrie suggested.

'Sherrie, I've got an idea. Between us, we could put her to the test and see if I'm right about her. Why don't I ask her to meet me in Hong Kong – I could do with her help anyway – and then she can fly back with us. If she doesn't take the bait, well, too bad.'

'Good idea. I'll get a fax off to her if you like.'

'Yes, do that. Book her into my hotel. Would you mind doing that?'

'Not at all.' Sherrie smiled and made a note.

'Thanks. But before you do, can I see your bottom please? See if it's recovering?' Sherrie dutifully bared her bottom and showed it to him. 'Good heavens, it's almost back to normal.'

'It's tougher than it looks!'

'It must be. Now why don't you lie down on the floor so that I can do to you what Sophie did to Fiona.'

He kissed and licked her with all his new-found expertise, flipped her over onto her back, held her legs up and got to work on her sex until she came. She then undressed him, they slipped easily into the *soixante-neuf* position and, when she sensed that he could take little more, she turned him onto his back, straddled him, guided him to the entrance of her body and lowered herself slowly onto him until he was deep inside her.

Chapter 9

After dinner – an excellent Scampi Provencale, followed by a fruit salad and then Stilton, a glass of vintage port and another cigar for Sir James – a sure sign of contentment – the sun had set and they were comfortably enclosed in their intimate capsule.

'Well, Sherrie. If Carol does join us, this could well be our last story. On this trip anyway.'

'True. Any thoughts?'

'Let me think . . . the last two were a bit similar, in mood if not in background . . . let's have something a little more strenuous. Go out on a high note.'

'Yes of course.'

'And from the little I know, men are just as likely to enjoy being passive. Could you bring that in?' he suggested.

'No problem.'

We'll stick to the present day and stay in England. And set the scene by describing the final rather than the opening scene. At the same moment – albeit 150 miles apart – there are two bare bottoms on display. Both are female, both extremely pretty and the owners of both are kneeling up, knees well apart and with their hips pushed up and out so that the clefts are wide open. Both bottom-holes are clearly visible and both are glistening.

Two men are studying one while the other is occupying the undivided attention of a man on his own.

We will start with the second, because it isn't quite as lovely as the first and I prefer to leave the best until last. It belongs to a woman in her late twenties, who we will just call Miss. A couple of hours before it was bared and bent, she had been hurrying down a very ordinary street in Fulham, dressed in a rather drab raincoat, with an umbrella in one hand and a shopping bag in the other. Nobody following her would have taken much notice, unless he or she was discerning enough to spot that there were definite signs of mobile and full buttocks beneath her clothes. And that she had nice legs.

Cursing the rain, she arrived at the front door of an ordinary Victorian house, opened it and trotted down the stairs to her basement flat, where she stripped off and dived into the shower. Naked, she presented a very different picture to the rather drab and unexciting figure of just a few minutes previously.

Her dark hair was cut short and only a full and warm mouth prevented her from looking unusually severe. Her eyes were dark brown and bold. Her body was lovely and white – she quite clearly was no sun-worshipper – and in terrific shape, with firm breasts, a narrow waist, long but curvy legs, round hips and a nice, broad and womanly bottom. Her pubic hair was dark, thick and extensive but when she dropped the soap and bent down to find it, her parted cheeks revealed an anus which was completely hairless.

She finished her shower, dried herself briskly and walked into the kitchen to make herself a cup of tea, standing while the kettle boiled and stroking her naked bottom thoughtfully. She took her tea into the bedroom and spent a few minutes exercising. Nothing vigorous, concentrating on deep-breathing and stretching, watching herself in a full length mirror. Then she applied a scent spray to all the usual places first of all, before carefully applying a dab to her most intimate crevice and the cleft of her behind.

She had dressed – in a loose dark skirt and white blouse – had done her hair and make-up and was just fastening a studded leather wristlet when the doorbell rang. Smiling tightly, she moved to the speaker, nodded to herself when her visitor identified himself and pressed the button to open the front door, waiting in her narrow hall until there was a nervous knock on her door. She waited until her visitor had to knock again before she opened it.

'Good evening, Jeffrey.'

'Good evening, Miss.'

'Follow me.' She led him through the kitchen and through a door leading off it, which took them into the room which made this particular flat perfect for her. The previous occupant had been a professional violinist who had divided the original kitchen and turned one half into a soundproof room big enough for his string quartet to practise in comfort.

Miss had furnished it with threatening simplicity. There was a two-seat sofa, a solid, armless chair in the centre, a padded kitchen stool and a much longer and lower footstool, also well padded. An array of wall-mounted spotlamps lit the whole room brightly.

Jeffrey looked around at the familiar surroundings, shuddered and then stood to attention while Miss walked slowly round him, eventually coming to a stop facing him.

'Go and stand up against the wall, Jeffrey. The gallery wall.'

Swallowing hard, he obeyed and forced his eyes to focus on what she called her 'Rogues' Gallery.' Neatly arranged in four rows of three were the dozen expensively framed, colour photographs of bare bottoms. All taken in close up, all red and freshly wealed, eight obviously male, three equally clearly female and one which could have been either.

He recognized a couple from his last visit, but all the others were new. The male victims were too sharp a reminder of his immediate fate, so he concentrated on the girls, especially the one in the middle of the second row, who was outstandingly pretty. Well, her bottom was. Miss came up behind him, resting her chin on his shoulder and whispered at him.

'Look at that one in the top left hand corner, Jeffrey,' she said softly, 'he was a *very* naughty boy. I had to take his trousers right off to deal with him . . . and with him as well.' A well-manicured finger reached over his shoulder and touched the bottom in question. 'But now it's time to deal with you, Jeffrey. Come over to my chair and we can have a little talk.' She sat down on the armless chair, spread her knees and, taking his hands, pulled him forward until he was standing between them. 'Now, you wicked little boy, what's this I hear about you being caught behind the bike sheds? With Cynthia, wasn't it?'

'Yes, Miss.'

'And you had your nasty, grubby little hand up her skirt, Jeffrey, didn't you? Were you trying to touch her little bottom?'

'Y-Yes, Miss.'

'Well at least you haven't lied to me, Jeffrey. I hate boys who tell fibs.'

'Will you let me off then, Miss?' There was a note of hopeful pleading in his voice.

'Oh no, Jeffrey. You've still been naughty. I'm sure that Cynthia didn't want your hand on her little bottom. I'm also sure that you don't want my hand on your bottom but you're going to have to put up with it. Do you understand, Jeffrey?'

'Yes, Miss. You're going to give me a spanking.'

'Quite right. Now take your jacket off – put it on the sofa – and come back here. No, round to this side. That's it. I'm going to have to take your trousers down, Jeffrey, so undo them and then bend over my knee. Good boy. Legs straight, arms straight. Good, now lift your bottom up so I can pull down your trousers. And what have we here? Thick winter pants? Do you mean that you went up to the dorm and put these on in case I gave you a spanking?'

'Yes Miss.'

'I see. Well, it's quite simple. Down they come and you get the lot on your bare bottom. Don't whine, boy. And *another* pair underneath! That does it! Extra. A lot extra.'

With practised skill, she slipped her left hand underneath him, eased the second pair of pants over an impressive erection, pushed the front clear and moved her hand back up for a good feel. 'Mmmm, getting to be quite a big boy, aren't you. Still, I'll soon have you crying like a baby.' Still holding his cock with her left hand, her right one tugged the pants down, revealing a chubby, white bottom, relatively hairless which could easily have belonged to a young lad rather than an elegant, forty-year-old merchant banker.

She spanked him soundly for almost five minutes, each smack making a noise like a pistol shot in the enclosed room and, by the end, he was crying out for mercy. He was made to stand in the corner, his red bottom was carefully photographed, then he had to bend over the back of her chair for twelve crisp strokes of her whippiest cane. That was for putting on the thick pants. He was then made to strip naked and go back in the corner for another photo.

Finally, he had to kneel on the long footstool, hands on the floor. 'And your bare bottom right up, Jeffrey. Higher than that. And spread your legs. I want to see your balls. Good boy. Right, you've had a good spanking on your nice little botty for putting your hand up Cynthia's skirt and a good caning for putting on thick pants. I'm now going to give you six of the very best with my riding crop. Firstly for having on two pairs of pants, secondly because you're a nasty, dirty little boy and thirdly because you've got such a nice fat little bottom. Are you ready?'

After he had shuddered his way through the six, she made him stay in position while she straddled his back and flicked the leather tag at the end of the crop into his cleft, concentrating on his anus. Not hard enough even to hurt much, but the persistent tingle restored his erection.

'Back in the corner for one more photo. Good. Smile please . . . I was joking, you silly boy! Right, that's it. Now on your knees in front of me and thank me for punishing you properly . . . Fine, now as you took your beating very well, I'm going to give you a special treat. You stay where you are, I'm going to turn round and let you kiss my bottom.'

'Oh thank you, Miss,' he replied fervently.

Jeffrey slowly rested his sizzling buttocks on his heels and with trembling hands, lifted her skirt, gasping in delighted surprise when he saw that she was wearing nothing underneath it.

'Oh Miss, you're all bare.'

'I know. You are allowed to have a quick look but then you must start kissing. No, Jeffrey, you begin on the outside of my left cheek, at the top ... that's it ... and work down. Very good. Keep going until you get to the middle, then move across to the other side. Now down the crack. That's very nice. Now go over it all again, this time with your tongue ... Well done, boy, I enjoyed that.'

'So did I, Miss. Is it all right to tell you that your bottom is really pretty?'

'Of course it is – and thank you. Stand up and let me see your willy. Yes, you *are* growing up,' she purred. 'Right, you can do one more thing for me and then I'll show you what a stiff willy's for. I am going to kneel up on the sofa, stick my bottom out so that the hole's showing and you are going to kiss and lick me there.'

'Miss?'

'Don't argue!' He stared at the neat hole, his nose wrinkled in distaste, but obedience was all, so, taking a deep breath, he bent forward and kissed her as commanded. It turned out to be far from unpleasant and he let his breath out, opened his mouth and applied his tongue with enthusiasm. Miss sighed. 'Oh, Jeffrey, you *are* a quick learner!'

At the same time that Miss had been hurrying home, in a large, old and very handsome manor house in Yorkshire, Lady Constance Galbraith was walking back from the stables, flushed and glowing after a couple of hours on the back of her favourite hunter. It was much hotter than in London, so she was only wearing a blouse and jodhpurs. She saw her husband in the rose garden, apparently in deep conversation with a tall man whom she did not recognise, waved as she passed them but carried on into the house, longing for a hot bath. She did not notice that they stopped talking and silently watched her rear view as she sauntered elegantly out of their sight.

She was a very striking young woman from any angle

but her rear view was outstanding, especially in her skin-tight, pale jodhpurs, which revealed far more than they concealed. The two men watched her in silence, both pairs of eyes glued to the movements of her hips as she walked slowly up the steps to the front door.

'What do you think of her, old boy?' asked her husband, Sir Rupert Galbraith, twelfth baronet and reckoned by Lady Constance's friends to have been the catch of the century when she announced her engagement. Tall, as fair-haired as she was, very rich, a brilliant horseman and with a double first at Oxford.

The other man turned to face him. Mr Frobisher was a new neighbour with whom Sir Rupert hoped to co-operate on a number of projects. He was even more striking than his host. Taller, at well over six foot, dark and with the lean good looks one tends to associate with glamorous adventures. In fact he had made his fortune in property, had retired on his forty-fifth birthday and was now concentrating on life's pleasures.

'Probably the most luscious rump I've come across.'

'Quite agree, dear boy. Glad you're a bottom man. So am I. Come in for a drink. You will stay to supper, I hope? Nothing formal, I fear – Cook's day off.'

'Delighted.'

Comfortably ensconced in Sir Rupert's study and with the second whisky and soda to hand, the subject of Lady Constance's bottom was raised again and the gleam in Mr Frobisher's eyes at the memory of the brief glimpse of it was unmistakable. Sir Rupert knew a fellow enthusiast when he saw one and leaned forward.

'Tell me something, Frobisher, if you were given a free hand, what would you do with my wife's arse?'

Mr Frobisher laughed, stretched his legs out, held his glass up to the light and stared into the amber depths as he collected his thoughts.

'Let me think. I'd start off by making her wear those jodhpurs. That walk of hers is quite fantastic, so I would parade her. Up and down the Ballroom – there's a decent amount of space there. Then I'd roll the jodhpurs down a bit, just far enough to bare her bottom and parade her again. Lastly I'd make her strip to the buff and do it all over again. Got decent titties, has she? I couldn't see.'

'Not bad at all. I say, that's pretty good. Like a horse at the Newmarket sales, what?'

'Exactly.' Mr Frobisher smiled inwardly. He had met men like Sir Rupert before, men who broadcast their ownership of wife or mistress by tantalising relative strangers with the remote prospect of possessing her. His host was staring at him, red-faced and open-mouthed, apparently caught on the hop by the brutal and unabashed frankness of his guest's reply. Then it was Mr Frobisher's turn to be taken aback.

'Tell you what, old boy. Promise to help me with the sale of that land I was telling you about, and I'll let you. Parade her, I mean.'

'I told you, I've retired.'

'Far too young to retire. You'll need the odd bit of work even if it's just to keep your hand in. And it'll help you get to know some of the local people.'

'I don't know . . .'

'Look, I need your expert help. Is there anything else you would like her to do? I know it all sounds a bit strange, but this sort of thing does her good, you know. Being told what to do.'

'You'll be there to watch, I assume?'

'Of course.'

Sir Rupert was even redder and beads of sweat stood out on his forehead. Mr Frobisher sensed that there was more to the proposition than met the eye but knew that he would never forgive himself if he let caution overrule his instincts. He took a deep breath. 'Yes there is something else I would do to her. Look, be a good chap, will you?' He held up his empty glass and Sir Rupert leapt to his feet. 'Give me a chance to collect my thoughts . . . thank you very much . . . good health.'

'Bottoms up!'

Mr Frobisher grinned. 'Yes, it will be. Right, even from the brief glimpse which is all I had of her, I could see that your wife is a remarkably lovely girl. And as her rear view was the part of her most in evidence, I shall continue to concentrate on that. Now I have a pet theory about the female bottom – I am convinced that you can tell quite a lot about the owner's character from even a quick glance, as long as the circumstances are favourable. It isn't the size, but the general shape and the movement as she walks which are significant. Now the shape of Lady Constance's bottom is superb, more apple than pear in shape, beautifully curved and I would imagine with a lovely tight groove down the middle. But there was a challenging cockiness in her walk. The way she was obviously exaggerating the sway and adding a little twitch to her movements. What she needs is a sound thrashing. So, when I had paraded her to my satisfaction, I would make her kneel on all fours for a dozen or so with her crop. Her bottom would be nicely striped, with the skin in between the individual weals a distinct pink, so that from a reasonable distance – let's say from your standpoint – her whole bottom would look quite red. Then I would make her drop her head right down, spread her knees and stick her backside right up in the air. In all probability you would be able to see her anus, in spite of the plumpness of her cheeks. Then I would lay into her with a belt until she was glowing like a Turner sunset!'

Sir Rupert looked at him in amazement. 'I wouldn't have believed it possible, old boy, I really wouldn't. You've got her down to a T.'

'So if I agree to help you over the land, you'll let me do all that to her.'

'By God, yes.'

'Sir Rupert, you've got yourself a deal.'

Mr Frobisher slipped back home to change for dinner and Sir Rupert told his wife that they had an unexpected guest, reassuring her that it was informal and that Mr Frobisher was not expecting anything other than a normal family supper. He then left her in the bath and she rested her head against the back, almost afloat in the deep water as it eased the stiffness from her muscles.

There had been something in her husband's expression

which had made her just a bit suspicious. A glitter in his eye? Yes, and the sight of her naked breasts peeping through the bubbles had held his gaze for longer than usual. Much longer. She ran her hands over her firm stomach and her nerves began to flutter, so she distracted herself by hauling herself to her feet and washing, unaware that she lingered even longer than normal on her pink, shiny bottom . . .

Later, she brought coffee into the small family drawing room and poured it as her husband offered Mr Frobisher brandy and a cigar, both of which he declined. Dinner had been surprisingly successful and their guest had proved to be easy and entertaining company. She looked at him surreptitiously over the gold rim of her cup. Apart from his striking looks, there was an inner composure about him. Knowing nothing about his background, she assumed that he was basically a self-made man, but he showed nothing of the tension one would expect from someone a little unsure of himself in unfamiliar surroundings.

He met her eye, and something in his look sent a thrill of fear through her. Nothing had been said, but she knew that her husband was going to set her up. Resentment boiled up inside her. Then she began to savour the acid taste of her fear. Part of her hoped that she was wrong and that it was just another, innocent encounter. But she also knew that if she was wrong, the disappointment would be sharper than physical pain. Memories of the last time flooded back.

She had been made to bend over the back of that armchair, her skirt had been whisked up and her knickers torn painfully off. Hands had pawed at her buttocks and then she had felt a hardness between her thighs, urgently probing for the suddenly moist entrance of her cunt. With a low cry of shame and excitement, she had dipped her back and parted her legs until the stranger was able to thrust in up to the hilt. Would Mr Frobisher be as crude and direct? She hoped not. Or was that what she really wanted? She squirmed in her seat, her mind in a whirl.

She offered the men more coffee and was refused with

normal politeness. Desperate for something to take her mind off her dilemma, she collected the cups, put them on the tray and dipped her knees to pick it up, horribly aware that she was treating them both to a clear view of the tightened seat of her skirt. She froze as her husband's voice smashed through her brain, slightly thick and hoarse, as it always was when one of his specials was imminent. She felt sick. Oh God, she thought, here we go.

'Don't bother to wash up, my dear. Gladys can do it in the morning. Leave the tray, go up to your room and change into your riding kit. Mr Frobisher was most taken with the sight of you in it this afternoon and would like a closer look. You won't be too long, will you?'

'No.'

'We'll be waiting for you in the Ballroom.'

The cups clattered loudly as her hands shook and she walked blindly out of the room to do her husband's bidding, hesitating briefly before deciding that as she never wore knickers when she was riding, she would probably get into serious trouble if she put them on now. She stood in front of her full-length mirror, adjusting her stock, then quickly brushed her hair and touched up her make-up. Her legs were so shaky that she went down the long staircase one step at a time, not daring to hurry. Her bottom felt lively in the stretchy covering, especially when she walked quickly along the corridor to the Ballroom. The door was shut. She knocked firmly and waited, her heart hammering away in her chest and her breathing laboured. But there was the usual insistent tingling in her sex and buttocks.

'Come in.' They were sitting at the far end, side by side and this time Mr Frobisher seemed to have accepted the offer of a brandy. Feeling like an aristocrat marching to the Guillotine for her execution, Constance held her chin up and walked firmly towards them. Then she noticed the riding crop on the table between their chairs and she wanted to scream as every nerve-end in her bottom flared into life. She didn't want to be beaten. But again, she savoured the hot acid flow as the fear spread through her. Her husband glanced across at Mr Frobisher and nodded.

She met the handsome guest's eyes but could read nothing in them.

'Walk across to the door, turn and walk back.' His tone was low, even and almost bored. Tears of humiliation sprang into her eyes as she turned to obey, more aware than ever of the jostling of her buttocks. She reached the door, turned and walked back, wanting to see approval and admiration in his eye. There was nothing, even though his gaze never shifted from her crotch.

He made her do it again and again, until her confusion was so pronounced that she retreated into her shell and obeyed like an automaton until he brought her out of her reverie.

'Come here, Lady Constance, and stand right in front of me please.' His calm politeness was far more threatening than the usual bluster she encountered. She found herself standing between his parted knees, staring out of the window. Her mouth was dry and she would have given her right arm for a brandy. His hair was sleek and thick. No sign of balding. Unlike Rupert. His hands were on her hips turning her. She stared at the distant wall. She jumped as he touched her bottom and began to squeeze the flesh. At last she could sense the desire in his touch and she began to relax now that she was on more familiar ground. She liked bottom men.

Mr Frobisher was certainly that. And if his eyes failed to show his feelings, his heart was singing. He forced his thumbs into the tight elastic and began to take down her jodhpurs, feeling her shudder as a couple of inches of cleft came into view, dividing a pair of buttocks which showed every sign of being as firm and smoothly white as he had hoped. Then she delighted him even further by giving out a strangled squawk of protest and snatching them up again.

In one easy movement, he whirled her round, shifted her to his right and flung her across his knees, pinning her down with his left hand in the small of her back, underneath her shirt so she could feel him against her bare skin.

'That was not very sensible, Lady Constance, and you will be punished for it. Bare your bottom.'

He kept his voice steady and low, confident that he already understood her well enough to know that she would find his unemotional approach far more intimidating than anything else. Struggling delightfully on his legs, she managed to heave the jodhpurs down, then slumped back into the traditional position with an ease that suggested long familiarity. Her bottom proved to be every bit as lovely as he had thought and he toyed with it thoughtfully until it softened as she relaxed. Then he patted the crown of each cheek, only just firmly enough to produce a little shimmy in the ample flesh. And then told her to get up and stand with her back to him again. As she staggered to her feet, he saw the surprise on her face and knew that after screwing herself up to be spanked, she was almost disappointed.

He adjusted the rolled down jodhpurs until they hung just below her gluteal folds, then tried to tuck her shirt up. And failed. With a sigh of annoyance, he found his Swiss army knife, extracted the little scissors and cut some four inches off the bottom, vaguely aware of the look of stunned horror on her face as he did so. Ignoring her when she seemed to thrust her pubis into his face, he turned her round and slapped her bottom.

'That's better. Now walk up and down again. Until I tell you to stop.' She stumbled off, blinking back tears of humiliation, and the two men sat back comfortably and watched in silence. After a while, she began to get used to the constricting jodhpurs and the exposure and realised that she was walking with something approaching her usual stateliness. The thought pleased her.

Sir Rupert was very pleased with Mr Frobisher's performance. While his eyes were locked onto his wife's jostling bottom as she walked away from them, on the return journey, he resisted the pleasure of looking at her neat, golden bush and watched her face. Pale, apart from a bright red spot of embarrassment on each cheek, her mouth compressed to little more than a thin line, she looked as resentful as one would expect. It was her eyes which gave her away. There was a gleam in them as they focused on some distant point.

At last, the worthy Mr Frobisher beckoned her to him and pointed to his lap. Sir Rupert turned his chair as she slid into position, then stood up so that he could look almost straight down on his wife's chubby buttocks as they quivered under the rain of crisp spanks.

Not that they were being hit hard. Effectively certainly, as the spreading red stain testified, but she had wailed in distress almost from the first and he knew that it was the degradation of such a childish punishment which was affecting her most. Frobisher's clever ploy of putting her over his knee, getting her all screwed up and then letting her go to get on with the parade had been the mark of a true genius.

Just as he sensed that the pain was beginning to excite her, Mr Frobisher stopped and lifted her to her feet.

Sir Rupert almost protested. Constance's bottom had never looked so vulnerable and sexy and he had been enjoying every minute. Then he heard Frobisher's level voice ordering her to strip naked, so sat back grinning evilly.

She was made to parade again, her pink rump contrasting beautifully with the flawless white of the rest of her body and, as she walked towards them, they had the added pleasure of seeing her firm little boobs gently bobbing up and down. Then it was time to move from the hors d'oeuvre to the main course.

Lady Constance was told to kneel on the seat of a chair and stick her bottom out, ready for the crop. She looked at Mr Frobisher pleadingly, then turned to her husband. Neither showed the least sign of compassion. In fact, both were thinking the same thing, that naked, with her hair in some disarray, her face flushed, her mascara running and her tits heaving as she panted, she looked utterly gorgeous. Resigned to her fate, she turned, walked to the chair and slowly took up the required position. Both men were experienced enough to notice the clear signs of her reluctant arousal – the red flush on her throat; the softness of her expression and, most telling of all, the way she presented her bare bottom for the punishment, thrusting it openly toward them, before shifting her knees apart and exposing the glistening pinkness of the inside of her cunt.

195

Mr Frobisher picked up the crop and tapped the naked bottom spread out before him. Several times, until she began to moan in anticipation. At last, he drew his arm back and drove it stingingly down, making her cry out as the thick red weal sprang into view, starkly vivid against the salmon pink of her freshly-spanked flesh. He heard her gasp, saw her waggle her bottom from side to side, then she impressed him further by immediately sticking it out again.

Even Sir Rupert was impressed by the way she took her medicine. Each lash was severe enough to make her heave her bottom about and to increase the duration of her lamentations but Mr Frobisher never had to tell her to present herself properly before administering the next stroke. More significantly, from his seat directly behind her, Sir Rupert could clearly see that her excitement was increasing with every lash. Her pubic hair was darker and glistening and the pinkness getting more and more visible as the whipping progressed.

Mr Frobisher may not have been able to see this but he was far too experienced to miss the signs. After a sound dozen, he put the crop down and squatted behind her, making Sir Rupert get to his feet and move to where his view was once again unobstructed, so that he could assess the damage more accurately. With a little grunt of satisfaction, he slapped each cheek, then resumed his stance and continued with the next dozen.

By the time they had landed, Lady Constance's bottom was wealed from top to base and she was clearly reaching the end of her tolerance. After another examination, Mr Frobisher decided that a little break would do them both good, so the poor girl was once again subjected to the humiliation of another parade. Then she was directed back to the armchair.

'And this time, I want you to stick your bottom out properly. When I say properly, I mean so that we can both see your arsehole.'

She stared at him, her mouth open in horror. He stared back and for the first time, smiled at her, deliberately crinkling his eyes to add warmth and enjoying the puzzled look on her face as she turned to walk back to the chair. He saw Sir Rupert rather awkwardly groping at his fly, obviously trying to adjust his erection and grinned. His wife reached the chair and paused, then turned to face them, her breasts still shifting firmly from her laboured breathing, her tear-stained face still red, her eyes blotchy and her mouth wet. She stood upright, her hands by her side, with no false modesty. Quite the opposite. She seemed quietly proud of her essential femininity.

Mr Frobisher understood. 'Lady Constance, you are quite simply the most beautiful woman I've met. And your bottom is quite outstanding.' He stretched out and trailed the soft leather tab at the end of the crop over her cheeks and mouth, down her neck, around each breast, her tummy, each thigh in turn. Then he carefully pressed the crop itself against her slit, slowly moving it in and out until it all but disappeared between the fat sex lips. Her eyes were closed, her fists clenched and she moaned and trembled.

'Turn round please.' She did so, on shaking legs and her scarlet buttocks quivered as she staggered into position. He repeated the treatment over her shoulders, back, thighs and bottom cheeks before slipping the leather covered whip into the deep cleft and working it up and down. She moaned again and bent at the waist to make the invasion easier. At last he pulled his weapon out and let his arm fall to his side. With a shuddering sigh, she moved forward a pace, rested her knees on the seat and slowly bent her head down until it was forced into the join of seat and back.

He watched as she paused, assessed her position, realised that she had not exposed herself as ordered, arched her back and paused again, uncertain. There was now a slash of white separating the redness of her buttocks, her sex was on view but only a slightly darker patch in her cleft indicated the location of her anus. Obviously she could feel cool fresh air on it, for she stayed still until he cleared his throat rather pointedly. A hand crept into view, rested on her right cheek and the tips of her fingers slipped inside the division, moving around and checking to see how much further she had to go. She sighed and her knees edged apart, she pushed her bottom further back – and there it was. Small, hairless, a lovely pinky-brown and as pretty and sexy as the rest of her.

Mr Frobisher straightened up, picked up the crop and began the finale with six moderate strokes across the full width, before shifting until he was in the right position to bring the crop vertically onto her bottom, starting on her right flank, moving steadily towards the centre, crossing the divide and finishing by her left hip. He could sense that even the tolerable force he was using was enough to re-kindle the blaze and felt genuine admiration for the way she did all she could to keep her bottom still.

'Well done, Lady Constance. You may straighten up and give it a good rub if you like.'

'Thank you, Mr Frobisher.' Her voice was strained and unnaturally high-pitched, but remarkably steady. She shot upright and her hands flew back to tend her burning flesh. He moved out of her way and bent forward for a better view, immediately joined by her husband.

'Right, that'll do. Bend over again please.'

She bent, stretching and straining until her little hole was again on display. Mr Frobisher resumed his stance and began to flick the leather tag into her open cleft. The first made her squeal in fear and hunch her back, closing the division, but almost immediately, she sobbed an apology and stuck her bottom out again.

He flicked away tirelessly and she obviously found the strange sensations very much to her liking, for there was a different tone to her little moans and wails and her bottom got noticeably wider as he moved in towards her anus. In time, though, he knew that it began to get painful – from repetition rather than increased force – and he knew that she was having to call on her reserves again.

Eventually, he stood up, tossed the crop down and bent down for a final look. She was an amazing sight. The skin of her cleft was a lovely bright pink, with even her anus glowing redly in the centre. Her buttocks were still a rich crimson, with the dark weals only distinguishable at close quarters. He nodded at Sir Rupert in satisfaction. 'I think that'll do – no need for the belt. There's just one more thing, old boy. Could you lay your hands on some Vaseline? Or baby oil perhaps. Butter would do at a pinch.'

Sir Rupert frowned back, clearly puzzled. Then realisation dawned and his face broke into a wide grin. 'No trouble, dear boy. Hang on a moment – be right with you.'

They had spoken quietly, but in any case, Lady Constance was so preoccupied by the sizzling waves of heat which were spreading out from her bottom, that she had not heard a thing they had said. As she had not been told to move, she kept her rear end jutting into the air and quietly revelled in her total exposure. It was not until her guest tapped her on the shoulder and handed her the jar of Vaseline that she realised that it was not yet over.

Mr Frobisher's soft voice made it all horribly clear. 'I want you to put it all over your anus and then cover your finger and push it right up your bottom.' Gulping, she reached out a trembling hand.

In complete silence, they watched her prepare her own bottom for its violation, the shining tip of her middle finger tentatively extended and groping for the entrance to her virgin orifice, slowly spreading slipperiness all around before vanishing to reload. Her hand reappeared, the finger found the opening, paused and then slid in as far as the first joint, swivelling as she tried to spread the ointment as widely as possible. They heard a whispering rasp as she screwed the cap back on and then saw her knees shift and her multi-coloured bottom wriggle and spread just a little more as she braced herself for the unknown, her heavy breathing loud in the stillness.

Mr Frobisher walked up to the nervously waiting bottom, undid his flies, extracted six inches of thick manhood, guided the head towards its target, took a deep breath and pushed. Luckily, he had gripped her firmly by the hips before doing so, because as she felt her little ring stretch intolerably as it yielded to the pressure, she tried desperately to squirm free. In pretend anger, he slapped her flank.

Hard and ringingly, then pushed another inch or so into her.

She had been in two minds about his intended taking of her remaining virginity. Her first thought had been horror at the prospect. But then the insistent tingling left in her rectum and anus from the flicking tag had aroused her curiosity, and slipping her finger in had been rather pleasing. Then she discovered the difference between a slim finger and a thick cock and had immediately suspected that her poor bottom was being split open. She shrieked in pain and desperately tried to tuck her tummy inwards, but his grip was firm and the slap had hurt. Then the burning prickle in her stretched anus began to fade and she just felt filled to bursting. At last, everything seemed to get used to the intrusion and her bottom thrust backwards to welcome him.

As he watched their hips begin to churn in unison and felt able to peer closely enough to see the glistening shaft piston in and out of her pointed bottom, Sir Rupert's left hand disappeared into his flies and jerked away to their rhythm.

Mr Frobisher came with dignified restraint, Sir Rupert with understandable inhibition and Lady Constance with loud cries of delight and surprise.

Afterwards, the two men slipped into various cloakrooms to tidy themselves up, leaving Lady Constance still slumped in the chair. They returned, made her serve them a final brandy and Mr Frobisher said goodnight and went home, shaking her hand as though it had been a perfectly normal evening and taking no notice of the fact that she was still naked and that her bottom was still extremely red.

Sir Rupert had another brandy before locking up and joining her in her bedroom. He looked down at her lovely sleeping face, kissed her cheek, undressed and slipped into bed beside her. Then he carefully took off his artificial right hand and turned out the light.

Sir James looked at Sherrie in amazement. 'That was a story to end stories,' he announced, rather pompously. Then grinned. 'Seriously, Sherrie, it was fantastic and I liked the bit about the false hand – explaining why he didn't beat her. You still look tired, my dear. Pity we haven't got a nice big bed.'

She smiled warmly at him. 'Probably wouldn't be a good idea. Too much like domestic bliss.'

'You're right. As usual! Anyway, we can't be far off now, so perhaps it wouldn't be such a good idea. Back to the story. I take it that 'Miss' was a pro?'

'Yes. But specialising in spanking.'

'She was obviously good at her job!'

'Very ... would you like to try it, Sir James? Being spanked?'

'I'm not sure ... OK, why not?'

'Right, come here. Let me just sit up straight. That's better. Now James, you realise that I am going to take your trousers down and do it on your bare bottom? Good. It's the only way. I'll just undo this button ... and unzip you. Over my knee. Good boy. Lift your hips, please. No, stay like that until I've pulled your pants down at the front. That should do, so down you go and I'll get your bottom nice and bare for you. You *have* got a nice bottie, James. Nice and firm ... but it still trembles and wobbles when I smack it. Can you feel it? Good. Right, settle down and we'll get on with it. Yes, I know it stings – it's supposed to! Well, that's got it all a very pretty red now. Yes, I think that'll do you. Up you get. Oh dear, your willy's looking all crushed and shrunk ... er, I take it that it didn't do an awful lot for you, Sir James!'

'Afraid not, Sherrie. But I promise you that if you failed, not even Miss would have succeeded. No, it's the active role for me. So, my turn to sit down. Hang on, let me take my things off first, so that we're both starkers ... there, across you come. Hey, it's very nice feeling your bare tummy and legs against mine. Now, I think just a nice long spanking will do the trick. I don't want you to worry about a marked bottom spoiling your fun in Hong Kong ...'

Sherrie squirmed happily on Sir James's naked lap, the growing warmth in her bottom giving her more pleasure than usual for one who generally liked stronger measures. But as she lay there, gazing at the thick blue carpet, she was relieved that he was not going to cane or strap her. She had an old friend in Kowloon, Hin Sui, a Chinese girl a little older than her. She was delicately gorgeous and, best of all, a keen student of traditional tortures and had promised Sherrie that the next time she came, she would demonstrate the subtle art of Chinese Bastinado. Apparently this worked on the same principle as the old and better-known water torture, with the maddening drip replaced by light taps on the naked buttocks with a short, thick cane. Hin Sui had assured her that at first, the sensation was pure pleasure and that the pain increased so slowly that the victim was able to savour it to the full.

'As a punishment, Sherrie, it gives so much time to think over one's crime before the pain is all. And for pleasure, there is nothing I know quite like it. The pain washes all the way through you, like a tidal wave of lava. You can really lose yourself in it. Tell me next time you come to Hong Kong, Sherrie, and I will arrange for three strong assistants to help me. Your beautiful bottom demands at least three of us to do it justice.'

So Sir James's steady spanking was providing the perfect preparation for the real ordeal ahead of her. Her bottom was already quite hot and bothered and the pain was increasing with every spank. She gritted her teeth and went with the flow. Eventually he came to a stop and helped her to her feet, and she pleased him by standing with her back to him so that he could watch her rub herself better. Then she knelt in front of him, took his erection in her mouth and satisfied him completely.

After which he sat her on his knee. 'Sherrie, tell me something – where do you come from . . . and how come you were on this flight?'

'Just my good fortune, Sir James!'

'No, the fortune is all mine . . . all right, I won't ask again. But I do appreciate everything you've done. Very much.'

'I know – and you've been the most rewarding passenger I've ever had, Sir James. But it's not over yet. We've got to sort out how we handle Carol . . .'

Chapter 10

Sherrie finished her usual pre-flight checks in good time and then sat down in her own seat near the galley to wait for Sir James and Carol. She could still feel a deep ache in her bottom after Hin Sui's treatment, but after frequent references to a variety of mirrors, she knew that not one bruise spoiled the smooth creaminess of her best feature. She kept her growing excitement at the prospect of meeting Carol in check by reliving that extraordinary session in her friend's penthouse ...

One room was furnished as a punishment chamber, with thick blinds to shut out all natural light. A wall covered with the most impressive array of implements – leather, wood, whalebone, plastic, rubber and even plaited horse-hair. She had walked up to the display and greeted some old friends, running a finger over the business end of each and her bottom tingled as memories flooded back, before concentrating on the present. There was only one piece of furniture. A long, low padded bench in the centre. Hin Sui looked delicious in her traditional cheongsam, with an occasional glimpse of smooth, ivory thigh through the long slit. Her three female assistants stood patiently against a wall, in equally traditional white shirts and baggy black trousers. She had smiled nervously at them and then lain face down on the bench, feeling her knickers tight against her buttocks as they fastened her wrists and ankles with strips of silk.

Peering over her shoulder, she had watched them crowd eagerly round as Hin Sui had knelt at her side and bared her bottom with deliberate sensuality. The admiring audience had made it all as exciting as it had been in her early days, making her rest her cheek on the bench, close her eyes and enjoy the simple pleasure of being bare bottomed. Then they had placed two canes in front of her, so that she could study them while they studied her buttocks. They were about as long and thick as drumsticks, but without the taper, and did not look in the least threatening. Not that she relaxed, knowing Hin Sui far too well to underestimate her promise of real pain.

And that promise had been fulfilled to the letter. The first minutes had been pure pleasure, with the light taps making her relaxed bottom quiver incessantly and producing no more than a warm tingle. The change to pain had been so gradual that it had crept up on her – partly, Hin Sui had explained afterwards, as her bottom was considerably larger than the average Chinese one, so that it took much longer for each bit of it to receive the necessary accumulation of taps.

Under Hin Sui's careful and expert direction, they had played her with masterly skill. As soon as she had showed signs of slipping into that reverie which only the truly submissive can achieve, they had either rested or done something different. Her favourite change had been when they had untied her, whisked her over onto her back and then lifted her legs right up so that her knees were pressed against her breasts, leaving her naked rear high and wide and – from the little coos of appreciation – very handsome. Hin Sui had taken a foot-long bamboo twig and flicked it against her bottom-hole, making her smile to herself as she remembered her last story, about the crop and Constance.

When they turned her over again, the sharp but minor throb in the middle of her bottom had blended in superbly with the boiling ache in her buttocks.

They had finished her off on her back again, with her knees up and spread wide. Not smacking her anus but taking turns to kiss and lick it, while another mouth did the same to her sex. She had lost count of her climaxes and the continual stimulation had been not far short of a torture session on its own account.

Semi-conscious, she had been put to bed, face down and with a lovely cold compress on her behind. She had slept for hours and, when she finally awoke, there was no more than a dull ache to remind her of the previous evening's activities. Until Hin Sui showed her the photos, when she had been shattered by the colour of her bottom.

Then Sherrie had summoned the four of them, stripped them naked, spanked their tight little bottoms and explored every inch of their bodies, loving the neatness of their tiny brown bottom-holes and their sparsely-haired fannies. The session had ended up with all five of them rolling around on the enormous bed.

The experience had left her feeling like a new woman. Now she got ready to meet the new woman in her life!

Dead on time, Sir James's car appeared at the foot of the steps and she stood at the doorway and put on her best air hostess smile. Noticing that Sir James beckoned Carol to go up ahead of him, she saw that his eyes were glued to the seat of the other girl's skirt.

She closed and locked the door, told the pilot that he could start the engines, bustled about putting jackets and briefcases safely away and then went forward to her own seat for take-off.

As the aircraft rocketed down the runway, she turned her mind to Carol's seduction. Her first impression had been that she was the sort of girl one would expect to see as a PA to a successful man – brisk, quietly efficient, neatly and soberly dressed – but Sherrie had seen the warmth in the bright blue eyes; the tight blouse and the low-cut bra underneath it; the swing of her big bottom and a broad smile which hinted that she could well greet life's pleasures with her heart, mind and arms open wide. Time would tell, thought Sherrie. But then she was not proved wrong all that often. They levelled out of their steep climb, the engine note softened to a dull rumble and she unbuckled her belt, checked her hair and make-up and joined Sir James and Carol.

They were already deep in a discussion about the various matters arising from the Hong Kong section of the tour but broke off as she approached. Sir James casually introduced them, accepted the offer of a pot of coffee and when she brought it, asked her to sit in on the meeting. 'Don't look so surprised, Carol. Sherrie has made some tremendous contributions already and I value her input. Now, what we were discussing, Sherrie, was the problem of the hand over to the Chinese in 1997 – it's only ten years from now after all. At the moment business is booming but, given the time scale and the probability of, at the very least, a sharp dip in all the world's stock markets, how do we play it?'

Sherrie thought hard for a moment. 'Keep away from the new airport. It could work out but it's risky. I think the best thing to do is to increase your investment but spread it around a bit more widely. Now, I was talking to . . .'

By lunch time they had covered all the immediate issues and Sir James gave a strong hint that a bottle or two of champagne would be a perfect way to end the meeting. Sherrie went off to get the first one open and, to give herself time to think, made up a plate of canapés.

The last hour or so had proved beyond doubt that her mission had been a success. Sir James had been on superb form. Incisive, far-seeing and creative, in complete contrast to the weary and uninterested man who had stepped into the aircraft at Heathrow. What had impressed her more than anything was the way he had listened to her and Carol. He had never been too proud to concede that they were right and to change his viewpoint accordingly. Not that it had happened very often as his intellect and experience were a powerful combination and more often than not, he prevailed. But he had never pulled rank and dismissed their contributions as trivial.

Carol had also impressed her. She knew her limitations as an executive but had a great deal of quiet self-confidence within those limits. She had, at the same time, won Sherrie's respect for the way she had accepted her as a temporary colleague rather than a rival. It had been stimulating and fun. And she was so attractive! It was time to take the relationship to the next stage.

206

They nibbled, drank and chatted for some ten minutes and then Sir James smoothly took the first step.

'It's a shame you weren't with us on Tuesday, Sherrie. Mr Chung insisted on taking us to a very discreet night club and they had one of the best cabarets I've ever seen. Not that I claim to be any sort of an expert on that sort of thing, of course!'

'Of course not, Sir James,' interrupted Carol primly.

'Don't look at me like that – you enjoyed it as much as I did! Come on, admit it.'

Carol blushed and then gave a sheepish grin as Sherrie tut-tutted in sorrowful disapproval. 'Well,' she admitted, 'the girls were gorgeous and so professional. The costumes were amazing . . . and haven't Chinese girls got funny little bottoms? Make mine seem enormous.'

Sir James looked at her speculatively. 'Personally I find them just a little too petite.'

Carol shot her boss a shy glance and smiled. 'I'm glad to hear it.' Encouraged by the other two, she described the evening in terms which left them in no doubt that it had been a bit of an eye-opener for her and the conversation gradually moved to the personal.

She had just admitted that she found bottoms 'rather nice – all soft and squishy' when Sherrie put her plan into action. As she opened the second bottle, she pretended to stumble and spilt about a quarter of the foaming contents over Carol's skirt. Before she could react, Sir James whipped out a handkerchief and rubbed away at the wet patch, carefully making sure that the liquid penetrated all the way through and spreading it around.

'Bad luck, Carol, you're soaked. Better take it off and change. I'm sure Sherrie can dry it.'

'But my spare ones are in my suitcase. In the hold.'

'Oh dear. Well, never mind, take it off anyway. I won't object.'

'I'm sure you won't Sir James. But . . .'

'What's the problem? You are wearing knickers, I assume?'

'Of course I am!' She blushed again. 'Oh well.'

She slipped the soggy garment off her very shapely legs and handed it to a contrite Sherrie, who trotted up to the galley to deal with it. When she returned she found a beaming Sir James and an embarrassed Carol, sitting down, with her legs firmly crossed. With an obvious effort, Sir James frowned at her.

'Sherrie, that was very careless indeed. You will of course pay to have Carol's skirt properly cleaned and I don't think that's enough ... Be quiet, Carol, I'm talking! Now, in view of one of our earlier conversations, I'm seriously tempted to give you a good spanking. Just to teach you a lesson. Let's face it, it's not the first time you've been clumsy.' Sherrie hung her head, just managing to suppress a giggle at the outrageous lie. 'Actually now I come to think about it, I don't see why you should get away with anything less. Do you a power of good. Come here and bend over my knee.'

Sherrie risked a quick glance towards Carol and was encouraged to see that for all her obvious embarrassment at the unexpected turn of events, there was definitely a gleam in her eye. She smoothed her skirt over her hips and moved forward, lowering herself onto the waiting lap with all the grace she could muster.

Sir James squeezed, prodded and poked and then gripped the hem of her skirt and hauled it all the way up, carefully leaving her slip in place. He then rested his right hand on the prominent bulge and frowned at his bemused Personal Assistant. 'Actually, Carol, I'm having second thoughts.' To his relief, there was an unmistakable look of disappointment on her face as she tore her eyes away from Sherrie's scantily covered bottom and met his. 'You're the one she spilt wine over, so it's only fair that you should spank her. Yes, I think it would be an even more pointed lesson for her. Up you get, Sherrie. Carol, you come and sit here – there's more room to swing your arm in this seat.'

Sherrie clambered up and whisked her skirt back down. Sir James shot up and stood by Carol's seat. The newly-appointed spanker rose with nervous diffidence and, while the two girls stared questioningly at each other, Sir James sat down. The sight before him produced an immediate erection.

Carol had her back more or less towards him, but at a slight angle, so that he could just see her face. Her bottom was right in front of his eyes; Sherrie was facing him. His eyes did a quick sweep of the whole scene and then settled on Carol's behind, neatly encased in plain white knickers. Considerably bigger than Sherrie's, plump and firm, it was irresistible. As though feeling the intensity of his scrutiny, she dropped her hands to the tops of her thighs and quickly ran her forefingers along the leg elastic, covering the little bits of cheek which had been peeping out.

He transferred his attention to their faces. Sherrie's mouth was curved in a tiny smile and her willingness to offer Carol her tender bottom was obvious. His PA looked far less assured. Her lips were parted and he could just see her breasts shifting up and down as she tried to get her breathing under control. The two women made a startling contrast. Sherrie with her dark, almost black hair, falling in soft waves to her shoulders; her neat but deceptively curvy figure, brown eyes, broad mouth and faintly olive complexion. Compared with her exotic beauty, Carol was the classic English rose, with lovely blonde hair, styled fashionably short, blue eyes, a peaches-and-cream complexion and a broader, plumper and more obviously curved body.

In the moment or two that the girls took to size each other up, Sir James had completed his inspection, had thanked his lucky stars that Sherrie had somehow flitted into his life. He had also just come to the conclusion that he actually found Carol more appealing even than Sherrie when she moved to take her place and he snapped out of his reverie, not wanting to miss a thing.

Even the two little paces which took her to the seat were enough to show him the firm mobility of her big bottom, but then she turned and sat down in one flowing movement. Looking up at Sherrie, she pointed to her lap, the round thighs close together, plumped up by the pressure of her weight against the seat and looking superb in the light stockings.

Sherrie was clearly as attracted to her legs as he was, because after she had moved to Carol's side, she rested both hands on the bare top bit of the further one, her fingers digging in, before slowly lowering her middle into position and slipping her hands from warm flesh to thick carpet, finally straightening her legs and digging her toes in. She turned her head to him, smiled her most impish smile, winked and then focused on the floor.

He sat forward, elbows on knees, chin resting on hands and concentrated on Carol. She was blushing again and staring down at the rounded seat of Sherrie's skirt, her hands out of sight. He was about to tell her to get on with it, but then thought it would be better to let her take her time. Her left hand appeared and settled on Sherrie's back, high up, between the shoulder blades. It trembled noticeably at even the slight intimacy but then she seemed to find the touch reassuring, for it slipped down the spine, rested on the small of the back before moving across to hold the hip. Then her right hand appeared, hovered, touched the rounded part of the left buttock and began to move over the twin mounds.

Suddenly conscious of his eyes on her, she looked up and blushed. He smiled encouragingly and her reservations seemed to vanish, because she suddenly began to move with proper authority. Her expression changed from tentative restraint to happy determination, pulling Sherrie's skirt up to her waist, helping herself to another quick grope, and then giving the slip the same treatment, her movements getting less brisk as Sherrie's knickers came into view. The familiar red stain spread over her cheeks, her lips parted and her eyes widened as she absently folded the thin silk on top of the skirt.

Sir James stretched up in his seat to get some sort of downward view and immediately sympathised with Carol's hesitation. Sherrie was wearing the most seductive knickers he had ever seen on her – black, tight, modestly cut so that they covered her bottom completely, but so thin that her cleft was visible. Carol was therefore faced with the reality of another girl's bottom at very close quarters and it had obviously come as a bit of a shock. He watched intently, seeing the tension leave her face as what was evidently a natural fascination with that part of the human anatomy overcame her inhibitions. Her right hand moved down onto the back of Sherrie's knee, then stole upwards until it reached bare thigh, where it lingered, the fingertips stroking the satiny skin. Then with growing conviction, it inched upwards, onto the knickers and ended up on the plumpest part of the right buttock. He saw her knuckles lift up a fraction as she pressed her fingers in, saw her mouth tighten, sensed her growing excitement. She looked at him, with a new sparkle in her eyes.

'How many can I give her, Sir James?'

'As many as you want, my dear.' Once again, he was tempted to interfere and suggest that she pulled Sherrie's knickers down, but held back. Apart from anything else, he was rather enjoying the novel view of Sherrie's patiently waiting bottom more or less in profile, although his line of sight was high enough to let him see the inward curve of her buttocks as they dipped in to the division. Carol's right arm moved slowly upwards and then flew down. Her stiff palm landed across both cheeks, right across the very centre, making a duller sound than the flesh on flesh contact he was used to and sending a ripple through Sherrie's bottom.

Sir James sat back and concentrated on Carol's face, seeing how she rapidly found the process very much to her liking. She began to smack harder; she dished out a dozen or so without stopping, then stroked and kneaded away. Her hand drifted down onto the bare thigh and she tugged Sherrie's knickers up, just far enough to expose the gluteal folds and an inch or two of buttock. She took a hefty pinch of naked bulge, squeezed and blushed.

Once she had got over her initial discomfiture, Carol began to enjoy herself, in spite of a growing conviction that she had been set up. Sherrie was far too bright and sophisticated to accept the pain and humiliation of a spanking under normal circumstances, but had bent over without the slightest protest. Neither had she uttered a single sound so

211

far – and there was a definite pink stain gleaming through those indecent knickers, so her bottom had to be hurting her. And such a luscious bottom! The pinch had proved how smooth it was. Even though she could see it clearly through that filmy material, she began to want to have it properly bare. Her last boyfriend but one had always smacked her bare bottom, so it was not exactly unfamiliar to her. Wanting was one thing, though, doing was another.

'Sir James, she doesn't seem to be feeling it properly and her knickers are a bit on the thick side. Would it be all right if I took them down?'

'You had better ask Sherrie,' Sir James replied, 'it is her bottom, after all.'

'I suppose it is! Sherrie, you don't mind if I bare your bottom, do you?'

Sherrie sighed. A deep, loud, sorrowful sigh, full of woe and misery. And so obviously phoney that Carol giggled and aimed a sharp slap at the bare part of the right cheek, which produced a loud 'Ow', a wriggle and a lifting of the hips in unmistakable invitation. Still smiling, she tucked her fingers into the tight waistband and slowly tugged, feeling the blush in her face as Sherrie's bare bottom popped into view, quivering gently.

It looked bigger, softer, more vulnerable and even more tempting than before. She sneaked a quick look at her boss, and seeing the friendly warmth of his expression, suddenly realised that she was being tempted rather than tested. Somehow he must have sensed her interest in bottoms and spanking and somehow had persuaded Sherrie to play the sacrificial lamb. Looking down again, she remembered that she had often wondered what it was like to dish out punishment and now here she was with a truly beautiful bum spread out in front of her, all lovely and bare, patiently waiting for her to get on with it. But she just *had* to stroke it first, so she smoothed her hand over the warm curves, loving the softness of it all. So much nicer to handle than a man's, if not as sexy. She trailed the tip of her forefinger down the tight groove and felt a flutter in her stomach as Sherrie gave a little groan of pleasure.

She liked the girl. Very much. But that made the desire to give a really sound spanking even stronger. Drawing a deep breath, she gave her a final squeeze, followed by a couple of affectionate pats, then set to work with a will.

Sir James watched with growing contentment. Carol had clearly taken a bit of time to get used to the idea, but now that she had made up her mind that it was a perfectly reasonable thing to do in the circumstances, she was going about it in fine style, reddening Sherrie's bottom most efficiently and making it bounce and quiver with each blow.

He stood up to get a different view and it sudddenly struck him that the whole thing was incredibly sexy. He couldn't really explain why he found the sight of one lovely girl spanking another on her bare bottom so erotic. The gracefulness of both participants had something to do with it, but it was far more complicated than that. He focused on Carol's face again. Pink from her exertions, her eyes gleaming, her lips in that lovely upward curve, her hair shining, she looked wantonly delicious and the smooth curve of Sherrie's body was perfect. Submissive, perhaps, but not reluctant. Moving round to see how Sherrie was getting on, he noticed a few small signs of distress. Her breath was whistling between her teeth; she was shaking her head around, whirling the waves of dark hair around her face; her hips were bobbing and weaving on Carol's plump thighs. He was just about to suggest that she should stop when some sixth sense made him sit down again and see how they sorted things out for themselves.

To her surprise, Sherrie realised that she was on the verge of coming. Normally it took far more than what Carol had dished out to bring her on, so the combination of her lovely face, soft thighs and sensitive hands and the exciting atmosphere must have worked together to good effect. She cocked her bottom up, spread her legs and offered herself blatantly.

Unfortunately, Carol just did not have the experience to understand the real reason for the sudden change in Sherrie's posture and assumed that Sherrie had had enough which, considering the state of her bottom, was hardly surprising. She slumped back in her seat breathing heavily, nursing her stinging palm and contemplating the red buttocks with awe.

Swallowing her disappointment, Sherrie took charge. She stood up and turned her back on Carol, holding her skirt and slip well clear so that she had an uninterrupted view of the damage she had wrought. It was then quite simple to wriggle around while she rubbed tenderly away and let her knickers slide down her legs till they fell to her feet. After a few moments of this, she bent slowly down as though planning to restore her decency, her bent back keeping her skirt well clear while she groped clumsily round her ankles. Not many people had been able to resist her bottom in that distended state and, to her relief, Carol was no exception.

'Could you hold it there for a second, Sherrie?'

Sherrie stayed put, with the tingles starting up all over again, then looked up at Sir James and nodded. He picked up his cue smoothly.

'Are you sure that she's had enough, Carol? From where I'm sitting, she looks remarkably unrepentant.'

She peered round her legs and saw that Carol was looking steadily at her proffered buttocks with obvious desire. Confident that she was going to be spanked again, Sherrie dipped her back and sighed in relief when she felt a hand running firmly over her rear, squeezing and pinching. Winking at Sir James, she waited patiently.

By now, Carol was convinced that the other two were working in concert to lead her astray. Right, she said to herself, even if I am wrong, I've thoroughly enjoyed it so far, so why not get stuck in and enjoy myself even more? The only problem was that she couldn't decide on the best course of action.

Once again Sherrie took over. 'Would you like me to stay like this, Carol? It would make a nice change.' There was no answer, but she saw her new friend stand up, move beside her and then her tight bottom was set on fire again. Later, Sir James suggested an application of cold cream.

'That would be lovely, Sir James, I'll go and get it.'

Kicking off her knickers but leaving her skirt up, she trotted up the aisle, found the cream and rejoined her smiling passengers, noting that Carol looked far more at ease. 'Look, would you mind if I took some of my clothes off – being spanked always makes me terribly hot.' Taking their silence as approval, she stripped naked, then knelt on the floor by the nearest seat, rested her torso on it and stuck her bottom out.

Sir James and Carol stood side by side, looking down at the enticing sight before them. He heard a little sigh and sensed that Carol was blushing again. Smiling inwardly, he slipped his arm round her waist and she rested her head on his shoulder, sighing again. His hand dropped to her hip, slid down her flank until it reached bare skin, lingered there briefly before tucking her knickers up into the cleft of her bottom and cupping her bare buttocks in turn.

He looked at Sherrie's tight bottom, felt Carol's relaxed one and then slapped her into action. She gave him a quick grin, knelt down behind Sherrie and began to spread the cream, giving him a splendid view as she did so.

She was, of course, fully aware that her buttocks were bulging out behind her, but Sherrie's fully exposed charms demanded her full attention. She dipped her fingers in the cream, spread it around and rubbed it in gently, with her last inhibitions fleeing when her movements moved the two halves sufficiently apart to expose the neat little anus in between. After a pang of embarrassment, she decided firstly that she wanted a longer and closer look and secondly that Sherrie had actually pushed her bottom against her hands, so quite obviously was more than happy to have her bottom-hole studied.

Sir James watched the action for a while, happy to see them both so obviously enjoying themselves but as his nostrils flared at the mingled scents of their excitement, he stepped forward to try to choreograph the most erotic cabaret in history!

The first priority was Carol. The sight of her rounded cheeks bulging out of her knickers had been most promising and as he stared down at her kneeling figure, he told himself firmly that it was high time he exercised his authority.

'Right, Carol, that's enough. Up you get.'

Dizzy with a combination of lust and champagne, she was putty in his hands, placidly obeying his every command. She stood in front of him while he sat and eased her knickers down so that he could admire her bottom, both standing up and bending down.

Carol stripped naked and stood next to Sherrie while he compared them, and clutched her hand.

She walked up and down the aisle, watched by them both. He told her to put her blouse and knickers back on. Then announced that he was going to spank her.

Carol returned Sherrie's sympathetic smile as she did up her buttons and winked at her, seeing no reason to disguise the fact that she had no objections whatsoever to proffering her naked bottom to the man she respected and admired more than any other.

As her soft weight settled on his legs, Sir James looked down on the scantily covered rump of his favourite employee and resolved to introduce her fairly gently to what was now his favourite hobby. Sliding his hand under the waistband of her rather virginal knickers, he ran it over her, revelling in the feel of her skin and the quality of her flesh, then pulled them down and enjoyed the view. She was bigger, plumper, rounder and whiter than Sherrie. Her cleft was deeper and tighter. Strawberries and cream compared with pure, clear honey. Two outstanding girls, two superb bottoms, and to his relief, he found that he preferred Carol. He began to spank her, lightly and with the greatest pleasure, loving the way she coloured so quickly.

Carol realised immediately that he was going to take his time and relaxed completely. Her previous boyfriend had not shown anything like the expertise that Sir James was demonstrating. She lay there, eyes closed blissfully, the rhythmic clapping noise of flesh on flesh lulling her as much as the rippling waves in her bottom. The warmth built up slowly and steadily; her sex lips began to flutter and soft moans echoed in her brain.

216

A soft hand cupped her cheek. She looked up into Sherrie's face, her warm brown eyes full of sympathetic affection and they smiled at each other. She saw the full mouth purse and come closer and knew that she was about to experience her first proper kiss from another girl. To her surprise she did not draw back but pursed her own lips in welcome. Sherrie was soft, sweet and skilled, slipping her tongue in, then drawing Carol's into her mouth and nibbling the tip.

The pleasure from Sir James's hand at one end and Sherrie's mouth on the other was too much and Carol's climax was quick and shattering.

With her head still swimming, they helped her to her feet and stripped her naked again, making her stand still, legs apart and her hands on her head. Hands roamed freely all over her, stroking her back, tummy and thighs, kneading her glowing bottom. Hot mouths clamped on her nipples. Her buttocks were pulled firmly apart and a finger tickled the little corrugations surrounding her anus. Another cupped her sex and a finger wormed its way into her slit. She was moaning again. She knew that the hands on her rear end were Sherrie's and, in among the stars she was seeing, images of her buttocks and bottom-hole floated and swirled.

With a little cry, she whirled round and grabbed Sherrie, pulling her close so that their breasts squashed together and their mouths locked. Her knees gave way and they sank to the floor, rolling around, and she could not get enough of the unaccustomed feeling of feminine softness against her.

Sir James stood up, looking down at their writhing bodies, his prick bursting. Unconsciously, he began to wrench at buttons and zips until he was as naked as they were. As he tossed his last sock aside, they settled with Carol on top, her pink bottom dimpled as she ground her pubic mound against Sherrie's. There was only one course of action and he took it, spanking her hard, right across the tight cleft and she screamed with pleasure. Pressing his hand into her back, he spanked away, much harder than before and Sherrie's cries of delight at the rhythmic press-ure on her sex added to the din. Carol's bottom began to jerk spasmodically as the waves crashed through her and he helped her on her way by squeezing her cheeks in time with her spasms. Then she slumped again and he gently rubbed the sting from her red bottom while she recovered and rolled over on her back. As he looked down at them, the difference between them struck him even more forcibly. He bent to kiss them both, with Carol first and last before she asked if she could slip away to freshen up, leaving him alone with Sherrie.

She was smiling softly. Her make-up had vanished, her hair was a tangle and her bush was damp and matted from Carol's attentions. She looked good enough to eat, so he knelt between her thighs, tucked his hands under her knees, lifted them until they were resting against her breasts and applied tongue to open bottom-hole. She writhed in his grip, panting. He moved slowly up the neat ridge of her perineum and into her slippery passage, flick-ing his tongue all around the glistening coral-pink folds. She moaned. Moving up a bit further, he found her clitty, drew it all into his mouth and sucked away, flicking his stiffened tongue against the hard little knob. She screamed.

Pleasing the two of them had temporarily satisfied him, so when Carol came back, neat, tidy and pink from her shower, he suggested that Sherrie should follow her, then make up some sandwiches and open another bottle. When she had showered, he took his turn, absurdly happy when Carol insisted on washing his back!

Still naked, they ate and drank with easy companionship and Sherrie cleared away. Carol had taken his usual seat and he noticed that her eyes were glued to Sherrie's retreat-ing back.

'She's got a lovely walk, hasn't she?'

'She's lovely all over. How did you find her?'

'It would be more accurate to say that she found me! Sheer luck, I think. Ah, coffee.'

As he sipped, he considered the next move and decided that the time had come to test his PA more rigorously. He drained his cup, Sherrie collected them and trotted up to the galley and he watched Carol watching her, then caught her eye.

'Slide your bottom forward until it's on the edge of your seat, please.' She blushed at the authority in his voice but obeyed without hesitation. 'Good. Now put your feet on the seat.' The remnants of her self-consciousness made her blush even more acutely, but again she did as she was told, first one foot, then the other until her anxious face was framed by her raised knees. He smiled at her reassuringly, then dropped his gaze.

The combination of her innocent looks, great body and abandoned posture was fantastic. The focal point was obviously her golden-haired sex, contrasting vividly with the smooth whiteness of her tummy and thighs. Below it, about three inches of tight bottom-cleft separated the dimpled mounds, squashed under her weight. He remembered how Sherrie had looked and tasted in a similar position not long before and got up, knelt down and lowered his head to make a comparison. Amazingly, as soon as she realised what he was going to do, her slit opened. Not much, but enough to reveal a bit of glistening pink. He kissed the inside of each thigh, starting at the knee and moving down until her soft and scented pubic hair tickled his nose, moved to her cleft and ran his tongue up the tight, soft groove until it slipped of its own accord into her slit.

She came as Sherrie returned and he stood up and helped Carol to her feet, supporting her with a steadying arm round her waist.

'Right,' he asked them, 'what now?'

The two girls looked at each other, trying to sort their desires into some order of priority.

Sherrie broke the silence. 'You choose, Carol.'

Carol frowned. Her hand longed for the feel of Sherrie's bare bottom; her bottom ached for their hands even more. She looked down at Sir James half-erect cock and realised that she wanted him inside her most of all. But he was the boss, so that was up to him. At last collecting her thoughts, she bared her soul.

'I'd love to give Sherrie another spanking first. Then I'd like the two of you to spank me again. After that . . . well, I'm in your hands.'

So she sat down and Sherrie floated across her bare legs, soft and yielding fore and aft. Her fantastic bottom was just asking to be soundly spanked and was scarlet by the time it had been.

Carol was made to kiss it better and Sherrie knelt up on the seat, thrusting out so far that her little anus winked at her from the middle of the white centre and she ended up licking her there after only a moment's hesitation.

Sir James put Carol over his lap, his prick digging into her tummy, and spanked her even harder. Then she had to kneel up on the seat and she found herself wanting to expose her all, forcing her hips back and up until a waft of cool air told her that her most private part was on view. The spanks felt very different on drum-tight buttocks.

Sherrie made her bend over the back of a seat and steadily added to the fires in her bottom. She was crying by the end and gasping when the hot wet tongue eventually slipped into the entrance of her anus, while Sherrie's finger busied itself on her clitty.

They made her walk up and down the aisle and said such nice things about the way her bottom moved that for the first time in her life, it pleased rather than embarrassed her.

Sherrie produced an instant camera and devoted a whole film to Carol's bare bottom in a variety of positions, the last one with her anus exposed. Even Carol found them quite exciting and insisted on snapping Sherrie. Then Sir James grabbed the camera and shot the two of them.

They found a sports bag, full of an exciting range of implements and, nervous at first, Carol tried them all, ending up in the middle of the aisle, clutching her ankles as Sir James used the cane on her with surprising skill.

Then Sherrie slipped away and Sir James laid Carol on the floor, tucked her knees up to her tits and got to work between her legs with mouth and tongue, so that the thrills from there combined with the burning ache in her buttocks to send her into orbit.

No sooner had she recovered from that, when she felt his weight on top of her with his prick nuzzling briefly at the entrance to her sex before thrusting in and at last fulfilling her.

After a decent interval, Sherrie re-appeared with more champagne and the first glass revived them to such good effect that she felt free to introduce them to one of her favourite ploys. She put a thick towel on the floor and told Carol to lie down, bottom up and with her middle on the towel. She carefully dribbled some of the chilled wine over both buttocks and, ignoring her shrieks, the two of them lapped away. Then Carol was made to kneel up and stick her bottom out, Sir James knelt behind her and when Sherrie poured some more onto the jutting tailbone and it trickled down the cleft, he was there to catch it with his tongue. They changed places and Carol's shrieks changed to squeaks at Sherrie's more subtle licking.

'Your turn now, Sir James.'

'Certainly not, Sherrie. Ladies first. Up you get Carol and I'll be Mother. Right, are you both ready?'

And when it was his turn, the combined effects of cool liquid and hot tongue were nearly too much. The girls sensed this the moment he staggered upright and in a trice, he was back on the floor, facing up and wondering what on earth they were up to. Suddenly Sherrie was standing over his head, one foot on either side and treating him to a wonderful view of her bottom. He was staring open-mouthed at the dramatically different aspect when it descended, the cleft slowly opening, until she was squatting comfortably with her two most intimate orifices in easy reach of his mouth. Raising his head a little, he got to work.

Then a soft hand folded round his prick, lifted it and it was nudging against something softly-haired and yielding. Just as he realised that Carol was squatting over his middle, it was enveloped in a clinging tunnel and he felt her buttocks spread softly on his thighs. Reaching down to take hold of as much bottom as possible, he guided her up and down and buried his tongue in Sherrie.

Finally sated, and with the snow-covered Alps looming

221

under the starboard wing, it was time to tidy themselves up. Carol realised that Sir James wanted to say a proper goodbye to Sherrie and tactfully slipped off to the toilet. Smiling at her retreating back – and promising himself that it would certainly not be his last sight of her bare bottom – he folded a happy-looking Sherrie in his arms, reaching down for a final reminder of the feel of her bottom.

'As you can imagine, there are lots of questions I could ask. But I'm not going to. I'd just like to repeat my thanks. And to tell you that I had planned to offer you a job with the Group. A very good job. But I know that you wouldn't take it. Whoever you really are – and I know that you can't be an air hostess – good luck. And perhaps we'll meet again.'

She smiled at him and kissed him warmly. 'Thank you, and I hope that you and the Group prosper. I'm sure you will. And look after Carol. She is rather special.'

'I know. And I shall, I promise.'

Half an hour later, Sherrie stood at the door watching them walk to the waiting Rolls Royce, grinning as Carol rather pointedly rubbed her bottom before climbing in.

It had all worked out far better than she had hoped.

Postscript

Sherrie stood patiently as she waited for him to speak. The usual gloomy red glow suffused the room; she could only just make out the shadow of his head and shoulders as he sat behind the huge desk. The strange incense made her nostrils flare and, as she breathed it in to fill her lungs, her head swam. It was hot and the silk blouse clung to her breasts, so clearly naked beneath the light material. At last he spoke, his voice deep and with a peculiar resonance.

'You think that Sir James is now a convert?'

'Yes Sir. And MacGregor shares are up.'

'I know. You have done well. Again. You have earned your reward. Prepare.'

'Thank you, Sir.'

Her hands fluttered at the fastening of her skirt. The metallic hiss of the zip sounded loud in the oppressive silence, then the beautifully cut garment slithered down her legs and lay in limp disarray at her feet. Her self-supporting stockings indented the flesh of her thighs, some six inches above her knees, leading his eyes up the smooth, pale curves to the neat triangle of hair and then to her fingers fumbling with the buttons of her blouse. Soon this joined the skirt and she was all but naked, shining in the dull light.

Until she was bathed in brilliance as a spotlight lit her up, making her blink. The tight little slit of her sex, the perfect circle of her tummy button and the dark-pink points of her stiffening nipples emphasised her flawless skin. She waited, counting one hundred and twenty seconds to herself, giving the Master two minutes to enjoy her front view

223

before turning to show him her back. She stood, stock still, for a further two minutes, almost able to feel the intensity of his gaze on her curves.

She then stepped out of her clothes and walked gracefully over to the far end of the room, deliberately making her naked bottom sway and wiggle more than usual. She reached the padded bench set end-on against the wall, paused to take a deep breath, then laid the upper part of her body on the leather surface, gasping at the coolness against the warmth of her flesh and inhaling the rich scent. Her hands grasped the side and she stared at the wall, her eyes glazed in concentration as she bent her knees in a little to achieve the required degree of curved projection in her buttocks. She moved her feet apart. Only a little. He liked a glimpse of her sex at the end of her cleft, but no more. She was ready.

Some considerable time later, she heard a faint swishing hum as the thick strap cleaved the sultry air and wrapped round the plumpest part of the target area. She felt her cheeks quiver at the impact and a hot swathe of pain made her gasp. Twelve strokes later, her bottom was glowing all over and had been perfectly prepared for the acidic bite of the springy rattan cane.

Her favourite. But she knew that he would make her wait for it. The first fluttering waves from between her legs quietened and she tucked her knees further under the bench to present a tighter, firmer bottom.

It was a perfect ending to a successful operation.

NEW BOOKS

Coming up from Nexus and Black Lace

Sherrie by Evelyn Culber
May 1995   Price: £4.99   ISBN: 0 352 32996 3
Chairman of an important but ailing company, Sir James is having trouble relaxing. But in Sherrie, seductive hostess on his business flight, he has found someone who might be able to help. After one of her eye-opening spanking stories and a little practical demonstration, money worries are the last thing on Sir James's mind.

House of Angels by Yvonne Strickland
May 1995   Price: £4.99   ISBN: 0 352 32995 5
In a sumptuous villa in the south of France, Sonia runs a very exclusive service. With her troupe of gorgeous and highly skilled girls, and rooms fitted out to cater for every taste, she fulfils sexual fantasies. Sonia finds herself in need of a new recruit, and the beautiful Karen seems ideal – providing she can shed a few of her inhibitions.

One Week in the Private House by Esme Ombreux
June 1995   Price: £4.99   ISBN: 0 352 32788 X
Jem, Lucy and Julia are new recruits to the Private House – a dark, secluded place gripped by an atmosphere of decadence and stringent discipline. Highly sexual but very different people, the three women enjoy welcomes that are varied but equally erotic.

Return to the Manor by Barbra Baron
June 1995   Price: £4.99   ISBN: 0 352 32989 0
At Chalmers Finishing School for Young Ladies, the tyrannical headmistress still has her beady eye on her pretty charges; the girls still enjoy receiving their punishment just as much as Miss Petty enjoys dispensing it; and Lord Brexford still watches breathless from the manor across the moor. But now there's a whole new intake for Miss Petty to break in.

BLACK
lace

The Devil Inside by Portia da Costa
May 1995   Price: £4.99   ISBN: 0 352 32993 9

Psychic sexual intuition is a very special gift. Those who possess it can perceive other people's sexual fantasies – and are usually keen to indulge them. But as Alexa Lavelle discovers, it is a power that needs help to master. Fortunately, the doctors at her exclusive medical practice are more than willing to offer their services.

The Lure of Satyria by Cheryl Mildenhall
May 1995   Price: £4.99   ISBN: 0 352 32994 7

Welcome to Satyria: a land of debauchery and excess, where few men bother with courtship and fewer maidens deserve it. But even here, none is so bold as Princess Hedra, whose quest for sexual gratification takes her beyond the confines of her castle and deep into the wild, enchanted forest . . .

The Seductress by Vivienne LaFay
June 1995   Price: £4.99   ISBN: 0 352 32997 1

Rejected by her husband, Lady Emma is free to practise her prurient skills on the rest of 1890s society. Starting with her cousin's innocent fiancé and moving on to Paris, she embarks on a campaign of seduction that sets hearts racing all across Europe.

Healing Passion by Sylvie Ouellette
June 1995   Price: £4.99   ISBN: 0 352 32998 X

The staff of the exclusive Dorchester clinic have some rather strange ideas about therapy. When they're not pandering to the sexual demands of their patients, they're satisfying each other's healthy libidos. Which all comes as rather a shock to fresh-faced nurse Judith on her first day.

NEXUS BACKLIST

All books are priced £4.99 unless another price is given. If a date is supplied, the book in question will not be available until that month in 1995.

CONTEMPORARY EROTICA

THE ACADEMY	Arabella Knight	
CONDUCT UNBECOMING	Arabella Knight	Jul
CONTOURS OF DARKNESS	Marco Vassi	
THE DEVIL'S ADVOCATE	Anonymous	
DIFFERENT STROKES	Sarah Veitch	Aug
THE DOMINO TATTOO	Cyrian Amberlake	
THE DOMINO ENIGMA	Cyrian Amberlake	
THE DOMINO QUEEN	Cyrian Amberlake	
ELAINE	Stephen Ferris	
EMMA'S SECRET WORLD	Hilary James	
EMMA ENSLAVED	Hilary James	
EMMA'S SECRET DIARIES	Hilary James	
FALLEN ANGELS	Kendal Grahame	
THE FANTASIES OF JOSEPHINE SCOTT	Josephine Scott	
THE GENTLE DEGENERATES	Marco Vassi	
HEART OF DESIRE	Maria del Rey	
HELEN – A MODERN ODALISQUE	Larry Stern	
HIS MISTRESS'S VOICE	G. C. Scott	
HOUSE OF ANGELS	Yvonne Strickland	May
THE HOUSE OF MALDONA	Yolanda Celbridge	
THE IMAGE	Jean de Berg	Jul
THE INSTITUTE	Maria del Rey	
SISTERHOOD OF THE INSTITUTE	Maria del Rey	

EROTIC SCIENCE FICTION

FANTASYWORLD	Larry Stern	
WANTON	Andrea Arven	

ANCIENT & FANTASY SETTINGS

CHAMPIONS OF LOVE	Anonymous	
CHAMPIONS OF PLEASURE	Anonymous	
CHAMPIONS OF DESIRE	Anonymous	
THE CLOAK OF APHRODITE	Kendal Grahame	
THE HANDMAIDENS	Aran Ashe	
THE SLAVE OF LIDIR	Aran Ashe	
THE DUNGEONS OF LIDIR	Aran Ashe	
THE FOREST OF BONDAGE	Aran Ashe	
PLEASURE ISLAND	Aran Ashe	
WITCH QUEEN OF VIXANIA	Morgana Baron	

EDWARDIAN, VICTORIAN & OLDER EROTICA

ANNIE	Evelyn Culber	
ANNIE AND THE SOCIETY	Evelyn Culber	
THE AWAKENING OF LYDIA	Philippa Masters	Apr
BEATRICE	Anonymous	
CHOOSING LOVERS FOR JUSTINE	Aran Ashe	
GARDENS OF DESIRE	Roger Rougiere	
THE LASCIVIOUS MONK	Anonymous	
LURE OF THE MANOR	Barbra Baron	
RETURN TO THE MANOR	Barbra Baron	Jun
MAN WITH A MAID 1	Anonymous	
MAN WITH A MAID 2	Anonymous	
MAN WITH A MAID 3	Anonymous	
MEMOIRS OF A CORNISH GOVERNESS	Yolanda Celbridge	
THE GOVERNESS AT ST AGATHA'S	Yolanda Celbridge	
TIME OF HER LIFE	Josephine Scott	
VIOLETTE	Anonymous	

THE JAZZ AGE

BLUE ANGEL NIGHTS	Margarete von Falkensee	
BLUE ANGEL DAYS	Margarete von Falkensee	

Please send me the books I have ticked above.

Name . . . .

Address . . . .

. . . .

. . . .

. . . . Post code . . . .

Send to: **Cash Sales, Nexus Books, 332 Ladbroke Grove, London W10 5AH.**

Please enclose a cheque or postal order, made payable to **Nexus Books,** to the value of the books you have ordered plus postage and packing costs as follows:

UK and BFPO – £1.00 for the first book, 50p for each subsequent book.

Overseas (including Republic of Ireland) – £2.00 for the first book, £1.00 for the second book, and 50p for each subsequent book.

If you would prefer to pay by VISA or ACCESS/MASTER-CARD, please write your card number and expiry date here:

. . . .

Please allow up to 28 days for delivery.

Signature . . . .
